THE QUEEN OF LISBON

Malcolm Havard

Oakbrook Press

Copyright © 2024 Malcolm Havard
All rights reserved

The characters and events portrayed in this book are fictitious. Any similarity to real persons, living or dead, is coincidental and not intended by the author.

No part of this book may be reproduced, or stored in a retrieval system, or transmitted in any form or by any means, electronic, mechanical, photocopying, recording, or otherwise, without express written permission of the publisher.

ISBN: 9798343407976

Cover design by: Malcolm Havard

THE QUEEN OF LISBON

by

MALCOLM HAVARD

CHAPTER 1

21st OCTOBER 1941 - 2350 HRS

THE '*SS NORMAN GIBSON*' AN HOUR OUT FROM LISBON

Edward Jenkins wished he'd gone with his gut instinct and worn his duffle coat. It was as cold as he'd expected and, even up on the end of the wing bridge some 30 feet above the water, he and the other duty watch were periodically pelted by spray whipped up by the strengthening breeze.

It wasn't the done thing though. There was a tradition on the 'Gibson' - no, more than a tradition, almost a sailors' superstition, and there was nothing more sacred than one of those; on the first watch out of port on the 'Norman Gibson' you didn't don your wet-weather gear. As a result, the other three watch members were dressed in civvies like they were still out on the town. At 16, Edward was the youngest member of the crew. The kid, the boy, the powder monkey, he was the butt of all the jokes, the ribbing, the pranks, everything was fired towards him already. He wasn't going to give them any cheap shots, so he did the same.

He was dressed like he was going out on a night on the town.

Like he was last night.

Edward couldn't help smiling at the memory; last night. What a town, what a night, the best of his life! The whole city lit up, like Liverpool used to be when he was a kid before the war and the blackout. But his hometown was never like Lisbon, fragrant with the scent of flowers, heady, a melting pot of people like any port city, but far more exotic. And the women, oh, the women! Well, one woman, Ana Maria, a Brazilian. His first, though no one knew that but himself and Ana Maria, his teacher, his muse.

She was so beautiful. Perfect.

Edward looked across to the southeast, up the Tagus estuary, where there was a glow in the sky, the lights of that wonderful city reflected on the clouds. She was there. When would he see her again? How many men would she see whilst he was gone? He hated the sick feeling that thought brought.

Something hit him on the back of the head.

Hard.

'Ow! Soddin' hell! What you do that for?'

His reaction to the blow was more shock than pain but still, he turned, furious, to face the culprit. His anger instantly vanished. It was Ellison, the Second Mate.

'Stop daydreaming, boy!' Ellison yelled into Edward's face. 'You're on watch. Keep your fucking eyes on the sea.'

'Sorry, sir,' Edward muttered, putting his binoculars to his eyes and turning to look out over the darkness.

'I'll give you bleeding sorry if I catch you again. You'll be in the brig.'

'Leave the boy alone, mon. Can't you tell the lad's in love.'

The rich, deep golden voice could only be that of one man; Swanny, the Jamaican. Laid back, languid, Edward had feared the towering black man when he'd signed on but Swanny, real name the magnificent Lancelot Lionel Earnest Swan, had become first a protector and then a friend, sheltering Edward from the worst of the teasing.

Ellison, all five-foot-three of him, now squared up to the six-foot-four West Indian, 'And you watch yourself too, Swanny.'

Now there was a distinct chuckle in Swanny's voice, 'Yes, mister mate, mon. I will be watching myself, mon.'

Edward saw the other watch members turn away and knew they were hiding their laughter.

Ellison was no fool, he could tell he was being mocked. He backed away. 'Alright, alright, enough. This is no sodding pleasure cruise. There's U-Boats out there,' he pointed to the west, towards the Atlantic. 'And we've got a hold stuffed with wolfram that Hitler's boys would love not to get back to Blighty, so all of you, keep your wits about you and your eyes on the bleedin' sea, understand?' He turned back to Edward. 'And you, boy, you keep your thoughts off whatever cheap whore took your drinking money and filled your head full of lies and promises last night.'

Furious, Edward took the strap of heavy binoculars from around his neck and stepped towards Ellison who'd turned his back to step inside the shelter of the wheelhouse. He was going to smash the mate's head in with the binoculars, not caring what would happen to him afterwards.

He didn't get far. He was grabbed by a seemingly immovable force.

'He's not worth it, Eddy mon,' whispered Swanny. 'Just leave it.'

Edward was skinny, no more than nine stone sopping wet, and his Jamaican buddy was not only tall, but had the physique to go with it. Swanny, whilst holding Edward to him, took the binoculars out of his hands as easily as picking the head off a flower

'But Ana Maria is... '

'I know, I know.' Swanny's tone was like honey and a soothing balm all at once. 'She's a sweet little lady. Ellison's just jealous, he's trying to make you lose your rag, mon. Don't let him get to you.'

Edward stopped struggling. 'Alright, alright, Swanny. Let go of me.'

Swanny didn't release him.

'You sure? You looked to have murder in mind, mon.'

'Yeah, yeah, I'm fine. Let me go.'

Swanny did.

'Give me those back.' Edward held out his hand for the binoculars. 'I've got a job to do, ain't I?'

'Job?' muttered one of the other watch members. 'Some bloody job, the Jerries never come this close in.'

'Yeah,' Charlie, the fourth watchman on duty spat onto the deck. 'It's out in Biscay where it gets serious, not 'ere.'

Edward brought the binoculars up to his eyes and started scanning the horizon. His ability to focus was limited by the tears that had come with his anger at Ellison's insults about Ana Maria, but Charlie was right; there was nothing to see anyway.

Everyone knew the U-boats never came in this close to the Portuguese shore, that's what everyone said.

He let his binoculars track away from his assigned quarter to the glowing lights of Lisbon. He missed her already. Yes, he knew what she did. Hell, he'd handed over his money on that first night, hadn't he? But after that, it was different; she was his, he'd taken her out for the next two nights, she hadn't seen anyone else. He'd told her everything, of Liverpool, of growing up, of his mum insisting he went into the merchantmen instead of the Royal Navy because she thought it would be safer, of her horror when she realised the truth. He also repeated proudly what Swanny had said about their cargo when he'd asked what the hell wolfram was; that it was the stuff that would win the war against Hitler, that when added to steel it turned into something that could punch right through tanks, something that both sides desperately needed it. 'We've got our holds full of it, Ana Maria. I'm helping win the war,' he'd told her, and she'd nodded and kissed him and then listened to how he'd take her home to see his mum in Liverpool once the war was won, but that he had to go because his ship, the 'Norman Gibson,' was leaving on the next night's tide, but he'd be back, with a ring.

Him and Ana Maria. Forever.

That was going to happen. He'd make it happen.

He remembered the job he was supposed to be doing. Swanny was right, there was no point letting Ellison win. He'd do his duty, get his pay, buy that ring and then, one day soon, put it on her finger.

He swung the binoculars back to his assigned quarter.

There was something there.

He couldn't process what he was seeing. A white line in the water, filling the lens from top to bottom. Spray on the lens? A crack in the glass? He checked, first the lens and then the eyepieces. Nothing. Which meant…

He looked out to sea again, without the binoculars this time.

He could see it. Clear and stark. Just like he'd been told to look for.

It was coming.

'Tor…' he croaked. His words wouldn't form.
'Torpedo.'
He managed barely a whisper
Somehow, he was flying.
How could he be flying? He was though, he could see clouds, the lights of Lisbon, a large blaze, the waves that —
Red.
Black.
Pain.
Cold, cold, so cold.
He gasped. He didn't take in air, it was water. Pain. Choking.
He fought, panicking, what was holding him?
Swanny again?
His scrambled brain started working.
He wasn't being held; he was deep underwater, drowning. He had to stop fighting to take a breath and kick up like he had at New Brighton when he had jumped off the pier with his pals.
How far down was he? Too far, too far!
Might as well give up.
Take a lungful.
End it.
Suddenly he could see — and breathe, he could breathe!
Edward took in deep, luxurious breaths of air, glorious air, coughing his way back to life. Where was the 'Gibson?' Did they know he was overboard? Had they stopped?
Where was it?
He trod water, turning slowly.
And there was his ship. The bow at least, sticking straight up out of the water, illuminated by flames that ran all the way up from the new waterline up to the forward anti-aircraft gun position.
Just the ship. No people. No sign of life. Where was Swanny, Charlie or even the Mate Ellison, or any of the other 30 or so people in the crew? He looked around for a life raft, a boat, anything?
There was nothing.

A flash of light was followed by a rolling roar like thunder and the sea suddenly fizzed and hissed. The magazine!

Edward dived down, forcing himself deeper into the cold sea, anything to get away from the rain of bullets and fragments of steel. Only when his lungs cried for mercy did he kick back up to the surface again.

It was dark. Of the 'SS Norman Gibson,' his home for the last two months, there was no sign other than the debris that he was now floating in.

Abruptly, something white shot out of the water next to him. A cork lifebelt ring, the ship's name in peeling black paint on the side.

Gratefully, he ducked under the water and came up inside it, letting it support him.

He was alive.

For now.

CHAPTER 2

22nd OCTOBER 1941 - 0002 HRS

25km NORTH OF ESTORIL, PORTUGAL

Lopes, his back to the wall of the ruined farmhouse, stared into the darkness of the fields beyond.

His senses were confused; around him were the scents of the countryside so familiar from his youth, yet here overlain with the iodine notes of the sea. He should be hearing the rustle of the breeze through the trees, but these were drowned by the crash of the waves from a few hundred metres downhill where the restless Atlantic pounded the coast.

He checked his watch. The luminous dials told him five minutes had passed since he'd last done so. Two minutes past midnight. He pulled a face.

'They're late, sir,' said Costa. Lopes realised that his assistant must have sensed his impatience as they crouched in the darkness.

'They are, Alvares, they are.'

'The informer's always been reliable, sir,' said Costa. 'They've never let us down before.'

Lopes didn't reply. He knew Costa was right but still, he checked the holster tucked under his jacket, ensuring he could draw his weapon quickly if needed. That he had it at all said so much; he hated carrying a gun, he was, after all, the famous unarmed Inspector Lopes, late of the Portuguese police.

Sometimes though, there was a need to carry one. Like now. He and Costa would be even less popular with some dangerous people after tonight.

If it went as expected.

If they weren't targets already.
If they hadn't been set up.

He stared out into the darkness again, straining his eyes to see something. In his imagination, he could picture men stealthily moving down the hill, guns raised, shotguns to bring himself and Costa down, pistols to finish them off. Their men were too far away to help. The little PPK would be of little use if this *was* a trap.

Costa also peered around the wall of the farmhouse. 'I can hear something, sir. It sounds like a truck.'

Lopes could hear nothing over the sound of the waves crashing into the rocks surrounding the little cove, but he trusted Costa was right; a good 15 years younger, his hearing would pick up much that Lopes would miss.

'Good. Ready the signal.'

'Sir.'

Lopes looked down towards the cove and the sea. If the information *was* right then there should be *something* waiting there, a boat certainly, but the informant had said U-Boat. It was dark, of course, yesterday had been the new moon, and that was certainly why tonight had been chosen; conditions where it was easier to come in unseen by the casual observer. But Lopes was *not* a casual observer, he *was* looking for it and yet he could see nothing.

It was puzzling. And unsettling. It was more suggestive of a double-cross.

He could now hear the truck. It *was* coming.

A few seconds later it bumped past them in low gear as it descended the rough track to the cove.

'Wait until they stop, Costa,' he whispered unnecessarily as his assistant knew what to do.

As if on cue, the engine noise abruptly ceased. Straining his eyes he could just make out men getting out of the cab. A torch flickered on and off. That would be the signal and the last thing Lopes wanted was to face a landing party as well, and not just because of the extra firepower - he was under strict instructions to avoid a diplomatic incident.

'Now, Costa, now!'

Costa raised the 'Very' pistol to the sky and pulled the trigger. A green flare shot into the air. At the same time, he blew a whistle hard.

Lopes had his expected reaction; a clutch of fear in his gut and he knew why. It wasn't the current potential danger; it was a throwback memory to going over the top from the trenches that always started with that soundtrack.

Costa's whistle was answered by others from the brushland below. There were shouts, a couple of shots, then more yells.

The firing stopped.

'Come on, Costa,' said Lopes, drawing his pistol.

It took a couple of minutes to reach the truck, and by the time they did so it was over. Four men were lying face down, and around them were a score of well-armed men, a mix of soldiers and police. One looked up at the sound of footsteps, and a torch was shone into their faces. Lopes shielded his eyes.

'Put that light down, boy, it's the boss.'

The light moved down.

'Any problems, Sergeant?' asked Lopes.

The squad leader shook his head. 'Not really, sir. They pulled guns on us, but they soon changed their minds when they saw they were outnumbered and outgunned'

'Good. Have you checked their load?' Lopes walked to the back of the truck. The sergeant went with him and pulled back the canvas.

'A few tonnes of high-grade wolframite, sir, all ready for Hitler.'

'You're a dead man, Lopes,' growled one of the men on the ground. 'We know who you are and… '

The man grunted in pain as a soldier kicked him in the ribs.

Lopes turned back to the truck. Another threat, not the first he'd encountered. It didn't bother him much, but Costa was a different matter. The lad had a family, a wife to support. And he was Costa, his friend.

But this was their job. It was what they had accepted.

'Right, let's get… What the?'

The flash had lit up the sky.

A few seconds later a dull roar of an explosion rumbled over them.

Lopes became aware of Costa standing alongside him, staring out to sea as he himself was doing.

'What was that, sir?' he said.

'I guess now we know where our U-Boat went to,' murmured Lopes. He pointed. 'There was a ship there. It went down quickly.'

'Torpedo?'

'Looks like it.'

'Why did they do that, sir?'

'I don't know, but I'm guessing it must have been more important than picking up two tons of ore. And it probably means a lot of trouble for us, Costa,' Lopes murmured. 'One hell of a lot in fact.'

CHAPTER 3

22nd OCTOBER 1941 - 1035 HRS
Costa looked up from his desk.

'Morning, sir. Did you see the news? It was a British ship that was sunk. It's all over the morning papers.'

Lopes nodded and sat down at his desk. 'There's going to be hell to pay for this, the British will be furious. In fact, I'm surprised that... '

The telephone on Costa's desk rang. Lopes gave a little chuckle. 'Right on cue,' he smiled.

Costa answered it. 'Yes, yes, I'll tell him.' He put the receiver down and was about to speak but Lopes was already on his feet.

'Oliveira's office?' he asked.

Costa returned his grim smile. 'Yes, sir. He wants to see you right away.'

Lopes gave a resigned sigh. 'Hopefully, I'll be able to keep us on the cases we've already got and not add to our workload.' He paused at the door. 'But don't count on it,' he added.

*

'Lopes. Sit down.'

Oliviera was wearing his distracted, put-up face that Lopes was getting used to. It meant his immediate superior was being put under pressure. And if the Tenente was being pressed for action, that meant Lopes was going to be too.

'You heard what happened last night?' Oliveira said even before Lopes had settled into his chair. 'The ship?' He pointed at the morning newspaper on the desk in front of him.

'British, I understand?' Lopes replied. 'Carrying wolfram?'

'Do you honestly think I'd mention it if it was a tramp steamer carrying coal?'

Lopes didn't react to Oliveira's sarcasm.

'I imagine the British are quite annoyed,' he said.

'They are fuming, The ship was torpedoed by a U-Boat just outside our territorial waters and was the only one sunk last night,' Oliveira said.

'Ah, I see.'

'Exactly,' said Oliveira. 'It means it's likely the ship was specifically targeted. They knew it was there, and they want to know how. They want action. Their ambassador demanded to see the Prime Minister this morning. Dr Salazar had to make an excuse. He was forced to fob him off with the Defence Secretary who explained that the German ambassador had assured him that no U-boats were operating within 50 kilometres of Portuguese waters and... '

'Which is hogwash.'

'... and that the explosion must have been caused by carelessness on the ship.'

'Also, rubbish.'

'Of course. The British were not satisfied and... '

'With not seeing Salazar. or with the explanation?' asked Lopes.

Oliveira glared at him. 'Lopes, I am your superior. I would thank you to remember that and not keep interrupting me if you know what's good for you.'

And I should remind you, Tenente, that you know, and I know that you are little more than a messenger boy, thought Lopes, but kept silent.

Oliveira gave up waiting for a conciliatory reply. 'They are not satisfied with anything. Not with the German explanation, but they expected that, nor with the response of the Estado Novo. They know information has been passed to the Abwehr and they are not going to be satisfied until they get to the bottom of the leak.' Oliveira stared straight at Lopes. 'Which is one of the reasons why you are here.'

Lopes met his stare and returned it with interest. It was as expected.

'How is this our problem? This is an issue that only concerns the British,' he said.

'You're not that naive, Lopes, so don't pretend you are.'

'And what about my job, Tenente? The one you gave me. Disrupting the local organised crime gangs moonlighting into unlicensed wolfram smuggling for the highest bidder and killing each other at the slightest excuse, remember? The one you said had the highest priority for Portugal's security and its standing as a neutral state? Has that changed?'

Oliveira scowled at Lopes. 'Of course not,' he replied. 'But this is even more important, and it's not as simple as you say. I wish to damnation that it was. The British are convinced that there is something more sinister going on. They think there is a fully trained agent operating in Lisbon.'

Lopes shrugged. 'I'm sure there is, in fact, more than one and not just German ones, Tenente. The city is full of them. Anyway, a fully trained agent is unnecessary. Essentially, the problem lies in Britain's own hands.'

'How?'

'Simply stop their Tars visiting the brothels. Or rather stop them from visiting one particular brothel, the one financed by the Germans where the girls earn extra escudos for reporting back the poor sods' pillow talk. Or at least get them to keep their mouths shut and their minds on the job at hand.'

'Our Prime Minister disagrees,' said Oliveira. 'He does not want to upset the delicate balance he has worked so hard to achieve between the British and the Germans regarding wolfram exports, and this threatens it.'

'As does the organised crime problem,' Lopes remarked. 'If you put me on other things, how does that get tackled?'

'You're always singing the praises of your assistant. Costa can continue your work. He has to earn his pay somehow now.'

'You mean now he's not spying on me for you.'

Lopes cursed himself for letting his mask slip and showing that Oliveira was getting to him. The satisfaction on the Tenente's face was obvious.

17

'Watch yourself, Lopes. You may have Dr Salazar's approval for now, but that protection does not extend to your assistant. Remember Costa's got a family to support.'

There was no point holding back. Lopes was on his feet.

'You didn't care a jot about him or his wife and daughters when you were willing to let him bleed to death in May. And, Oliveira, you know, if he goes, I go too.'

'Yes, you can go but it's easier for you. You've got your wife's money to fall back on, don't you? He doesn't.'

'That may be so but don't think you'd escape the consequences if I go. I can't imagine you lasting long when your actions reach Salazar's ears.'

Oliveira rose to his feet, so the two men were facing each other over the desk.

'Don't you dare threaten me, Lopes.'

'Why not? You're threatening me.'

Lopes was pushing things, he knew that, but there was no going back now. He thought about what he'd turned down in May, a life with Elena in the States. That seemed ever more appealing now and even more remote. If he were to be dismissed today, he would not enjoy a new life with his lover. Instead, it would be a lonely, internal exile, reviled by the state.

He was going too far.

Fortunately, it was Oliveira who blinked first.

'Enough,' he muttered, sitting back down. 'This is getting us nowhere and it's unnecessary. All Dr Salazar is asking of you is to meet with the British and listen to what they have to say, to be seen to be looking into their claims, nothing more.'

Lopes also sat back down. 'That's all?' he said. 'Then why put Costa on my work?'

'Because, as I said, this was only one of the reasons I called you in. There is another job the Prime Minister wants you to do.'

Oh God, thought Lopes. 'What?'

'The Doctor is unhappy about a certain organisation which is now operating in this country. He wants it closed down.'

Lopes frowned. 'Organisation? Which one?'

'The AMR. Have you heard of it?'

Lopes thought. 'I don't think so. What is it? Some political movement?'

'In a way, it is the Apoio a Mulheres Refugiadas. As the name suggests, it assists women refugees.'

'What? How is a refugee organisation political? And why does Salazar want it closed down?'

'Dr Salazar believes it to be anti-Portuguese.'

'How exactly?'

'It is an affront to family values.'

'How?'

'For one thing, it encourages and helps these women into work.'

'So?'

'Some of it is illegal and immoral work.'

'But... '

'And it also employs lawyers to defend women in actions against Portuguese citizens.'

Lopes was genuinely puzzled as to why this was an issue but then understood. 'Ah, you mean defending women against attacks by our citizens? And let me guess, most of the attacks are by our men?'

'Innocent family men who've fallen foul of the wicked ways of these foreign women'.

'Pah! Wicked ways...really?'

'Lopes, you've been given your instructions. Now, go and carry them out.'

'But I'm not political. I deal with crimes. I don't do jobs like that.'

A sardonic smile played on Oliveira's face.

'You work for us now. That makes you political. We say what a crime is. As for you, Lopes, you're also used to dealing with the fairer sex. I'm guessing Dr Salazar thought you'd be the perfect person to investigate a group of troublesome females.'

Lopes stayed silent. He wasn't going to rise to that particular fly. Oliveira waited, Lopes was sure he had prepared some smart comment about his complex love life and the affair with Elena. At last, his superior tired of waiting, commenced on a more conciliatory track.

'Lopes, you were chosen because this needs both your policing skills and your contacts. We need to know who is behind this. It also requires someone with tact and patience.' He looked shrewdly at Lopes. 'Would you rather someone from Da Souza's old crew, do it? Because they are the second choice.'

'No, I wouldn't. But these women surely need help.'

'Your country needs help, Lopes. It needs protecting.'

'From helpless refugee women?'

'From myriad outside forces including fascism, communism and a thousand other movements that challenge our way of life. These overseas women with their lax morals and dangerous fashions are already causing problems.' He nodded at the newspaper on his desk. 'There was another killing last night. This man they're calling the 'Hemline Killer' has struck again.'

'Are you seriously suggesting that these poor women are to blame for being butchered.'

'Of course it's their fault. The way they dress, the things they do. Totally unlike Portuguese womanhood. They bring it on themselves, and their malign influence is turning the heads of young, impressionable local girls. You experienced this influence yourself earlier this year, didn't you?'

Lopes's restraint vanished.

'That s none of your damned business, and as for blaming the women for this...' Lopez shook his head. 'That's disgusting.'

Oliveira opened his hands wide. 'This is out of my hands, Lopes. I have been instructed to give you these two tasks; placate the British and investigate and close down the AMR. These are your orders. You know the alternative for you and your assistant.'

Lopes took a few seconds to think. This might not be as bad as he thought; a single meeting with the British, maybe he'd have to produce a brief, desultory follow-up report, and, as for the AMR investigation, it wouldn't be difficult to give the impression of progress without actually doing very much. Still, he ought to go through the motions of protesting.

'So now I have three jobs.'

'That should be nothing for a man of your abilities, Lopes. A little diplomacy with your English friend and looking for some troublesome women. Right up your street.' He smiled.

'And shall we say you should report on your progress on the AMR matter, what, every day at 4 pm?'

Lopes's smile faded. His idea of procrastination until the problem had gone away had now vanished. He shook his head. 'I'll never get any work done on anything if I have to come here every day. How about once a week?'

'We'll settle on every other day then. As for the British, I've arranged for you to see Armstrong at their Embassy at 11 o'clock' He looked at his watch. 'Which is in precisely 35 minutes. Plenty of time for you to get there.'

Oliveira rose. The interview was over.

And Lopes had again been railroaded into an impossible situation.

He swore on the way out of Oliveira's office. Working for the PVDE was a gift that went on giving.

CHAPTER 4

22nd OCTOBER 1941 - 1145 HRS

Lopes checked his watch. He had been late, but had now been kept waiting even longer. Was that deliberate? Possibly, but as the British had asked - no not asked, demanded - this meeting, then probably not. What was there to gain from it? Still, Lopes found the waiting irritating.

He was, at least, comfortable. He'd been in this room a few times before. For a waiting room it was exquisite, exuding the feel of a gentleman's study. To one side was a small dining table with four elegant chairs set around it. Bookshelves lined the room, and the gold leaf of the titles on the spines glinted in the autumn sunshine streaming in through the tall, south-facing windows. A crystal chandelier hung from the ceiling over three comfortable armchairs set up to invite convivial conversation. To complete the décor, an Ormolu clock ticked loudly on the mantelpiece above the fireplace. The contrast with Lopes' own office in the basement of the PVDE couldn't be more marked. He and Costa had no comforts, not even a window.

Finally the door opened, and Armstrong strode in. He looked surprised.

'Lopes,' he said, looking puzzled. 'I was expecting...' He paused, then shook his head. 'Oh, never mind.'

'You were expecting someone more senior?' said Lopes. 'I'm sorry, you've got me.'

Armstrong pulled a face. 'I was hoping that your government would take this matter more seriously. It's crystal clear that our ship, the 'Norman Gibson,' was targeted deliberately. A wolfram shipment rarely leaves Lisbon, yet the German Navy knew. God knows how they had a U-boat so close in though.' He sighed, 'Sorry, Lopes, that wasn't meant as a personal insult to you. It's just...well, we're locked in a life-or-death struggle with these bastards and when things like this happen...'

Lopes nodded. 'That's alright. It wasn't taken as an insult and, as for why the U-boat was so close, I think I can answer that.'

Armstrong frowned. 'You can?'

'Yes, it was there to pick up a smuggled load of wolframite from a cove north of Estoril. We seized the gang after a tip-off last night but there was no sign of the pick-up. I did wonder why at the time. Well, now we know.'

Armstrong nodded slowly. 'Because they were called away to a better offer. That's the first bit of good news we've had. It means that the agent, whoever they are, are only getting information from the sailors and not someone deeper in the supply chain.'

'Doesn't that mean that the problem is simply to do with loose lips by your sailors in the brothels? Surely that's simply down to keeping your men out of them, or at least getting them to keep their mouths shut?'

Armstrong shook his head. 'I wish it were that simple. Certainly, we do have a problem there, but, no, this is something more sophisticated.'

Lopes couldn't hide his doubts. 'Really? Isn't that a little, how do I put this delicately, paranoid?'

'No, the level of information gathered and how quickly it was relayed suggests that a trained agent is at work – someone who is used to extracting the maximum from the subject as well as targeting the right individuals.'

'Oh, come on, this is just one ship, one load.'

Armstrong remained impassive. 'Take my word for it, it's more than that.'

Lopes shook his head. 'I think you should tell me what you know and not hold anything back, if you want our help, of course.'

Armstrong took a deep breath and then exhaled slowly whilst he thought. 'Alright. We've had an intelligence report that gave us a warning last month that just such an agent had been sent to Lisbon. Last night's events were the first proof that the intelligence was correct.'

'What intelligence? What was the source?'
'That I can't tell you because, to be honest, I don't know. Not even the ambassador is given that information. It is reliable though. London assures us of that.'
'Alright, I'll have to take that on trust. The question is, what do you want us to do about it?'
Armstrong looked amazed. 'Well, find them, of course! What else?'
'Why?'
'I thought that was obvious. They're causing ships to be sunk.'
'British ships?'
'Yes.'
'Then this is just a British problem. Look, Armstrong,' Lopes held up his hands to forestall further argument. 'I realise what you're going to say about this issue risks upsetting the balance of power in the Nazi's favour, but you must realise our powers are limited. I'm not sure that any crime has been committed on our soil. How can an arrest be made?'
'You're the PVDE. You don't need a crime to arrest people.'
'You've been talking to Oliveira, I see.' Lopes muttered. He stared at Armstrong for a few moments then gave a little laugh. 'Alright, that's true but...' Lopes stopped. This discussion could go round in circles without getting anywhere, arguing that Portugal was neutral and not an ally of Great Britain was both true and a lie at the same time. It was time to bring this interview to an end so he could get back to his proper work. He would offer Armstrong something. 'I'll ask some questions of my former and current colleagues to see if we can find this person.' He took out his notebook. 'Can you give me a description?'
'No, sorry.'
'What?'
'We have no idea what they look like.'
Lopes sighed. 'Nationality?' Armstrong shook his head. 'Do you even know their sex?'
Armstrong shrugged. 'Probably female,' he said.

25

Lopes closed his eyes and muttered. 'God, give me strength,' to himself.

At that moment there was a knock on the door. 'Come,' called Armstrong.

It was a young man, presumably one of Armstrong's staff. 'Sorry to bother you, sir, but the survivor has arrived. You said you wanted to speak to him.'

'Indeed, pray ask him to wait outside. I've nearly finished with the inspector here.' Armstrong turned back to Lopes. 'You'll have to excuse me; I do need to chat to this chap while everything's fresh in his mind. I doubt he'll know anything but it's worth a try.'

'Is he the only survivor?'

Armstrong nodded. 'I'm afraid so. He was lucky, he was picked up by a fishing boat within half an hour. They were a couple of miles away and saw the explosion. I understand he's shaken up, naturally, but physically he's alright.' Armstrong stood and held out his hand. 'I'm sorry I've not given you much to go on but, we'd be very grateful if you could find something.'

Lopes also stood but didn't shake Armstrong's hand. 'Wouldn't it be better if I stayed to hear what he has to say? It might help my investigation.'

Armstrong shook his head. 'No, I want him to meet him alone. If he says anything useful, I'll pass it on.'

Lopes understood the reason; Armstrong's instinct for secrecy. He was a diplomat in name only, Lopes could only guess at the man's real job. He rose, shook hands and then allowed himself to be guided out.

In the hallway was a boy, well at least he looked like a boy, Lopes put him at 15 or 16 at most, dressed in old, tatty, and mismatched clothes. This had to be the survivor, a man-boy, cast into the sea and lost everything but his life. He looked shattered; the lad had the hundred metre stare Lopes had seen so often in Flanders. His heart went out to the young man.

'Mr Jenkins. May I call you Edward?' asked Armstrong. 'You poor chap, what an ordeal you must have had. Come through so we can talk. Can I get you some tea?'

Armstrong led the young man into the meeting room. 'I'll expect to hear from you in due course, Lopes,' he said, as he closed the door.

Lopes nodded to himself. Another impossible job.

CHAPTER 5

22nd OCTOBER 1941 – 1425 HRS

I wondered where you'd got to, sir,' said Costa with a wry smile, after Lopes had explained where he'd been.

'Well, now you know.' Lopes sighed. 'Hopefully, both of these jobs will be temporary. I'm sure they just expect me to be seen to be doing something and that will be enough.'

'I hope so, sir." Costa was opening letters sent down to their department from the mail room, The correspondence had all been previously opened - the PVDE liked to keep an eye on their personnel and their contact with the outside world - but it was an important part of their current operations, much to Lopes' distaste.

Most of the letters were from informers. This was what Portugal had become under Salazar and the PVDE; a nation of snoopers, of whispers, of tittle-tattle, of informing on your neighbours, of gossip, of criticism of the state, or the police, sometimes the leader himself. Some was done for reward; despite the economic improvements made by the Estado Novo and the boost that the spike in prices for wolfram that the country was benefitting from because of the war, Portugal was still beset with poverty and a few escudos received from the state in exchange for snippets of information was very welcome. Most, though, was done out of fear. Failing to pass on what you knew could, and often was, punished.

Much of the information was useless, but even Lopes had to admit that some wasn't. Some of their best leads had come from these letters. Still, it was still distasteful, and he was happy to leave the task of wading through them to Costa.

'Anything worthwhile today?' he asked, pressing tobacco into his pipe.

'No not really.' Costa frowned deeply at a letter, then screwed it up and threw it in the wastepaper bin.

'What was that?'

'Nothing, sir.'

'It didn't look like nothing.' Lopes put his pipe down, rose, and walked over to the bin. He removed the screwed-up letter and opened it up, 'Ah, another threat.'

'Yes, sir.'

'It mentions you by name, Costa.'

'And you too, sir,' shrugged Costa. 'So why bother about it? We get at least one a day.'

'You can't just ignore them; they should be reported.

Costa sighed. 'What's the point, sir? I used to, but nothing ever happened, either from the powers-that-be or to us. I just throw them away now.'

'But Costa…'

'I know, sir, but it is what it is. We're interfering with a business that makes serious money. Wolfram has become like gold. When we seize a shipment, it hurts the crime bosses.'

'But…'

'Threats are part of the job, sir.' Costa opened his jacket to show his pistol. 'You know I always carry this. Perhaps you should do the same.'

Lopes stared at the gun, then glanced down at the desk where his own Walther PPK sat in the drawer. He'd put it back that morning, after the raid up in Estoril. Maybe Costa was right, but he'd managed his entire career without carrying it. 'Perhaps I should, Alvares, but... well, you know my feelings. I just don't feel comfortable carrying one all the time.'

'I'd feel better if you would, sir.'

'And I'd feel better if you dropped the sir, Alvares. I think by now we're beyond that. It's Dinis or Lopes, whatever you prefer.'

Costa smiled. 'I know, but I prefer sticking with the 'sir', sir. It feels more comfortable.'

'Touche, Costa, Touche.' Lopes returned Costa's smile. 'Right, let's get the report written up on last night's events and then we can get you back to your family. You deserve some time with them after last night's late finish.'

'Thank you, sir.'

*

After Costa, reluctantly, had gone, Lopes headed up the stairs to, also reluctantly, carry out investigations connected with his two new jobs; finding out about the AMR and looking for the needle in a haystack that was the possible German agent. That meant dealing with both sides of an organisation which he'd rather not go anywhere near; the PVDE itself. The AMR would be in the domain of the domestic/political side of the organisation, the spy would fall into the remit of the international section.

This meant he would be treading on several sets of toes. He anticipated there was going to be a lot of resistance.

He wasn't wrong.

He tried the section head of the domestic side first; and ran straight into his first roadblock.

'Yeah, we know who you are,' he was told when he introduced himself. 'A bloody joke.' There was laughter in the room.

Lopes persisted. 'I'd like to see Sargente Diaz.'

'I'd like to see Marlene Dietrich in my bed, but I've got as much chance of that as you have of seeing the boss.'

'But...'

'Look,' said one of the others. 'Just accept it, Lopes. You're not welcome here and you're not going to get any help from us.'

Lopes decided to play his trump card. 'I've been told to investigate the AMR on the instructions of Dr Salazar himself.'

Instead of help, he received even more laughter.

'Fuck off, Lopes.'

'Bring the doctor with you next time and we might let you see our files. Probably not though. Now sod off.'

Lopes didn't get much further with the international section. He did at least get a hearing, but the reaction was similar.

'What? You haven't got a name, you don't know what they look like, you don't know their sex, you don't know whether there's an agent at all, do you?'

Lopes nodded. 'No,' he admitted.

The PVDE agent shook his head. 'This isn't worth wasting our time on, Lopes. And why are you looking into this anyway? This isn't in your remit, but it most certainly is in ours. If there's an issue, a serious issue, the bosses would have come to us, wouldn't they?' The section chief sat back in his chair with a condescending, self-satisfied smirk on his face. 'Doesn't that tell you a lot about your worth, Lopes? I almost feel sorry for you. You're what they wheel out when the State wants to be seen to be doing something.' He looked at his watch. 'It's getting late. I've got real work to finish.'

So that was that for cooperation.

Lopes resignedly headed down to the archives. He wasn't at all surprised by his reception; indeed it was what he expected, especially as many of Da Souza's allies were still active and resented Lopes - more than resented, hate would be closer to the mark, associating Lopes and Costa with their leader's fall. Lopes was sure that many suspected him of Da Souza's murder, which, of course, they were right to do. Lopes could live with that; he didn't regret Da Souza's execution[1].

It was still depressing how little help he was getting. This was an impossible job. Once again, he'd had shit shovelled onto him. He was getting heartily sick of it. At least the archives couldn't speak and add to the verbal derision. They were a last resort for help within the PVDE itself though because they were, by nature, out of date. If records had been archived it meant they contained stale information. He doubted that they'd provide much in the way of help.

They didn't.

But, also, in a way, they did.

He was searching for information related to the AMR rather than the spy as there was little point in looking in the archives. Armstrong's implication was the agent had only been active for a short time. If there were files on them in the PVDE they would still be active and located in the international section. Regarding the AMR, the influx of refugees had been ongoing since the war began, but it had peaked in May and June of the previous year. It was likely that the AMR had been established during that time, and if it had, there would be files on it. However, there were none. This suggested that the AMR had been set up very recently, within the last few months. Interesting. It was also, Lopes reflected, impressive that Dr Salazar knew about them already. The leader of the country's ability to keep tabs on the smallest detail in society was renowned. Salazar had a reputation for this. Judging by the AMR, this reputation was well-earned.

He checked his watch. It was getting close to 10 pm. More than enough for one day.

Wearily, he returned the last of the files to the archivist and headed for the door.

CHAPTER 6

22nd OCTOBER 1941 - 2213 HRS

Lopes stepped off the tram at his regular stop and began the long trudge up the hill towards his house. It had rained sometime that evening and, although the weather had improved, the jagged stone pavements typical of the city were slick and treacherous.

He hardly noticed that he was treading carefully; it was second nature to all Lisboas. This was useful, as his thoughts were elsewhere.

As was his habit, he'd used his tram journey to think through his work. He'd done this throughout his years in the police, thinking through his cases. Now he had a pair of them, both difficult, both unwelcome, neither of which he felt were up to him to solve, one because it wasn't the responsibility or concern of the Portuguese state but a problem for the British, and one he morally disagreed with. Could he make enough progress with both to keep his superiors happy whilst not actually solving either? Possibly, but how?

He'd tried to find evidence for the possible spy. He'd asked around the PVDE. Sure, he'd got nowhere. but he'd tried. The British would not be happy but tough, he'd tried. The more important question was would Oliveira be satisfied? Probably not but, again, tough. He'd tried.

So that left the AMR, which led him to a train of thought he didn't like. About refugee women.

One particular refugee woman.

Dark haired, dark eyed. Petite. Attractive.

'Get out of my head, Elena. I need to think,' he muttered.

He had to show evidence that he'd at least tried with regard to this case, but how was he going to find out anything about them if the active PVDE investigations were closed to him and the archives were of no use?

The answer was obvious; it was in what Olivera had said about them paying lawyers to defend the women against Portuguese men. That meant there would have to be a complaint made to the police from the woman who had been assaulted. That would create a paper trail that he could follow, including identifying the lawyers the AMR used.

So, there was his next port of call for the job he didn't want to do. He needed to talk to his old colleagues in the police. A place where he was as popular as he was within the PVDE.

Lopes sighed. He was at the bottom of the last hill that led up to his house. He should go home. It was part of the agreement he had with his wife. It kept up appearances for the neighbours that everything was fine in the marriage, that he kept normal hours - or what passed for normal in the PVDE - and wasn't staying away. He owed her that.

And yet.

He sighed to himself. Nothing good awaited him up there. He looked down the hill, towards the light. Down there would be sailors, merchant seamen from all nations eager to spend their money, and where the bars and women were equally as eager to relieve them of it. As well as German agents hungry for snippets of value to the axis. The sailors probably didn't care. Who was bothered if they were robbed blind if, for a few hours, they lived, and laughed and loved and forgot about facing the next sailing through U-boat infested seas?

Lopes could do with forgetting as well. And he could justify it as work. He took one last look back up the hill. He should go home. But it wasn't inviting. It wasn't truly home. He turned back towards the town. Time to investigate, and maybe, just maybe, forget.

He paused. Something was bothering him. What was it? Lopes didn't dismiss the feeling; his instincts had served him well in his years on the beat. He looked back up the hill straining his eyes against the darkness, trying to make out the frontage of his house. There was nothing he could see that caused him alarm but still, he lingered for a few seconds longer before turning back and walking towards the city's bars.

He tried but could not quite dismiss his feeling of unease.

A drink might help.

CHAPTER 7

23rd OCTOBER 1941 - 0045 HRS

The drink was helping, as was simply being out and around the city's bars in the small hours.

Yesterday, if he'd been asked, he would have said he knew all the bars and cafés. This was his patch. The majority, the more presentable side of the social scene, were familiar haunts. As for the more risqué, sometimes illegal establishments, the gambling dens, and brothels, they had been a huge part of his working life; many of the crimes he investigated happened in them, but now he admitted that the truth was that his knowledge was just like those PVDE records; stale.

The war had changed things. It supercharged the experience and intensified and extended the demand and need for entertainment and escape. New places in all the categories from bars to brothels had opened up across the city but especially in the usual hotspots; the Barrio Alto closest to the docks and where Alfama met the grander buildings in the centre. And despite the increased numbers of places, everywhere was crowded and the streets packed with bodies - men in the main, but some women amongst them - shuffling, singing, laughing, bouncing off the walls as they moved from place to place.

Lopes knew why this expansion had taken place; Lisbon was the last major city in the continent of Europe south of Stockholm that still had its lights on, where people could party freely. Even the big Spanish cities that shared the peninsular, Madrid and Barcelona were not like the Queen of the Seas because they had been wrecked and been left economically destitute by their fratricidal war. Lisbon was a breath of free, fresh air in a continent blighted by the clouds of war. But it was more than that; Lisbon was wealthy now; it had become a focus of the world in conflict because of wolfram.

Lopes drank some more of his beer, alone on a stool squeezed next to a table full of Danish sailors loudly carousing the night away and making plans for where they would go next, which seemed to focus on which cat house they would visit.

He reflected on another truth that had been, at first, hard to accept but became blindingly obvious as the night progressed; the changes had been a surprise to him because he'd got old and had left all of this behind long ago.

When was the last time he'd been out like this? Three years? Five? Yes, sure, he'd gone to enjoy Fado but the art form that had grown out of Lisbon's' working, striving, struggling poor was no longer that. It had become gentile, an entertainment for the middle-class pseudo-intellectuals. Like Lopes himself. He'd lost touch, and he was getting old. Maybe that was why Elena appealed so much to him. She was young, and being with him was good for his ego. It told him that he still had it.

He closed his eyes. No, it wasn't that, at least he hoped it wasn't. There was a lot more about Elena, an awful lot more than her youth. She was fierce in every way; fiercely vital, fierce of temper, fierce and confident in her lovemaking, yet combined all that with a beguiling vulnerability. That was why he loved her.

Loved? He'd never admitted that before, but he knew it was the truth.

'You old fool, Lopes,' he muttered. 'She was using you like she used Vogel.'

'Hey, darling, why you look so sad?'

The words, spoken in English, though with the intonations of a native Portuguese speaker, were accompanied by a wave of perfume.

Lopes opened his eyes to find he was staring into a pair of gentle brown ones set in a small, almost elfin face. The woman's skin was so golden-brown it almost glowed and her hair was a mass of jet-black curls. The woman's beauty was enough to make his heart thump hard.

He was not alone in this.

'Hey, love,' said one of the Danes in heavily accented English. 'Leave that bloke, come and sit with us. We'll give you a good time.'

This was accompanied by ribald laughter and comments in their native tongue from his table companions.

'Fuck off,' she said. 'I'm talking with my friend here. He's about to buy me a drink, aren't you darling?' she added, plonking herself on Lopes' lap.

He was going to protest, was going to tell her to give the Danish sailors a break, to explain, nicely, that he wasn't interested and, anyway, had not paid for sex since he was a teenage soldier in France but her light, lithe body reminded her too much of a certain person and his senses responded accordingly.

'See,' she said. 'I knew you'd like me, Captain.' She smiled coyly. 'Now about that drink you were getting me.'

'Of course,' said Lopes. 'What can I get you? I'm sorry, I don't know your name.'

'Angel; my name's Angel,' she replied, shuffling to one side to let the still-grumbling sailors pass as they left to go to pastures new. 'And I'll have a Martini.'

'There's a seat free now,' said Lopes nodding toward the vacant table and then signalling to the barman who was already pulling out a cocktail shaker. Lopes realised she had to be a regular, as he knew the drink she had ordered. He knew even more clearly now that this was unwise, but her squirming body reminded him how long it had been and also what that had led to last time.

'You want to get rid of me already?' she said. 'Don't you like me?' she threw her arms around his neck and nuzzled his neck. The drink arrived and Angel stayed. The vacant table was not empty for long; a group of British merchantmen took it, casting envious eyes towards Lopes and the woman on his lap.

'Of course I like you,' said Lopes.

'So,' said Angel, sipping her drink. 'How long is your ship in port, Captain?'

Lopes was momentarily puzzled but then put it all together. She assumed he was another merchantman. 'You've got it wrong, I... ' he began.

'Ana Maria! What are you doing?'

The voice was youthful, there was hurt in it, and despite the clamour in the bar, carried quite clearly over it all.

Angel turned her head and was instantly on her feet and away, heading, not to the street, but out the back of the bar.

'Ana Maria, wait!'

The young man was pushing his way through the bodies, not caring who he shoved. Lopes recognised him, he was the lad from the British Embassy.

'Hey, watch it!'

'Who do you think you're pushing?'

The lad was wading into deep trouble, Lopes could see that. To add to the shipwreck he was going to get a beating to his misfortune if he went on.

'Get out of my way. Ana!'

Despite the beer he'd put back, Lopes shifted into police mode. He took his badge out and moved towards the fray.

'Easy, Easy,' he yelled in English, 'Police, settle down now or I'll arrest the lot of you.'

'Who the fuck do you think…?'

One sailor had angrily turned to confront Lopes, but his mate, who looked a little more sober, took a good look at the badge and dragged the protester away.

'Sorry officer, I've got him,' he said, and whispered something in the other man's ear that sounded awfully like, 'He's Gestapo. Look at the fuckin' badge, you idiot!'

In the meantime, the barman, obviously used to trouble, grabbed the young man with the help of another local.

'Get off me! Get your hands…'

Lopes had now remembered his name. 'Edward, Edward, stop.' He held the badge up to the barman and then to the young man. 'Steady lad, it won't do you any good if you get arrested, will it? Will it?' The young man looked beside himself with anguish and was barely listening. 'Edward,' Lopes repeated. 'That's your name, isn't it?'

'Yes,' said Edward. 'How did you…?'

'I was at the Embassy this morning when you came in,' Lopes grasped the young man by his shoulders and shook him. 'Look at me! Come on, look. Do you recognise me?'

Edward struggled to focus on Lopes' face, suggesting he'd been drowning his sorrows for some time. At last, though, there was a spark of recognition.

42

'Yes. you were there,' he said. 'At the embassy.'
'That's right, good. Now come on, let's go, eh?' Lopes smiled warmly. 'Your lady friend has long gone. Let's move on, eh?' Lopes instantly knew he'd said the wrong thing.
'Ana Maria! You, she was on your knee.'
'Yes, but...' was all Lopes managed before Edward abruptly swung his fist at him. Lopes had no time to duck; his world suddenly went red, and the floorboards came up and hit him.
As he lay stunned, he heard police whistles.

CHAPTER 8

23rd OCTOBER 1941 - 0145 HRS

Lopes held the damp towel gently against his cheek, wincing in pain. It hurt more than he expected. Why hadn't he just gone home?

The door to the break room at the police station opened, and the duty sergeant peered inside. 'How are you feeling, boss? Any better?'

'A bit. Alex, a bit,' he answered.

The sergeant shook his head. 'Can't believe you got hit like that, boss. By a kid too. You're slipping.'

'A kid in love, Alex, a kid in love.' Lopes stood up and inspected his reflection on the glass of a picture of Antonio Salazar on the break room wall. He winced. He'd have a cracking shiner in the morning.

'The little sod got you good,' said the sergeant. 'But he'll pay for it in court.'

Lopes sighed and shook his head. 'There's no need for that. Let him go.'

'But he hit a cop!'

'An ex-cop, Alex, an ex-cop.' He touched his swollen face. The pain was easing. 'There's nothing hurt but my pride. I should have known better.'

Alex shook his head. 'There's a lot of things you should have known better. Like going in that place to begin with.'

Lopes was about to protest that he was on a case and was working, but he knew that wasn't the truth; he was there for his own reasons, even if he hadn't thought through what they were.

'Yeah, I know, you're right,' he muttered. 'But, whatever, the lad's young, he's only a kid and he's been through a hell of a lot. He deserves a break.'

'You want to let him go?' Lopes nodded; Alex puffed out his cheeks. 'On your head be it,' he said. He frowned, there was a commotion outside. 'What the hell's going on?' he muttered, 'Excuse me a moment.'

Alex was not gone long, he was straight back reaching for his cap and taking his gun and flashlight out of his desk drawer. 'Sorry, Dinis, looks like we've got another dead girl.'

'The 'Hemline Killer?'

'Dunno yet. but it's the right time for him. Mind you, I wouldn't give him any title other than bastard.' Alex checked the batteries in the torch and then looked at Lopes. 'Er, boss?'

'What, Alex?'

'You used to be in Homicide, didn't you?'

'Would you like me to come along, Alex?'

'Would you mind?' Alex looked relieved. 'I want to catch this sod and you've got the experience. Me and the lads do our best but…'

'No problem.' Lopes frowned. 'What about the murder squad? They have the experience.'

'Well, they aren't using it. When they turn up at least.'

'When they turn up? Does that mean sometimes they don't?' Alex's look said more than words could. 'Who's in charge of it now, I've lost touch.'

'Ribeiro. Need I say more?'

Lopes laughed. 'No. Alright, lead on.'

CHAPTER 9

23rd OCTOBER 1941 - 0215 HRS

Lopez knew a lot of the Barrio Alto but this was one area that he hadn't, to his recall, been in before.

It was dark, malodorous with the stench of rotting food and urine. Many of the houses were boarded up, and some looked on the point of collapse. It was not a place he would want to end up in. He was sure that the poor, bloodstained victim at his feet, illuminated in the light of their torches, had felt the same.

Next to him, Alex clearly agreed. 'The poor lass,' he said crossing himself. He reached out towards her eyes, intending to close them.

'No,' said Lopes sharply, slapping Alex's hand away. He immediately remembered who he was; yes, not a civilian but not a policeman anymore and apologised.

'That's alright,' said Alex. 'You're right. I should leave her just as she is until the murder squad gets here, right?'

'That's right, Alex.' Lopes checked his watch. 'Though they're taking their time about it, aren't they?'

'It's not unusual, I'm afraid,' sighed Alex.

Lopes frowned. 'They've been slacking lately? It's not that long ago that I left, and standards were good then. Surely Ribeiro hasn't made things that bad already?'

Alex shook his head. 'No. But they'll know from the time and place it's a low priority.'

'What? How can any murder be a low priority?'

'It's who she is.' He nodded at the dead woman. 'Or rather who she isn't. She isn't going to be some nice, Catholic, respectable Portuguese lady, is she? Not on these streets at this time of night. She's either a local whore or a foreigner, likely both. A refugee, That makes her a nobody.'

Lopes stared at his friend in astonishment. 'Bloody hell,' he muttered. He checked his watch again. Twenty past two. They'd been there 20 minutes or more already. 'Alright,' he said, 'Are you alright with us doing a preliminary look over ourselves?' he asked.

'Of course,' said Alex.

They turned their torches back on the body. Lopes still had his notebook on him, having not been home yet, so he took it out along with his pencil. 'Are you alright taking notes for me?' he asked Alex. 'I usually have an assistant with me, you see. It'll make examining the body and crime scene easier.'

'My writing's not the neatest but I'll do my best.'

Lopes handed over the book and pencil. 'So,' he said. 'The body is lying on its back propped up against the wall.' He knelt in front of the corpse. 'Her hands have been pressed together as if in prayer.' He gently reached his hand out and lifted the woman's chin. 'No rigor. She's still warm too. And her throat has been cut.' He caught a look at her face; she was older than he first thought, perhaps in her early 30s, handsome rather than classically pretty but there was one striking thing about her looks; her eyes were wide open and her pale blue irises displayed the pure terror of her final moments.

His heart went out to her. He was quite unable to speak for a few moments and he had to remind himself that he could best serve her by doing his job. He forced himself to give Alex her description. 'Fair hair, possibly bleached and dyed judging by the roots, which look a little darker. Eyes, blue, age 28 to 35 probably. Dressed in a skirt and blouse with stockings. Blouse has a label which…' He gently tipped the woman's head forward so he could see better. '…is from Le Marche.' He looked at Alex. 'That's a Parisian Department Store. Very fashionable.'

'Expensive?'

'They are usually the same thing, aren't they?' He looked at the blouse more carefully, trying to ignore the blood that soaked it. 'There are signs of repairs. She was proud of this blouse. She looked after it.'

He straightened up, his knees were protesting already. Getting older was not easy. That was something this woman wouldn't face.

Lopes flashed his torch around. 'No handbag, and nowhere on her to hold identity papers, but from her dress and appearance, I'd be willing to bet she was a refugee.'

'Most of this guy's victims are,' said Alex. 'And dressed like that too. Showing a lot of leg.'

Lopes looked at her again. To him, the woman's dress was quite modest but he was, perhaps, more cosmopolitan than most. He continued to look around.

'This appears to be a cut-through from the busier streets on either side.' He walked a little way from the body and crouched down to examine the ground. 'There are drag marks and...' he turned back and shone his torch on the body, then returned to peer closely at the woman's feet. 'It appears that one shoe has been jammed back onto the foot, probably after death.' He straightened up. 'Did you get all that, Alex?'

'Just about, I think.'

'She was dragged there after death and positioned in that way.'

'Yup,' said Alex, 'Most of them have been like this. She'll have a rosary bead in her hand, as all the other ones did. It's this guy's calling card.'

Lopes bit his lip, deep in thought. 'That's not been in the newspapers. That's good.'

'Why?'

Lopes smiled. 'Because it helps to find the person who didn't do it.' He saw Alex's puzzlement. 'You may find this hard to believe but with cases like this there's no shortage of people who walk into a police station claiming to be the killer.'

'Why on earth would they do that? They'd get life.'

'Who knows, Alex, who knows?' said Lopes 'Human beings can be stranger than most people can imagine.' He reached down and took the woman's hands and then opened them. Sure enough, a wooden bead rolled out into her lap. 'Yes, you were right,' said Lopes. 'And that little detail can be put to any of the misguided fools claiming fame and notoriety.' He checked his pockets but found nothing of use, so flashed his torch around the alley. 'Ah,' he said with satisfaction. There was a discarded newspaper in the weeds by a boarded-up door. He picked it up and took a double page from the centre, the cleanest part, tore it in half, then halved it again. Once he was satisfied he could pick the bead up without touching it with his fingers he reached towards it with the newspaper sheet and was able to examine it under the flashlight.

It was nothing exceptional, just an ordinary rosary bead worn smooth by years of prayers. 'It might have prints on it,' he muttered to himself. 'Probably not though, but it's worth trying.'

'What the bloody hell do you think you two bastards are doing? Get away from there, the pair of you.'

Lopes did not, at first, turn to meet the newcomer. He knew exactly who it was; Eduardo Ribeiro, arsehole of this parish. He made a show of carefully wrapping the bead before straightening to acknowledge the arrival of the homicide detective.

'Glad you could make it, Ribeiro,' he said. He flashed his torch around. Alongside Ribeiro was another detective Lopes vaguely recognised, plus a couple of men with a canvas stretcher. They'd be from the mortuary. 'And as for what we doing, I would say we were doing your job.'

'Fuck you, Lopes,' snapped Ribeiro. 'This is my case. You've no right to interfere. I should arrest you.' He turned angrily to Alex. 'You. It's Mendes, isn't it? Did you call him in?' He jabbed his finger at Lopes.

'Yes, that's right,' said Alex.

'You're a bloody idiot. You should know better,' said Ribeiro.

'Steady on, inspector,' said Alex. 'Dinis is an experienced detective. I thought... '

'You thought? You? You're a uniformed plod. That's getting way, way beyond what you're capable of.'

'Leave it, Alex,' sighed Lopes. 'As for arresting me, do you want to try?'

'Maybe I should, just to see what clout you have.' Ribeiro was right in Lopes' face now, so close he could smell brandy and cigarettes on the man's breath.

'Go on then, Eduardo, be my guest.'

He held out his wrists to be cuffed.

'Don't be so fucking childish,' grunted Ribeiro. He turned to look at the body. 'So who is she? Actually, don't bother, I can see she's some cheap foreign whore.' He straightened up. 'Alright, take her away.'

The assistants moved towards the body, but Lopes stood in front of them to block their path.

'Wait. What about photographing the scene?'

'Fuck that! What's the point?'

'The point? To record the murder scene.'

'What for?'

'To help catch the murderer, of course.'

'Catch them?' Ribeiro gave a bitter laugh. 'Really? How are a couple of snaps going to help? It's just a waste of time, a waste of *my* time to boot. Anyway, as far as I'm concerned whoever's doing this is doing us a favour by getting trash like this off the streets.' He turned to the waiting men. 'You have your orders, take her away.'

'Yes, boss.'

Alex, who was looking as cross as Lopes, moved to stop them but Lopes stopped him.

'Leave it,' he murmured. 'He's going to do it anyway, whether we cause trouble or not.'

Ribeiro was almost glowing with satisfaction. 'Good. Common sense at last. Perhaps you're finally learning.' He leant in close to Lopes. 'Doubt it though.'

'You're a disgrace, Ribeiro. You always were.'

'Sticks and stones, Lopes, sticks and stones. Remember I'm not the one that got the sack. I'm still a policeman. Come on men. Get a move on.'

Ribeiro's men had laid a stretcher on the ground next to the woman's body. Lopes had no desire to see her being manhandled.

'Come on, Alex. Let's get back.'

It was only when they had left the little alleyway far behind that he remembered the bead. He stopped, wondering whether he should take it back.

'What is it?' Alex said.

51

Lopes had already decided. If it was in his control he could do something with it. Once in Ribeiro's hands, it would probably end up in the fire. 'Nothing. Let's get back to the station. I don't know about you, but I could do with a hot drink.'

'Not sure about hot, but I could do with a stiff one.'

Lopes laughed, pushing the newspaper-wrapped bead more deeply into his pocket. 'Maybe we should have both, Alex,' he said. 'Lead on.'

CHAPTER 10

23rd OCTOBER 1941 - 0545 HRS

Alex reached for the bottle. 'Another one, Dinis?'

Lopes checked his watch and then groaned. 'Look at the time! I'm supposed to be in the office in a couple of hours.'

'You'll need another then,' laughed Alex, offering him the bottle.

'I'd better not... ' began Lopes, but Alex was already pouring. 'Just a small one then. Woah! Steady there.'

The two men sat back, glasses in hand. 'How many murders does this make?' said Lopes.

'Eight... I think it's eight anyway,' sighed Alex.

'You don't know?'

'I'm not sure all have been reported. We've had four of them on our patch, I'm sure there's been another three in Alfama and one just outside the docks themselves. The trouble is no one took much notice at first. To most, it was just another refugee who didn't matter. It was one less.'

Lopes stared at the golden liquid in the bottom of his glass, 'Seeing how Ribeiro treated it, that's no surprise.'

'Yeah, the good thing is it's in the newspapers now.' Alex shook his head ruefully. 'I can't believe I just said that. Normally I hate the press hanging around. They usually make our lives harder, but at least it's out in the open now. Maybe the powers-that-be will do something about it now. Dunno though, when the first story was splashed, all the command wanted to know was how the AMR had got the details of the killings.'

In the fuzzy haze fuelled as much by tiredness than by the brandies he'd downed in the last hour, it took a few moments for what Alex had said to register. 'The AMR? What did they have to do with it?'

Alex puffed out his cheeks and took another slug of brandy. 'What didn't they have to do with it?' he replied. 'As far as we can work out, they led the reporters to the story, provided crime scene photos, lists of victims, the works. God knows where they got hold of it all. But still...'

'But, as you say, the reporting is useful in that it's prodding the authorities to do something.' Lopes sipped his brandy. 'Actually, that explains a lot.' He realised that Alex was looking puzzled so he explained the job he'd been asked to do.

'God. I thought being a simple cop was hard enough,' said Alex, draining his brandy and offering the bottle to Lopes, who shook his head and put his hand over his glass.

'So you've had other run-ins with the AMR?'

Alex topped up his glass. 'Oh, God, yes,' he said. 'If we as much as pull in a foreign woman for questioning then an AMR lawyer will arrive almost before the cell door has clanged shut. And these aren't any old lawyers, these people are top-notch defenders. It makes it virtually impossible for us to hold them. Then once the women are released, they just melt into the city. Sure, most of them haven't done anything seriously wrong, they're either just after some money to survive, or have been assaulted themselves, but still...'

Lopes thought about this. 'Top lawyers. That implies a fair bit of money behind them. I wonder where they get that from.'

'Good question. I've no idea.'

'When did they start sending the lawyers in?'

Alex frowned, clearly thinking. 'Probably about three months ago. something like that.'

Lopes nodded to himself, so his original suspicions based on the PVDE records were right, This was a recent thing. So where had they come from?

There was a knock on the office door. A young policeman leant around the door.

'Sergeant, we've got a few drunks to process. We need more cells. Are we alright to release that British lad?'

'What, that boy Edward?' said Lopes.

'Yes, I guess so,' said Alex. 'I'd forgotten all about him. You still not want to press charges?'

Lopes could not help but touch his swollen face. 'No, let the lad go.' He checked his watch. 'In fact, I'll go with him. I'll need to at least freshen up before I go to work.'

Alex nodded towards the policemen. 'Yes, let him go.'

'Yes, sergeant.'

By the time Lopes had said his goodbyes to Alex, Edward was in the police station's reception. He was in front of the desk, filling out the paperwork. Or at least the desk officer was trying to.

'What address are you staying at?'

Edward looked at him blankly. 'What? 'he said in English 'I don't understand what you're saying.'

'Address! Address!' said the desk officer, stabbing his pen at the form.

Edward looked bewildered, clearly not understanding.

Lopes made his way over. 'I'll translate,' he said, explaining to Edward exactly what the officer wanted.

'I dunno, do I? I was torpedoed. I lost my ship,' said Edward. 'I just want to go home.'

'That could take a while,' said Lopes. 'Did Armstrong at the embassy offer any help?'

'He said something about the sailors' mission, that they'd find me digs, but I wanted to find...Hey, it's you! You're the sod that was with her. I'll...'

Edward raised his fists and would have launched himself at Lopes if the custody policeman had not grabbed him.

'Right, put him back in the cells,' said the desk officer

'No,' Lopes said, 'He's just upset.' Turning back to Edward he stood directly in front of him. 'Look, lad, calm down or else you're going to get yourself in serious bother.'

Edward still looked sullen. 'So what?' he replied.

'Back in Britain, wherever you're from...'

'Liverpool,' muttered Edward.

'Liverpool, yes, so if you hit a policeman in Liverpool you'd be in bother wouldn't you?'

'Yeah, of course I would, but... Oh God, you're a cop!'

Lopes took out his badge and showed it to him. 'A sort of cop. Perhaps a bit worse than being an ordinary one, actually.'

'I'm sorry, I didn't know, I didn't.' Edward looked desperate.

'Fine. So you understand what trouble you could have found yourself in - and will, if you try and attack me again?'

'Yes, I'm sorry. I am.'

'Edward, you're just a young man in love,' Lopes smiled. 'We've all been there. And listen, that girl you were looking for, I hadn't picked her up, she just sat on my knee because there were no seats. I wasn't in the bar for that, I was working on a case so nothing would have happened, alright?'

Edward just nodded.

Lopes turned to the desk officer. 'Edward here is going to be fine. He's not going to be any more trouble. Oh, and he'll be contactable at the sailors' mission on the Rua du Moda.'

The desk officer wrote this down. 'Alright, you can go.'

Edward looked blankly at him.

'He's releasing you,' Lopes told him.

'Thank you, Oh God, thank you.'

'Come on, I'll walk you out.'

Once outside he was about to say his farewells, but realised that Edward was looking confused. 'Do you know where the mission is?' Lopes asked.

'I'm sure I'll find it.'

'Oh, for God's sake. Come on, we've got spare rooms, you can stay with us – well, me actually, because my wife's away. I'm sure you'll be more comfortable there than at the mission.'

'Thanks, but I want to find Ana Marie.'

Lopes smiled. 'I thought that was what you had in mind. That's not a good idea, is it, Edward? No, no, just think about it for a minute, it really isn't.' The young man looked like he was going to make a run for it. 'It's after five in the morning. Even Lisbon is going to sleep and, I don't know about you, but I'd like to get some shut-eye too.'

Suddenly Edward seemed to accept what he was being told and his energy vanished. He looked like what he was; a tired young boy.

'Yes, I would too.'

'Good. Let's go and find a tram then.'

Lopes guided the young man up the street.
Like father and son.

CHAPTER 11

23rd OCTOBER 1941 - 0915 HRS

Lopes settled down further in the bath. This felt strange and he knew why; It was the wrong time of day, but he needed it.

He ached from the long night. It was more than the blow that young Edward had landed on him, it was to do with the fact that it was the second consecutive night he had been on his feet for hours. The first night had been the raid. Last night it was the murder. He must be getting soft, he used to be able to work night after night, but not now.

The trouble was he knew he wasn't getting soft. He was getting old. The realisation was way worse than the aches and pains. When had he last felt the joy of being young? That was easy; Maybe when he'd been with Elena. It had been a stressful time but she'd been able to help him forget things.

It had almost been the same last night when the girl had sat on his knee. Of course, she was a street girl but she was still young and lithe. She excited him then as she did now.

She'd called herself Angel. Yet Edward knew her as Ana Maria. Why had she changed her name? But then, why not? With what she did, why not use different names? Giving yourself a different name from your real one could give you a different personality to live in, one where you could pretend it wasn't you doing the distasteful things. He'd known other street girls do that.

But she'd run when she'd seen Edward. That wasn't like a working girl used to the life. They were usually hardened, streetwise, ready to stand up for themselves. They'd never run, never back down.

So why had Angel/Ana Marie run away?

The ringing of the phone brought him back to the present. He knew the maid would answer it, she would have even if his wife had not been staying at her mother's.

'Hello, yes this is the Lopes' residence. Yes, I'll get him for you. One moment, please.'

Lopes knew his soak was over. He was out of the bath and in his dressing gown by the time the maid had made her way upstairs and tapped lightly on the door.

'Thank you, Isobel. I'm on my way.'

It was Costa on the phone.'

'Are you alright, sir?'

Lopes explained about his long night.

'Sounds rough, sir, and I'm sorry to disturb you at home but there's been a development on the smuggling case. I'm afraid we're not going to be able to interrogate the men we arrested last night.'

'Why not?'

'Because someone poisoned them in jail. Two of them are dead, the rest are sick, They may not recover.'

Lopes struggled to take this in. 'How the hell did someone do that? No, forget that, it was a stupid question. Damn it. There'll be hell to pay for this.'

'Yes, sir, in fact, it's already started. The 'phone's been ringing all morning. The bosses are asking for you. I'm sorry, sir.'

Lopes sighed, 'Not to worry, Alvares. I'll get dressed and come in.'

'Shall I get the car and pick you up?'

'There's no need.'

'I don't mind, sir. It gets me away from answering the phone.'

'In that case, thank you, Alvares. I'll take you up on that offer.'

'See you soon, sir.' Lopes put the phone down.

This was something that had come out of the blue. Who'd want to kill the men who'd been arrested? A rival gang? Possibly, but that was less likely than the alternative; that they'd been silenced by their bosses. The stakes with wolfram were getting that large, the price of the ore had gone up fourfold since the summer and looked to go even higher now the war had spread into Russia. It was more than enough to kill for.

'Jesus Christ,' Lopes muttered to himself.

He turned to head upstairs to get dressed but the telephone rang again. 'I've got it, Isobel,' he called. He picked it up. 'Hello?'

'Don't use your official car. Not if you want to live.'

The line went dead.

Lopes stared at the receiver in shock for a moment before he forced himself to think and force action from his sleep-deprived brain. He pressed the keep button several times.

'Operator, put me through to the PVDE headquarters — urgently.' He waited. 'Come on, come on!'

'Caller, you're through.'

'PVDE switchboard.'

'Put me through to my... I mean, Inspector Lopes' office.'

Again he waited.

'Caller, there's no answer. Can I take a... '

'No! You've got to stop Adjunte Costa using the...'

The operator screamed as a rolling, ominous, boom came through the instrument. Lopes heard shouts before the line was cut. About a second later there was a second, more distant report from outside as the sound travelled across the city from the headquarters building.

'Costa, Costa, no!'

Lopes dashed to get dressed.

'Isobel! Call me a taxi.'

CHAPTER 12

23rd OCTOBER 1941 - 1045 HRS

Lopes paced up to the end of the corridor and then back to where chairs had been set up as a waiting area. He'd been doing this for the past half an hour, ever since he'd arrived at the hospital and been told to wait. He'd tried sitting, but had been unable to keep still.

Periodically a door would open, and a nurse or doctor would come out. He'd look expectantly at them, waiting for news, but so far every time the same thing had happened; the medical staff walked straight past him so he'd gone back to pacing the marble corridors with their evocative aromas of antiseptic and bleach. At last, though, a doctor appeared, looking for him.

'Inspector Lopes?'

The doctor was older than most, and overweight. He looked as tired as Lopes felt.

'Yes, that's me. How's he doing? No one would tell me.'

'He's fine, considering. He'll be a bit deaf for a while and he's got some cuts and bruises but he was lucky.'

Lopes sighed in relief. 'Can I see him?'

'Of course, though he's getting ready to go home.'

'Is that wise?'

The doctor shrugged. 'Probably not, but he insists. Perhaps you should tell him that.' He indicated to the door. 'Be my guest.'

Lopes found Costa gingerly fastening his shirt. He had cuts all over his face which was flushed rather red as if he'd had a really bad dose of the sun. Crusted, dried blood stuck to both his ears.

'Hello, sir.' Costa's voice was rather louder than normal. 'I seem to be making a habit of ending up in this place. Sorry about that.'

Lopes shook his head. 'Don't worry about that. I'm more concerned about you. What the hell happened?'

'What? Sorry, sir, everything's a bit..! he waved at his ears, 'fuzzy? dull?' He grinned. 'At least I'll be able to sleep through the baby crying for a while'.

'Don't joke,' Lopes shook his head. 'What. Happened? He mouthed.

'The bomb?' said Costa wincing. 'I went down to pick the car up and had my hand on the door handle and then I saw the wire. It didn't look right so I walked away. Then everything went black. He looked down at his trousers, the bottoms of which had been shredded. 'My wife's going to kill me. These were almost new.'

Lopes sighed, 'Come on, Costa, let's get you home.' He helped Costa to his feet. 'And then I need to go and have a long chat with Oliveira.'

*

'This is disgraceful. That some common criminals should have the nerve to plant an explosive device in an official car; a PVDE car no less!'

'I'm glad you agree,' said Lopes.

'Though what annoys me as much is the sloppiness and lack of basic security precautions you and your subordinate displayed.'

Lopes stared at Oliveira in astonishment. 'What? But…'

'Your work was bound to upset the criminal community. You knew there had been threats, yet your official car was left out in the streets where anyone could gain access to it.'

'But…'

'It's a dereliction of duty on your part, Lopes.'

'That's not on! We have to park outside the compound because certain members of this organisation refuse to let us have space inside. You know that.'

Oliveira shrugged. 'That you are not man enough to stand up for yourself to your peers within the PVDE is hardly my fault.'

'What? How dare you!'

'And how dare you spend your time which should be devoted to working on the tasks I set you, stick your nose into business that does not concern you.'

Lopes was puzzled for a moment. Then he got it. 'Ah, Ribeiro.'

'I see you know exactly what I mean. Yes, we have had an official complaint from homicide that you interfered in their investigation.'

Lopes snorted derision. 'Investigation? You could hardly call it that.'

'Don't you dare, Lopes, don't you dare!' Oliveira was on his feet now. 'What the hell were you doing walking the back streets of Lisbon in the small hours of the morning attending murder scenes?'

'I was helping them out.'

'Helping? It's not your job, Lopes. This is your job. What we do here. No wonder your assistant nearly gets murdered when you've been neglecting your duties like this!'

'You're blaming ME for the bomb?'

'For letting it happen, yes.' Oliveira pointed at Lopes' black eye. 'Did you get that in the early hours too, Lopes? What were you doing? Trying to forget your domestic problems with a night of drinking and whoring? Pull yourself together, man.'

The fact there was an element of truth in what Oliveira had said made it a lot worse.

'I resign,' he said.

'Not accepted,' snapped Oliveira. 'Get on with your jobs. The ones I and Dr Salazar gave you.'

'But...what about the threats from the gangs? The attack?'

'What about them?'

'Do we get more protection? Costa could have died.'

'Could have, but didn't. Look, Lopes, if you were doing your job diligently, the problem wouldn't exist because those who threaten you would be behind bars.' Oliveira got to his feet.

'This meeting is over. You have your orders, Lopes. Go and carry them out. Oh, and I expect a report on the progress you've made with the AMR to date on my desk first thing tomorrow.'

CHAPTER 13

23rd OCTOBER 1941 - 1210 HRS

Lopes stormed out of Oliveira's office, slamming the door behind him.

He had no intention of going back to his own office and working on his report; Oliveira could go hang as far as he was concerned. He needed to be anywhere else than within the walls of the PVDE. He strode out onto the street and started walking, he didn't care where.

He knew the respite was only going to be temporary. He'd have to go back eventually.

Or would he? What could they do to him if he did leave? He knew he'd seen it happen before. In a country like Portugal, when you displeased the State, not to the extent of needing to be locked up but annoyed them in some way, you became a non-person. You fell into a limbo where you could no longer work anywhere — not for the State nor for any private enterprise as the latter relied on the state for income. You were shunned, friends would no longer be willing to be seen with you, not if they didn't want the same treatment. This had happened to the diplomat, Ariste des de Sousa Mendes, who defied Salazar by giving out visas like confetti to all and sundry in Bordeaux thereby saving hundreds of Jews. He was recalled and even now was in internal exile, reduced to near poverty.

Wasn't that better than this though? He had nothing to fall back on. His wife already despised him but would never divorce him. Perhaps she'd pay to make him go away. No, no, there was a risk he might then find happiness, and she wouldn't risk that. He'd be made to stay, living out his days mooching around the house or eking out whatever pocket money he'd be allowed in some cheap bar.

Lopes stopped walking. He had to snap out of this blackness otherwise who knew where he'd end up. A bar probably, and he was already drinking too much. He was near one of his favourite viewpoints. He went over to the rails and looked out over the city.

'I should have gone to the States with Elena,' he muttered to himself. 'But if my aunt had balls she'd be my uncle,' he added savagely. He'd slammed that door shut even harder than he'd done with Oliveira's.

Lopes closed his eyes and let his head drop. This was quite enough wallowing. He'd go home and, tomorrow he'd go back to the office with his tail between his legs.

He started as something hard was jabbed into his ribs and an accented voice whispered in his ear. 'Don't say anything. Don't call out. This is a 38. If I fire, it'll blow your guts out over all those nice people below. You wouldn't want that would you?'

Lopes kept quite still. 'No, I wouldn't. But you might like to know you're robbing the wrong man. I'm a cop.'

'I'm not robbing you and you're not a cop any more, Lopes.'

What was the accent? Italian?

'So what is it? An assassination?'

The man laughed. 'If it was, you'd already be dead, Lopes. No, this is an invitation to a meeting.'

'One I can't say no to?'

'Exactly.'

Lopes heard a car draw up behind them. 'This is our ride. You're going to come quietly, aren't you?'

'I don't have a choice, do I?'

'That's sensible. Come on.'

A few seconds later Lopes was in the back of the car, and a hood was thrust into his hands.

'Put that on and duck down.'

The car pulled away with Lopes wondering how much worse his life could get.

CHAPTER 14

23rd OCTOBER 1941 - 1355 HRS

The car journey was not long, no more than 15 minutes, and most of that was spent in traffic. Finally, the car slowed, and turned sharply, The engine stopped and Lopes heard a heavy door behind the vehicle slam shut.

'Right, you can take that off now.'

Lopes pulled the hood off and blinked in the bright sunlight.

The car door opened.

'Out you get.'

He looked around him. The car had pulled into the yard of a large house. The yard was bounded by a high wall. Interestingly, this looked like the home of someone very wealthy. The sort of wealth that might come from legitimate business or old, inherited money but could also come from more disreputable sources.

Like smuggling something valuable.

Something like wolfram.

Lopes had no doubt; this was the property of a gang leader.

'Inside.'

'Who is it I'm seeing?'

'You'll find out soon enough.'

Lopes was pushed into a plush room. A library. Books lined the room in open cases, all leather-bound with gold lettering on the spines. Was this just for show? A demonstration of supposed intellectual capability? He was left alone in the room, so had a stroll around looking at the titles. There were some Portuguese volumes but more in other languages, a mix of German, French and British, on a diverse range of topics from science, through history to economics. There were some classics, but some were more recently published. Interesting. Something told him this was not for show.

'Do you like my library? It's my favourite room.'

The voice was familiar yet unexpected. It also gave him an unexpected jolt of pleasure. 'Elena.' He stared at her in astonishment. 'But... How did you get here?'

She smiled. 'How do you think?' She waved her hand at the room. 'This is my house.'

'Yours?'

'Yes. Well, it is now. Let's say I inherited it.'

'What? How?'

'Come on, Lopes, I thought you were sharper than that. You seem to be slow on the uptake today. Is that down to all the late nights you've been having recently? Must be hard on a man of your age.' She indicated the armchairs. 'Shall we sit? Would you like tea? Or something stronger?'

Lopes sank into one of the chairs. It was soft leather, old but immaculate and very comfortable. 'Tea would be fine, thanks.'

Elena sat in the chair opposite, picked up a small silver bell and rang it. Moments later a woman stepped into the library. 'The inspector here will take tea with me, please, Ines.'

The woman had the look of a local and when she spoke Lopes knew instantly that he'd been correct. 'Yes, madam,' she said, and seemed to hurry out of the library. Had that been an anxious look she'd just given Lopes?

'Hmm, looks like you've made an instant impression on Ines,' Elena had seen it too.

'Perhaps she doesn't like the police,' said Lopes. 'It's not uncommon.'

Elena nodded. 'You're not wrong there, though Ines isn't one of ours.'

'Ours?'

'A refugee. She came with the house. It's normally my women who've had bad experiences at the hands of your colleagues.' Lopes saw her turn her attention back to him.

'Anyway, thank you.'

'Thank you?'

'For not assuming the obvious.'

'Ah, that you found another male benefactor? I did briefly wonder I admit, but then I realised the obvious.'

'Which is?'

'You went back to the bank in Estoril and retrieved the rest of the contents of Vogel's safety deposit box?'

She nodded. 'I did, and thank God Uwe chose somewhere where they're used to dealing with female customers. The rest of this country's like the dark ages where women's rights are concerned.'

Lopes nodded. 'Salazar has a bit of a blind spot there. That and the deal he's done with the Church.' He looked around the room. 'So you picked up the deeds to this place?'

'I did. This and three others, as well as some share certificates that Uwe held. He invested in wolfram mines,' she laughed, 'Both the British and the German ones. That has proved to be a very wise investment.'

'I'll bet.'

'They give a decent income.'

'But still, you did this all by yourself? I mean, set up this house?'

'Not entirely, I admit. Ah, here we are.'

Ines had arrived with the tea. This gave Lopes the chance to look Elena over. She looked much the same as when he'd last seen her, which was, after all, just a few months ago, but she was also different. The fine details had changed. Everything about her had improved by degrees, her hair was in nearly the same style but was neater, and the cut was sharper, Her clothes, similarly, echoed the look she had in May, but the quality had improved. Her complexion was clearer, she positively glowed with health suggesting she was eating well. There was something else too; a new confidence. She looked like a wealthy, independent lady, which was quite clearly what she now was.

'You seem to like what you see,' she said as Ines left.

'I always did,' admitted Lopes.

'Lopes, that ship has sailed after what you did,' she said, suddenly looking serious.

'I know that.' He sipped his tea. 'So, what do you want? Why did you bring me here?'

'Straight down to business. Good.' she said. 'Firstly, how's Costa?'

'He's alright. A bit shaken, and temporarily deaf.' He glared at her. 'Tell me that wasn't your doing.'

Elena shook her head. 'Of course not. Poor Costa. He has terrible luck. Sorry, we couldn't let you know sooner. We only got the word about the attempt on your life a few minutes before.'

'We?'

She smiled. 'Haven't you guessed yet? Why do you think Salazar chose you to be the one to investigate and close down the AMR?'

'How did you...? Wait, the AMR is yours?'

'Not just mine. It was my idea, certainly, but there are lots of able women - and a few men, they have their uses in this country, I admit - who help me and run things day-to-day. I'll introduce you to some of them later on. Well, if they agree, that is. They are not too keen on the police and not about the PVDE, naturally.'

Lopes smiled. 'Naturally.'

'My role now is mainly to ensure that the funds keep coming in and are used most efficiently. After all, my father was a finance professor, so I might as well use my family knowledge.'

Lopes pulled out his cheeks as he exhaled slowly. 'Bloody hell,' he muttered. 'So this kidnap of yours is to make me stop?'

'Oh no,' said Elena, smiling. 'I'd much rather have you trying to bring us down than anyone else, especially not some of the other thugs in the PVDE.' Her eyes, fixed on Lopes, seemed to bore right into him. 'Anyway, you won't succeed.'

His heart thumped hard when she looked at him like that. It was distracting. He had to force himself to ask the follow-up question. 'What do you want then?'

Elena's serious look returned. 'The others hate this idea but I have no choice. I need your skills as a detective.'

'For what?'

'To do what the police aren't doing. I need you to catch the man who is killing my friends.'

CHAPTER 15

23rd OCTOBER 1941 - 1420 HRS

Lopes stared at Elena open-mouthed.
'But... I'm not...'
'Not what, Lopes? Decent? Not someone who doesn't care?' She gave a little laugh. 'Despite the way you treated me, we both know that's not true. You *do* care, and I think you care most for the helpless, those whom others aren't bothered about. That's the way Beatrix raised you.'
'You know what I was going to say; I'm not a policeman. Not anymore.'
She shook her head. 'Yes you are, fundamentally, and you always will be. You know that too.'
'Perhaps, but not officially, Elena. What I'm officially supposed to be doing is investigating your organisation and seeking to close you down.' He spread his hands wide. 'How am I supposed to do that and catch a murderer? Something that is most definitely my job.'
Elena's expression didn't change. 'I still want you to do it.'
'Why? Because I owe you?'
Elena nodded slowly. 'It's nice to hear you admit that. But no, for other, very good reasons.'
'What reasons?'
'One is because you know these women who are dying have no one in the State standing up for them. The police treat them like dirt, to them they are nothing, they are just trash, unimportant.' For the first time, Lopes could see real emotion in Elena. 'And that's not fair. You hate, unfairness, don't you?'
'Yes, I do, but...'
'Many of them have lost everything, they're displaced, homeless and penniless. We try, we can when possible, to give

them a roof over their heads, particularly if they've got children but our resources are limited. We can't do it for all of them, and those we can we have to move on after a while.' She swallowed. 'It hurts to have to turn people away. It hurts even more when I...we...send them to their deaths. Three of our women so far. You saw one last night.'

Lopes stared at her. 'Last night? She was...'

Elena nodded. 'When I heard that you'd been there it triggered this idea. Why were you there?'

'I was at the local station when the report came in. I offered to help. Then, as Homicide was slow in arriving, I had a good look at the scene until they finally turned up.'

'And what happened then? Actually, I know.' she looked straight at him. 'They did nothing, didn't they? They took her away like rubbish, didn't they?'

'Yes,' said Lopes.

'Her name was Beatrice, just like your mother. Well, almost. She was 25. She had only been in Portugal for a few months. She had been a teacher, but then she helped some shot down British pilots in France and was betrayed. She had to get out.'

'I'm sorry. And I do care. But...'

'I know. Not your job. Which is why I've got another reason why you'll do it.'

'Which is?'

'We can give something in return. Something from me - no, not that, in case you have any hopes. Something I can give, that the State is not giving you.'

'What's that?'

'Protection from the people who are trying to kill you. We have trained, armed personnel and intelligence resources in helpful locations. That's how we uncovered the bomb plot.'

Lopes noticed her biting her lip. 'There's something you're not telling me, isn't there?'

She nodded. 'Yes. The information we got came from a source from within the PVDE. One of their informants had told them about the bomb. All the details, in fact.'

He looked at her in shock. 'No. Surely not?'

'Dinis, I wouldn't lie to you about this, I promise. I have this information from a source I trust implicitly.'

Lopes looked at the ceiling and had to take a couple of breaths before replying. 'I believe you. The bastards! The absolute bastards! They'd let us die.'

Elena sighed. 'I know. Who needs enemies, eh? Whatever, whilst we can't keep several hundred women under guard we can two ex-cops.'

Lopes stared at Elena for a good 30 seconds. 'And Costa's wife and daughters? They are the most vulnerable.'

'Of course.'

Lopes rubbed his face thoughtfully. 'Apart from it being a breach of my orders, I just don't see how I can investigate properly. I haven't got access to the homicide files, and there's no way that the head of the investigation, Ribeiro, will let me anywhere near them.'

'That's no problem.'

'I'm sorry, but it is. I need to see them to investigate.'

'I know.'

'So, I…'

'I have them. Or at least photographs of them,' she smiled. 'I told you we had good intelligence. That includes in the police.'

'But how?'

'Can't you guess? Women are largely invisible in Salazar's Portugal. Often this is a handicap. Sometimes it's an advantage.'

Lopes shook his head in disbelief. 'No wonder Salazar's worried about you. You've done all this since May?'

'This and more.'

'If I agree, and I'm not saying I am, what if I don't succeed? There's no reason to believe I'll be able to find the killer. Do we lose our protection if I can't?'

Elena shrugged. 'We'll have to see, won't we? I'm sorry, Dinis, that's the best I can do.'

Lopes stared at her for a few moments. 'Alright, I understand. And I accept.'

Elena looked serious for a moment. Lopes could tell she was weighing something up. He decided to encourage her.

'It's better if you don't hold anything back, just lay it all out.'

She sighed. 'Yes, I know. Right, firstly the easy bit; you'll have to work here. There are a couple of reasons for that; for one, it'll ease the load on our watchers just to be on Costa alone in the evenings and nights. The other thing is we can't risk the State finding out about the leaks in their files. It would betray the women who trusted us.'

Lopes nodded. 'I see that. So I'll be staying here at night? If so, I'll need to get some things.'

'Of course.' Elena still looked troubled.

'Go on, tell me,' he said.

'Alright. My partners in this enterprise don't want you here. It was me that insisted we needed you.'

Lopes laughed. 'Elena, I'm used to working somewhere I'm not wanted.'

'I know but they've asked for some strict conditions. The main one is that you'll never know where 'here' is. We know you'll have to go to work as normal but, in the evening, you'll be picked up and brought here blindfolded. I'm sorry but this was something that Rosa insisted on.'

'Rosa?'

Elena looked cross with herself. 'Never mind, I'm sure you'll meet her soon enough. All I'll say for now is she's one of the people who've helped me set this up. Her men are the ones who provide the security.'

Lopes' mind was racing. He had a bad feeling about who these people might be, probably ones that the PVDE and the state would not like him associating with. But Elena was looking at him expectantly. He did owe her a debt and he knew the truth was she still had a hold on him.

'Alright,' he said. 'I'll do it.' He looked at his watch. 'I might as well start tonight. Can someone run me home? I can pick up my things then.'

Elena smiled and nodded. 'Of course. And thank you.'

Her smile gave him a jolt, but it was one of pleasure mixed with loss.

CHAPTER 16

23rd OCTOBER 1941 - 1705 HRS

It became obvious to Lopes after only an hour of looking at the photographed files that there was no way he was going to be able to work effectively that night. He was too tired, he needed rest.

He called Elena and confessed this to her. She agreed to get him home and called her driver as well as Pietro to take him.

He couldn't help but watch the way Elena looked at Pietro. Was there a hint of something there, a look, a lingering glance, a certain softness in the eyes of the pair? Then he forced himself to stop; it wasn't his business and even if his suspicions were confirmed then it would just hurt.

So he meekly allowed Pietro to put the hood over his head and to be led to the car. He lay down on the seat to get out of sight.

They'd been driving for about ten minutes when Pietro said, 'Alright, take off the hood and sit up.'

Lopes did so and recognised where he was, just a couple of minutes from home.

'So, Elena's place is in the suburbs then?' he said.

'None of your business, copper,' said Pietro. 'That's what the boss says and if that's what the boss wants, she gets.'

'It's alright, I don't need to know.' Lopes frowned. 'I know not to cross Elena.'

Pietro grunted. 'Yeah, her too.'

Lopes frowned at this. What did that mean? But he had other things to find out.

'I was trying to place your accent. Italian?'

Pietro didn't reply. The man, short and stocky and with dark hair, had a long scar on his cheek that resembled a burn, but Lopes recognised it as a near miss from a bullet, probably a high-velocity rifle. 'You had a lucky escape there,' Lopes said, pointing at the scar.

Pietro's finger touched the scar. 'Yeah. So?'

'I was wondering where you got it. You're too young to have been in the Great War, so I'm thinking Spain. Were you one of Mussolini's troops?'

Now Lopes got a reaction. 'Mussolini? that thug? I wouldn't piss on him if he were on fire,' Pietro pulled up a sleeve to reveal a tattoo, 'International Brigade. Volunteer. Though a lot of good it did us.'

'Indeed. Ah, here's my house.' Lopes pointed. The car drew to a halt. 'Are you coming in?'

Pietro peered at the house. 'Anyone else in there?'

'Just the maid.'

'The maid? I thought you were a man of the people and not a capitalist oppressor. My answer is no. You can bring your things out to me. And don't be long, bourgeois pig.'

Lopes laughed at that and left Pietro in the car with the driver. International Brigade, so at least a Socialist but more likely a Red.

'Elena, you don't half pick some dangerous company,' he muttered.

The one group that Salazar hated more than Spanish fascists was communists of any nationality and the ones operating in his capital city were the worst of the lot. It was fear of communists and communism that had led to the formation of the PVDE in the first place. And then there was the woman Elena had mentioned, seemingly accidentally; Rosa. He'd taken that name at face value, but Elena's reticence about revealing her name and Pietro's background caused him to think again. Rosa was an evocative name amongst communists, they revered the German Communist leader, Rosa Luxemburg. Was Rosa a pseudonym? It seemed likely.

He made a mental note to quietly check the records the next day, and to warn Elena if necessary. As soon as he opened the door to his house he heard voices. One was the maid, Isobel, but the other was male.

Immediately he found himself reaching for his gun, then cursing because it was on his desk at work. He thought about calling Pietro in but then dismissed the idea; if things did turn nasty then it would be hard to explain why he was seeking the help of a communist to his masters. No, he'd have to deal with this himself. Steeling himself, he opened the door to the kitchen - then breathed a sigh of relief.

'Edward, it's you! I'd forgotten you were here.'

Edward had been sitting at the kitchen table, watching Isobel work. He immediately sprang to his feet.

'Mr Lopes, sorry, I didn't know whether I should go but I didn't think I should leave without seeing you. Anyway, I'll get my things. I need to be out looking for Ana.'

'No, no, don't worry, Edward, there's no need to hurry off anywhere. I'm sure Isobel here will keep you company.'

'Hello, sir,' said Isobel. 'I hope it's okay, but I've been practising my English with the young gentleman.'

'Yes, yes it's fine,' he said to her then switched to English. 'Mr Jenkins, don't worry, you can stay here as long as you like. Now, if you'll excuse me, I just have a few things to do. You two stay here and I'll be back in a few minutes.'

He left the pair in the kitchen and went up to his bedroom As he packed, his thoughts drifted to the other job he'd been tasked with; tracing the spy, Edward had mentioned the woman again; Ana Marie. That reminded him of his train of thought before he'd got the call about the bomb. There was something odd about her and the way she'd picked him out. It was niggling at Lopes. He could kill two birds with one stone here. He made his mind up.

Closing his suitcase, he took it downstairs and straight outside where Pietro and the driver were waiting. He handed the case to Pietro - or at least tried to.

'I'm not your lackey,' Pietro growled, 'Put it in the car yourself.'

'Alright,' said Lopes, doing so. 'But there's a change of plan. I'm going to stay here tonight.'

'That's not what was agreed.'

'I don't care, it's what's happening. I have things to do here.'

Pietro stared in hostility at Lopes and then gave a huff of exasperation. 'So be it,' he said. 'I don't give a fuck if you get whacked. See you tomorrow. if you're alive.'

He got into the car and it pulled away. Lopes went back inside.

'Edward, would you like to stay?'

He saw Edward glance at Isobel. He could see why, although a good bit older than the boy, she was attractive and friendly.

'Yeah, if that's alright?'

'Two for dinner then, Isobel' he said. 'Edward, come on. Let's have a chat whilst we wait.'

CHAPTER 17

23rd OCTOBER 1941 - 1955 HRS

Lopes put down his fork and reached for the wine bottle. 'Another glass, Edward?'

The young Englishman shrugged. 'I dunno whether I should, Mr Lopes. Me Ma doesn't like me drinkin' an' I neva tried this stuff before I came 'ere,' He smiled. 'It's nice though. A bit like pop. just not fizzy.'

Lopes smiled and filled Edward's glass. 'You'll be fine, Rose is one of this country's specialities and isn't that strong. And please, call me Dinis.'

'Thanks, Mr Lopes. I mean, Dinis.'

Lopes felt a touch guilty about plying what was effectively a boy with drink but he had an ulterior motive. The lad was shy and it was difficult to make conversation with him so a little alcohol needed to be applied to make him relax, He told himself to be cautious; the last thing he needed was to have to clean up after an unwell teenager.

'So, tell me about this lady of yours, what was her name? Ana Marie?'

Edward blushed. He took a sip of his Rose'. 'Yeah. Dunno what to say about her. What do you want to know?'

'How about how you met?'

'The usual. We were in a pub, sorry a bad… You don't have pubs here, do you?'

'No, we don't. So were you with your mates?'

'Not when she appeared. I'd lost them, dunno where and then there she was. It was like a miracle.'

Lopes took a sip of his wine. That was sort of what he'd expected, it was how 'Angel' had operated with him. It might not mean anything, it might just be her modus operandi. Going with a solitary man gave her some security. Packs of men operating together could be dangerous for a working girl. But there was also something that reminded him of the wolf, separating the weakest from the herd. So what was she? Hunter or predator?

'I take it that it wasn't just that one night?'

Edward smiled. 'Oh no. It was great, she liked me. Dunno why, she was lovely and I'm, well, I ain't no film star, am I?'

'Don't do yourself down, Edward. Women go for more than looks. I know that only too well.' Lopes sipped his wine and then stared into the pink-hued depths. 'So, you spent all your time together?'

'Yeah, three days. It was fantastic.'

Lopes frowned. 'Where did you stay?'

'Her place. She had her own flat. It was a nice spot.'

Now that was a surprise. Working girls tended to live hand to mouth and only the best, most expensive hookers, had anything more than a room in a rough part of town.

'Nice, where was it?'

Edward gave a rough description. Now Lopes was very interested; it was in an expensive part of the city. 'I take it you went back there to look for her?'

'Yeah, but she weren't there, was she?' Edward screwed up his face. 'The caretaker said she'd gone and it weren't 'er place anyway. Stupid sod, it *were* 'ers, she had all her stuff there 'n there was no bugger else's kit lying around. I know 'cos I checked once when she were in the loo.'

Oh my God, thought Lopes. This was now shouting set-up.

'It must have been a lovely time. I bet you told each other everything, didn't you?'

Edward's face displayed the pleasure at the memory. 'Yeah, she was one of those people who were so easy to talk to.'

'Edward', he said, knowing he'd have to be careful with what he said. 'Did you tell Ana Marie about your ship?'

The reaction was immediate. Edward leapt to his feet. 'Oh, bloody 'ell, not you too. That stuck-up sod at the embassy were askin' whether I'd told anyone. 'Course I bloody didn't. We were told not to talk, weren't we?'

Lopes was also on his feet, but not in anger. Now was the time to talk the lad down. 'I'm sorry, Edward. I didn't mean anything. Come on, sit down and finish your wine. Come on, please. So what about your plans when you find the girl.'

Edward was still on his feet. 'Yeah right, like you wanna know.'

'I do.'

'Why? It's pointless, ain't it? She's vanished, ain't she?'

'Well, yes, but maybe I could help.'

'What do you mean?'

'I'm a cop, aren't I? It's one of my jobs to find people.'

Edward looked at him in astonishment. 'You mean, you'll help me find her? You told me before that I should forget her.'

'Yes, I know I did, but that was before I realised how important she was to you. Come on, sit back down, eh?'

Both of them sat down, and Lopes kept up the conversation although his mind wasn't fully on it now. The truth was he really wanted to find Ana Maria/Angel or whatever her real name was. He didn't need to ask Edward anything else. This wasn't a court of law, he didn't need to convict the lad or, indeed, make him suffer any longer. He knew what Edward had done and it was clear, from his reaction, that he knew and would never forgive himself.

But it looked like the German agent had, literally, landed in Lopes' lap.

CHAPTER 18

24th OCTOBER 1941 - 1350 HRS

Armstrong frowned as he read the report. When he finished it he tossed the slim manila file on the table in front of him.

'The stupid little sod,' he muttered.

They were in Oliveira's office, in the comfortable area laid out like a gentleman's lounge where Oliveira received important guests.

'To be fair, David, the boy didn't confess that he'd given this woman the information.'

Armstrong gave a grunt of derision. 'Yes, but you, me and the inspector here know very well that he did.' He looked at Lopes. 'That's your belief, isn't it, Lopes?'

Lopes nodded. He couldn't bring himself to condemn Edward in words.

Armstrong picked up the file again, opened it and turned to the sketch inside. It had been a busy morning. Lopes had got in early and arranged to have a session with the PVDE's resident artist whilst his memory of Ana Marie/Angel was still fresh. The result was a reasonable likeness, certainly better than most of the suspect sketches that adorned his former place of work. Added to the report that he'd written out and had typed up, it presented a flimsy but convincing case for the young woman being the agent the British were seeking.

'I know the boy is young and wet behind the ears but surely he should have realised he was being set up?' Armstrong put the sketch down and tapped it. 'I mean, look at her. How did that spotty little Herbert think that her going for him was real? And with the luxury apartment too. Unbelievable!' He looked up at them. 'Good work anyway. Impressively quick, Lopes. I don't know how you did it.'

Lopes, who had omitted the details of the incident with 'Angel' only mentioning that she'd been witnessed operating in the way she had with Edward, muttered that he'd been lucky.

'I'm sure it was more than that,' said Armstrong. 'So, when do you envisage there being an arrest?'

Lopes and Oliveira exchanged glances.

'We don't envisage making any arrest,' said Oliveira.

Armstrong looked astounded. 'But…' he began.

'What crime has she committed?' Lopes cut him off.

'She set out to gather intelligence. She's a foreign agent.'

'She is but, with respect, Mr. Armstrong, so are you.'

Lopes saw Oliveira frown at this.

'I am a diplomat.'

'That's what it says on your papers, but we all understand that the truth about your role is somewhat different.' Lopes kept his gaze steady. 'To claim anything else would be insulting our intelligence.'

Armstrong slapped the table in front of him. 'How dare you! You're suggesting I'm the same as this woman?'

Before Lopes could reply, Oliveira stepped in. 'Gentlemen, please, Mr Armstrong, I'm sure the inspector here meant nothing of the kind. Lopes, thank you, I think you should take your leave now.' Oliveira's tone left no doubt that this was an instruction and not a suggestion.

'Of course,' said Lopes, smiling to himself as he got to his feet. Armstrong had sat back in his chair and crossed his arms, still furious. Lopes nodded in his direction. 'Mr. Armstrong, a pleasure as ever.'

He turned to leave.

'Inspector,' said Armstrong. 'One more thing.'

Lopes turned back. 'Yes?'

'Mr. Jenkins is at your house still, isn't he?'

'Yes, he is.'

'As soon as you get back instruct him to come to our embassy immediately.'

Lopes felt his heart sink. 'He's only a young boy. Surely he…'

'He's an idiot who's managed to lose his country a ship, his crew and an essential war cargo. He's also a British citizen. We'll decide what to do with him.'

'He's right, Lopes,' said Oliveira. 'Given your work over the last few days, I think you deserve the rest of the afternoon off. Go straight home and send this Jenkins to Mr Armstrong.'

'Yes, sir,' said Lopes between gritted teeth.

He shut the door behind him. He needed to get out. He needed a drink. But he also needed to be Judas first.

CHAPTER 19

24th OCTOBER 1941 - 1930 HRS

'Alright, you can take the hood off and get out.'

Lopes had heard the gate slam behind the car and had already reached for the hood. The sun had set but there was still a reasonable amount of light to see his surroundings. He couldn't help himself; he tried to see some landmarks beyond the high walls.

'This isn't a time for sightseeing. Get inside.'

Pietro gave him a non-too-gentle push. Lopes didn't mind unduly; there was nothing to see anyway, either the walls were too high or the house was not overlooked by anything. He did curse himself for not drawing the files down on communist groups during the day but young Edward's revelation and the need to write and distribute the report on Ana Marie/Angel had taken longer than he'd expected, and then his day had been cut short by his instructions to send Edward to the embassy. He'd found him happily chatting with Isobel — it looked like the infatuation with the German agent was just that, a passing fancy for there was a definite attraction there. It was not pleasant to give the young Briton the news that he was to go and see Armstrong straight away. Lopes hadn't the heart to tell him why he was wanted.

It was almost a relief to receive the call to leave the house and walk to a place where he could be quietly and willingly kidnapped.

Now he was inside the house, his home for the weekend, ready to start work. At least this would take his mind off his problems.

It sounded like he wasn't the only one with them. As Pietro led him towards the study where the files were kept, he heard raised voices from upstairs. One of them belonged to Elena.

'That's not fair.'

'It's not. It's you being a child.'

'I'm not...'

'Yes, you are. One little look and you think the obvious. Well, honey, you got it wrong.'

'But...'

'Oh. be quiet, child.'

Lopes had stopped in the hallway. They were speaking English. The other woman was American. He had met many Americans in France so he could place her accent as being East Coast, possibly Boston.

Pietro also looked upstairs. He was scowling. Then he turned back to Lopes. 'What are you gawking at? Get in there.'

He pushed Lopes hard towards the study, sending him staggering. The limit of Lopes' patience had been reached, he recovered his balance, took a stride towards Pietro and gave him a hefty push in return that sent the Italian sprawling across the hall floor. Lopes could see the man's shock turned to fury. Pietro reached for his pistol, but Lopes was too quick for him, kicking the gun hand and sending the automatic clattering across the tiles. He hauled the man to his feet and slammed him against the wall.

Lopes got right in his face. 'Listen, sonny, I've come up against the likes of you so many times before, bullies who think they could push me around. Like those little punks, you don't impress me and you certainly don't frighten me. Understand?'

Pietro tried to free himself; the man was strong and a fair bit younger than Lopes but he had the advantage of anger and adrenalin coursing through his veins to boost his strength. This wasn't just the man in front of him anymore, he was Oliveira, Armstrong and all the others who'd frustrated and used him, Antonio Salazar included. He slammed Pietro's head back against the wall which had the desired effect of knocking the fight out of the man.

'Alright, alright,' the Italian muttered. 'Get off me.'

Lopes didn't let go.

'I'll get off you when I know we've come to an understanding. You'll treat me with respect, right? Right?'

He slammed Pietro even harder against the wall.

'Yes, yes, for fuck's sake!'

'Dinis, what are you doing?'

Lopes held Pietro for a few more moments before letting him go. He brushed himself down with his hands before answering. 'I was just having a nice little man-to-man discussion with your new boyfriend, Elena.' He walked across the hall and picked up the automatic, checked the safety was off and then held it out for Pietro. 'I think we understand each other now, yes?'

'Yes.' Pietro glared at Lopes, but took the gun and put it away. Elena went over to him.

'Are you alright?' she said, reaching out to touch Pietro's cheek, which was reddened by the contact with the wall. Pietro angrily pushed her hand away.

Elena took a deep breath and shook her head. She muttered something under her breath that Lopes couldn't hear. Then she turned to the Italian. 'Pietro, Rosa wants you upstairs. Lopes, shall we make a start?'

He followed her into the study. He waited until she'd shut the door before asking the question that had been burning inside him.

'Elena, what's going on? Who exactly are these people?'

'None of your business.'

'Elena, I'm worried about you. If these people are who I think they are, you could be in deep trouble.'

She gave a grunt of mirthless laughter. 'Trouble? Oh yes, I've not had that before, have I?'

'I know but...'

He reached towards her, but she slapped his hand away.

'What the hell do you think you're doing?' She stepped away from him and sat down at the table. 'Lopes, remember you're here to do a job, that's all, understand?'

'Yes, I do.'

'It doesn't include sticking your nose into my life. You don't have any right to do that, not after what you did to me before.' She crossed her arms. 'You certainly don't have the right to be jealous.'

That was all the confirmation he needed. He tried not to let it hurt. It was like trying to keep back the sea.

'No, I know.'

'If you can't accept it, you can go.'

'Yes.' He looked at the door.

'But that means you and Costa can face whoever's trying to kill you on your own.'

Lopes stood and watched her for a few seconds then nodded. 'Alright. This is the job, I understand that, but...' He bit his lip and sat down, changing his mind about adding anything more. 'Right, where were we?'

Elena spent a moment composing herself before replying.

'Putting the photos of the files in chronological order like you wanted.'

'Oh yes, right. Let's carry on with that.'

Despite making an effort, it still took Lopes some time before he could concentrate on the task at hand.

CHAPTER 20

24th OCTOBER 1941 - 21.25 HRS

Lopes reached for one of the few photos left on the pile they'd dubbed 'uncertain' and squinted at it.

'Could I borrow the magnifying glass?'

Elena was using it on another of the photographs. She carried on using it for a few seconds more, then, pulling a face, passed it over.

'I'm still none the wiser about that one,' she muttered, tossing the photo back towards the uncertain pile.

'Yes, the date on this one's blurred too,' he said moving the glass backwards and forwards hoping that his tired brain would, somehow, magically make sense of the dark smudges. 'Your lady spies could do with steadier hands.'

'That's not fair. You know what they were risking. Would you be that brave if you were in their place?'

Lopes gave a little laugh. 'No,' he admitted. He looked at the long table. There were perhaps 150 photos laid out on it, dwarfing the ten or so 'uncertain' shots and the twenty-plus 'unusable' discards now in the bin. 'I didn't mean to be critical, it's just frustrating; this record might be the one that provides the key detail.' He hesitated between the bin and the uncertain pile before deciding on the latter. 'They did well. I'm impressed.'

Elena gave a little nod before reaching for another photo from the uncertain pile again. She looked as tired as he felt.

'Let's leave those for now, eh? Look at what we've got.'

He got up and stepped away from the table. Elena joined him.

'So what's the next step? What are we looking for?'

Lopes smiled to himself. He'd been in this situation many times before; the experienced detective guiding a recruit in the art of criminal investigation. He'd never had a pupil like this before, one who, despite his best efforts, still distracted his senses.. It was difficult to put her perfume and the memories to one side and be the professional she needed him to be.

'First, we need to establish the killer's modus operandi.'

'Isn't that just a posh way of saying finding out what the killer's signature is?'

'Yes and no. The MO is what they do, how they work, the time the crime takes place, the type and characteristics of the victim and the like. That could be similar across several perpetrators; one cat burglar's MO will be very similar to another. The signature is what marks it out as theirs and theirs alone.'

She nodded. 'I see, yes, that makes sense. So here the killer's MO is that they attack foreign women in the early hours of the morning?'

'That's right.'

'And he cuts their throat to kill them?' She paused. 'I say 'he,' is that right?'

Lopes walked down to the end of the table and then back up to the end, going from the oldest to the most recent.

'Oh yes, sadly, most killers are men and the fact that his victims are who they are, well, that speaks for itself.' He picked up one of the pictures of the dead women. 'And, yes, he kills by cutting the woman's throat. It's done most skilfully too, a single, sweeping cut from left to right.'

'Isn't that more the killer's signature rather than their MO?'

His 'pupil' was as sharp as he'd come to expect of her.

'Sometimes there's a grey area where the two overlap. This is one of them; yes, this is part of the killer's signature. The cut is remarkably straight too, the start and the end of the wound are pretty much level on all of them. Interesting.'

'In what way is it interesting?'

'I just wondered whether the killer struck from the front.' Lopes shook his head. 'No, that's unlikely, that way they'd risk being soaked in blood.'

He looked at the photos again. 'There's no other violence involved, no punch to the face, no sexual congress.' He paused, frowning. 'Except...'

'Except for this one.' Elena beat him to it. She tapped her fingers on a set of photographed records.

Lopes joined her. The file included a postmortem picture of a dead woman. She, like the rest, had her throat cut but there was also swelling around her face and her genital area, suggesting she'd been raped.

'Yes,' he said. 'This one looks different. In fact...' he picked up the photos, stacked them together and placed them on the far side of the table. 'I think this is the work of an angry punter rather than our killer, so let's put it to one side for now.'

Elena was frowning. 'Looking at the signature again, that includes the prayer bead?'

'The rosary? Yes, that's right. That and placing the bodies in a position of modesty.'

'But then this one,' she walked to the beginning of the series and took the photo of the dead woman lying on a slab in the mortuary. 'There's no mention of — oh now what?'

There had been a light knock at the door. Elena walked over and opened it, still with the photo in hand. It was the maid, Ines.

'Yes, what is it, Ines?'

'Madam, I was wondering if you and your guest — oh, My God!'

Lopes could see that she had seen the photo, then had turned her gaze to the table and that its contents had shaken her. The maid crossed herself and looked anxiously towards him and then back at Elena.

'Ines, we're working,' said Elena. 'What is it?'

'I...I...was wondering if you needed some supper before I go home?'

Elena glanced at the clock on the mantelpiece. 'Oh, look at the time. Ines doesn't stay here overnight, she goes home. I'm sorry, Ines. I hadn't realised. Yes, I could do with some tea and something light to eat. How about you, Dinis?'

Lopes realised he was both hungry and thirsty.

'Actually, I could do with something. We've made a good start. Maybe this is the time to stop for now.'

'In that case, yes please, Ines...but don't go to any trouble. Don't delay yourself, you need to get home to your child.'

'Yes, madam. It's no trouble.'

'Thanks. Just put something out in the library. We'll be in shortly.'

'Yes, madam.'

Elena had turned back to the table, but Lopes was still looking at Ines and saw her expression briefly flick from nervous subservience to something else; a twisted anger, almost hatred. It changed so quickly that he dismissed it as passing annoyance at being delayed. He turned back to the table as the maid closed the door behind her.

'So shouldn't we dismiss this one? Oh, God, I'm treating her like a number, not someone I knew.' Elena picked up the photograph that showed the woman on the slab in the morgue.

'You knew her? Sorry, I didn't know.'

'I knew a few of them. Well, our paths had crossed. I didn't know them well. Except for her. Poor Sarah.'

Lopes came over to look at the photograph. It was very like the other postmortem images, where they existed at least. A naked body on a marble slab, its modesty covered by a sheet pulled up to just over the breasts, the eyes closed but with the stark paleness of death and the wound to the throat, neat but savagely deep.

'How did you know her?'

'I travelled with her for a while. We became separated. She was one of the first people I brought here when I set things up. I hoped she could stay, but she and Rosa fell out...and, well, a few days later I heard she'd been murdered.'

Elena's voice had tightened a bit at the end and Lopes saw her swallow. He started to reach out to comfort her but hesitated; would it anger her? But then the moment passed. Elena put the photograph back on the pile and stepped away.

'There's no mention of a rosary bead with her,' she said. 'Does that mean she's not a victim of our murderer?'

Lopes looked at the file photographs again and then at the date; August 4th, a good three weeks earlier than the next one. After that, the time spans between the killings were much shorter, sometimes only a day had passed between the murders. So did this one belong? Elena was right; there was no mention of a rosary bead as there was with all the others they had on the table. Yet the killing was otherwise so similar; Sarah was a foreigner, in her case Dutch, and was physically like the others, in build at least, and her throat had been cut. Certainly, it was enough for an otherwise unconcerned and, by the look of the records, generally sloppy homicide squad to include her in the possibles.

'I think she is a victim of him,' said Lopes.

'Really? Even without the rosary bead?'

'Yes, I think she might be the very first, which could explain its absence.' Lopes shrugged. 'I have no proof of that, I admit. I just feel in my bones that it's true.'

'Policeman's intuition?'

He smiled. 'Yes, but it's more often right than wrong.' He looked at the table again. 'This looks like a pattern. She — I mean Sarah — looks like the first. If it's the first time he killed then it would be a shock, something he'd have to process. That's why there was a gap. In between he found a reason to justify what he was doing, decide it was right but also that he needed something, some divine approval perhaps, hence the rosary beads, but that only came about when he started to kill again.' Lopes yawned. 'Come on, let's get something to eat. We've all weekend to finish this.'

Elena was still staring at Sarah's picture. It took a few moments for the spell to be broken and for her to lead Lopes to the library. He looked back at the table as she closed the door. It was going to be a long couple of days, and not just because of the investigation.

CHAPTER 21

25th OCTOBER 1941 - 0750 HRS

Lopes was awoken by the smell of coffee.

He lay in bed for a few moments processing the events of the last few days and the previous evening in particular.

They had eaten their supper in the library, sitting quite far apart, which was Elena's clear choice. Briefly, they had talked about the case and the direction they'd need to take over the weekend to make progress. All the time though, Lopes had wanted to ask one question; who was Rosa?

He'd not wanted to ask her directly, he was sure that would just have led to her ending the conversation then and there. Fortunately, he was able to link it to the case.

'You said that Sarah left after an argument with Rosa. What was that about?'

Elena had not answered straight away. She was being careful about her response. 'They had a difference of opinion. There'd always been some tension between them. They held rather different views. It came to a head and Sarah left.'

He'd tried to be casual about it, taking a mouthful of the bread, cheeses and meat that Ines had put out for them before asking the obvious follow-up.

'What was causing the tension?'

Elena folded her arms. 'You just can't stop being a policeman, can you, Lopes?'

'What do you mean? It was only a question.'

'Yes, and a very pointed one. You're trying to find out about her. Well, I'm wise to it. It's not happening.' She stood up. 'I'm going to bed, which means you are too. We're not having you wandering about the house.'

'What? I'm a prisoner? You're going to lock me in?'

'That's part of the deal I made to get you here.'

'Deal? That's not a deal you made with me. There was no mention of anything like that.'

'Tough. That's what's happening. If you refuse then I can get Pietro and his men here to make you. I'm sure he'll be more than happy to get a bit of revenge after what you did to him earlier.'

'So this is down to them, is it? Rosa and her cronies?'

Lopes was also on his feet now, and the two faced each other across the room. Elena was at her bristling best, something he'd seen before when she'd lost her temper. Like before, too, he saw the anger fade and her underlying character emerge. 'Dinis, please, just accept it. No, it's not because of Rosa. Well, not just her. There are another ten women here, a couple of them with children, vulnerable, scared. They are the ones that the regime wants to deport. This is their last refuge until we can sort papers for them and get them somewhere safe. They've been asked not to wander the house when you're here, so they're prisoners too, but they are doing it gladly because there was some panic when I told them that we'd have a serving PVDE officer here. You understand that?'

Lopes nodded. 'I do, yes.'

'This was the only way to stop them running off. They're on the floor above you and in the attic rooms, in case you were wondering.'

Four storeys then, thought Lopes, filing this away. Then a more practical problem came to mind.

'What if I need to...'

'There's everything you need in the room. Water, towels and a commode.'

'Right,' he had smiled. 'As practical as ever.'

She had returned his smile. 'Of course.'

And now here he was, awaiting the time when he'd be unlocked.

He put the bedside light on and looked around the room. It was as nicely furnished as the rest of the house. There were worse places to be locked up. And by less attractive jailers.

He sighed. 'Stop being an old fool. You're deluding yourself,' he muttered.

He got up and dressed. Then his eyes fell on the shutters, still closed. That would give him a view of the city, he could work out where he was then. Perhaps some people would have been satisfied to accept the terms of his confinement, but Lopes wasn't one of them. It was important to him to know. It might be useful, though how exactly he couldn't be sure.

It didn't matter. The shutters had been screwed shut. Without tools, he couldn't open them, not without forcing them. There were voices outside the door, softly spoken, female. People were moving. They receded.

They were heading upstairs.

A few minutes later he heard someone call. 'Alright, ladies, is everyone in their rooms?'

There were murmurs of assent.

'Alright. The prisoners are back in their cells. You can unlock him.'

The American woman again. That had to be Rosa.

He heard a knock on the door, followed by the turning of the key.

It was Elena.

'Alright,' she said. 'You're free to use the bathroom now. It's two doors down on the right. Then they'll be breakfast downstairs.'

'Thanks,' said Lopes. He couldn't help glancing upwards. A couple of faces were visible looking down at him. They quickly darted away.

'Please don't do that. They're nervous enough just with you in the house,' muttered Elena. 'And don't wander around up here and certainly don't make any move to go upstairs. It won't go down well.'

'Alright, I won't.' He looked at her. She looked like she hadn't slept and there was a suspicion of redness around her eyes. 'Are you okay?'

'Yes, of course I am, why shouldn't I be?' The snap was followed by a sigh. 'I'm sorry. I know you were just being you. And I'm sorry about this arrangement. It's not...'

Her words petered out.

101

'It's what it is.' He reached out and touched her arm in reassurance. He expected it to be shrugged off but it wasn't. For a moment she moved towards him but then stepped away.

'I'll see you downstairs,'' she said.

Lopes watched her go, then turned thoughtfully and headed to the bathroom.

CHAPTER 22

25th OCTOBER 1941 - 0830 HRS

Lopes looked around the dining room. He'd not been here before. Unlike the rooms he'd seen before, the hallway, library and study where the inquiry was being conducted, this one showed the adaption for its new use as a refuge. The period furniture had been removed and replaced by a long table and benches as you might see in the refectory of a monastery. The remains of the women's breakfast remained at the far end, whilst an area had been cleared so that he and Elena could eat. Ines served them and then moved to continue clearing up.

He remembered the fleeting look from the previous evening. Given the load of plates, cups and saucers she had to carry back into the kitchen, Lopes could now see a likely source of her anger; her workload.

Once she had left the room, Lopes remarked about this.

'Is Ines the only staff you have?'

Elena frowned. 'Why do you want to know? Lopes, just stop trying to find things out about us.'

'I wasn't, honestly. It was just an observation. She seems to have her work cut out if she is, that's all I was saying.'

He took a sip of coffee.

'Sorry,' Elena replied. 'I think I'm as on edge about having you here as everyone else. Yes, she's the only housekeeper, but we have a cook too. Ines used to do the cooking too when this was Vogel's second house, but it seemed unfair to ask her to take that on when all our people arrived. The new cook is one of our women. She used to be the cook in a boy's school in France.' Elena was just picking at her food, moving it around on the plate rather than eating.

'A Jewish school by any chance?'

'Of course. Why do you think she had to get out?' She chewed on some bread. 'We try to get everyone to muck in here. Your colleagues make it impossible for our women to work and support themselves without risking arrest, so it keeps them busy.'

Ines' return delayed Lopes' next question. She carried a coffee pot which she placed on the table by them.

'Thank you, Ines,' said Lopes, smiling at her.

Ines didn't return it. Instead, she hurried away to carry on clearing up. Lopes watched her. In many ways, she was typical of Portuguese womanhood; dark hair, dark eyes, small in stature and build, but wiry and strong nonetheless, the result of the hard manual labour involved in laundering a family's clothes and preparing food and simply getting around a city as hilly as Lisbon. Her age was hard to gauge, as with many women of her class given their toils; Lopes put it at anywhere between mid-thirties and mid-forties. Her face had lines around the eyes, ringed with dark suggesting insufficient sleep and there were flecks of silver in her hair.

When she retreated to the kitchen again, Elena made his unasked question unnecessary.

'It was a risk keeping her on. I know that, given what we do here.'

'Yes. The city's full of informers,' he said.

'Most of them working for your organisation.'

'Indeed.'

'Look, I couldn't let her go, could I? It wasn't fair. We are set up to help women. Her husband went off with another woman years ago, she's alone with a young boy to bring up. She needed the income.'

'It sounds like you're trying to convince yourself rather than me.'

She gave a little laugh. 'Perhaps you're right. Have you finished?'

'Eating, yes but I could do with more of this.' He drained his coffee and refilled it from the pot. 'Am I alright to take this with me?'

'Yes, I'll do the same,' she said. She got up, carrying her cup. Lopes followed. At the door, she turned and called, 'We're done, Ines, thank you,'

There was no reply.

Outside the door to the study, Elena stopped. 'I locked it last night, I didn't want anything disturbed. Do you mind holding this?' She gave him the cup whilst she reached for the key which she had on a cord around her neck. It was as they stood this way, facing each other, Lopes holding a cup in each hand and Elena reaching both of hers up to the top of her chest, that there was a soft but distinct click.

Both he and Elena looked upstairs. Other than a slight blur of movement there was nothing to see.

'It was probably one of the children,' said Elena turning to the door and unlocking it. 'A couple of the women have theirs with them. Don't worry about it, though it's another reason to keep this locked whilst we're working.' She stared at the photos on the table for a few moments. 'I wouldn't want any of them seeing this. Come on, let's get going.'

She went inside but Lopes waited for a moment, looking up at where the sound had come from. It was with a feeling of disquiet that he followed her.

CHAPTER 23

25th OCTOBER 1941 - 11.10 HRS

'There, that's the last one plotted.'

Elena stood back from the map on the wall. Lopes came over to join her.

It was a street map of the central districts of Lisbon concentrating on the Bairro Alto, Rossio, Estrella and Madragoa areas. There were nine pins placed on it with wool strands leading out from each one to a card. On each card were the details of the murder victim, including her name, where known, the date of the murder and outline details of the crime scene.

Neither of them said anything at first. It was a sobering sight to see the victims all laid out like this, knowing that these were nine lives snuffed out, nine sets of hopes and dreams destroyed.

Lopes blinked away his emotion. It was now up to them to solve this and ensure that no one else was added to the list. He needed to be a professional.

'There's a definite pattern here,' he observed. He tapped on the Bairro Alto. 'Five of them are here, that seems to be the main stomping ground of our man. Even this one.' He pointed to the northernmost pin. 'Sure, it's almost in Rato but that's essentially Bairro Alto too, so that's six of the nine.'

Elena nodded to herself. 'Except, Sarah's, the one we think was the first one, is a little further out in Estrela.'

Lopes could see that she was right. 'Yes, but remember the killer might not have fully developed his method or motivation then. We can't read too much into the first murder being a bit different.'

'Alright, so the Bairro Alto is the central area. Does that mean that he lives there? Is that the case with all killers like this?'

'Killers like this are, thankfully, rare. I only know them from records from abroad.' Lopes frowned. 'But from what I gather it can mean they do, but not always. Sometimes a pattern like this happens when someone deliberately comes into an area from elsewhere because it's somewhere where they can find what they're looking for.'

Elena pulled a face. 'So it may not help us to map things like this?'

'Everything we do is helpful. It gives us more of a picture.' Elena looked at him, her scepticism obvious. 'I think in this case it does point to them living in this area.'

'Why does it?'

'Think about how they get around without drawing attention to themselves. They cut the women's throats, there'd be a lot of blood. Even if it was done from behind, I can't see how they didn't get it all over themselves. How do they move around without being seen with all that on them? That suggests that they are somewhere close to home when they do it. It minimises the risk of being seen.'

Elena stared at the map. 'But it also raises the risk of being seen acting suspiciously by a neighbour,' she murmured.

Lopes couldn't help smiling to himself. His 'pupil' was impressive.

'That's very true,' he said. 'Though it is the early hours and if he works a job that, say, has shifts so people are used to him coming home at all hours, that reduces the chance of drawing attention to himself.' Elena had, at his request, brought a blackboard that had been sitting in the nursery unused into the study. Now Lopes turned to it and picked up some chalk. 'Let's summarise what we think we know.' He wrote down "Lives in Bairro Alto. Shift Worker?"

'You can add lives alone to that,' said Elena. He looked at her quizzically. 'If you're coming home with that much blood on you, you'd have to.'

'He could wash his clothes.'

'Really?' she raised her eyebrows. 'Can you name any man that does that? Willingly at least. If they haven't got a wife, they've got a mother that does.'

Lopes dutifully added "Lives on his own" to the list.

Elena had come and stood next to him. 'Sorry,' she said. 'That was thoughtless. I didn't mean to remind you of Beatrix.'

'That's alright.'

Still, she put out her hand and stroked his arm. Their eyes met.

The knock on the door was badly timed.

Elena turned and walked towards it. A sense of loss walked with her. She unlocked the door. It was Pietro.

'Yes? What is it?'

He looked at Lopes, then gave a little sideways movement of his head to bring her outside. Elena followed him into the hallway. He couldn't make out what was being said. He wondered but went back to examining the photographed files.

A minute or two later she was back. The look on her face told a worrying tale.

'What is it?'

'It looks like we'll have to cut this short,' she said. 'I don't know why but your bosses are looking for you. There's a bit of a flap going on. They've got men at your house. They've even been in touch with your wife.'

'My wife? But she's away at her mother's.'

'Not anymore, she's not. They've brought her home.'

'Oh, hell. She'll be furious.'

'Yes, I'm glad I've not met her.'

Lopes took a moment to think through the meaning of this news. 'It has to be because after what happened to Costa, they're twitchy about the wolfram gangsters. They can't know I'm here, or even think I might be.'

'No, but, in time they might guess, which wouldn't be good for either of us. It looks like we'll have to stop bringing you here. Don't worry. We'll still try and protect you. It'll be harder, but I owe you that.' Elena looked at the photographs. 'Damn your wife, and damn the PVDE. I thought we'd have longer. Just as we were getting somewhere.'

Lopes came and stood beside her. 'We still can.'

'What do you mean?'

'Just carry on with what we've been doing,' he said.

'Me? But I'm not…'

'Yes, you are. It's obvious you've got a good eye and an investigator's brain. You've also got the right motivation.' He nodded at the table. 'This was always just going to be the start. At some point, I'm going to have to use some real police to try and catch him.'

She frowned. 'But Homicide isn't bothered. You said that yourself.'

He nodded. 'You're not the only one who can do things outside normal channels. I know some good policemen who can do a proper investigation. As long as they have the right briefing and pointers about who to look for.' He pointed at the table. 'That's what this can produce.'

'Yes, but what do I look for?'

'Details. Things that link them. Things that stand out. Their backgrounds, people they know, places they've all been, things like that.'

She looked at the table. 'That's quite a job, They've probably all been here, for a start,' she muttered. 'But then so have a hundred others.'

'Elena, with your attention to detail, you sound exactly the person to do this. If you're willing of course.'

She grabbed his arm, linking hers through his and smiled. 'Of course I am. Thanks. I guess we can't risk picking you up from the street again. We'd better arrange a time and a place to meet.' She frowned, thinking.

'What about that cafe where you met Connolly? Remember it?'

She nodded. 'Yes. Gosh, that seems a long time ago now.'

'It does. We'll start there in a few evening's time.'

'Monday? At about seven?'

'That sounds fine. If I don't turn up, don't worry. It'll be that I've had a problem.'

'What, like being followed?'

'Exactly. The last thing I want to do is lead the PVDE to you.'

'I appreciate that.' Elena smiled again. 'I do appreciate you taking risks for me. Deal or not, I know you don't need to. But now…'

Lopes smiled too. 'Now it's time for the hood again.'
Elena nodded. She kept hold of his arm though.
He wasn't going to shrug her off.

CHAPTER 24

25th OCTOBER 1941 - 1430 HRS

Lopes had a five-minute walk to his house. Pietro, even more sullen than usual had dropped him off in a side street off the little park where Lopes sometimes sat smoking his pipe whilst contemplating the day's events after work. Now he delayed making his way back until his pipe was filled and lit.

He needed the calming effect of the tobacco smoke more than usual.

There were three PVDE cars outside his house. That told him how seriously they were taking this and, potentially, how much trouble he was in.

There were two of them outside his front door in their trademark macs. At his approach, one tossed his cigarette away and stepped in front of Lopes to bar his passage.

'Where do you think you're going?'

Lopes took out his badge. 'Get out of the way,' he said. 'I live here.'

The PVDE man didn't apologise. 'Oh, it's you, is it? You've turned up. Too bloody late to get to go and see Sporting kick off though.' He spat on the ground. 'Right, let's get you in. Go and tell the boss.'

Lopes arm was grabbed roughly, and he was propelled through his front door and into the hallway.

'Get off me!'

'Stay there.'

'No, I won't. This is my own house.'

The PVDE agent drew his revolver. 'If I tell you to stay, you damn well will.'

'Put it away, Rocha.'

'Yes, sir.'

Oliveira came down the stairs, looking as calm and elegant as ever but with a frisson of irritation about him.

'So, our prodigal agent returns at last. Are you alright, Lopes? Hurt at all?'

'Of course, I'm not hurt! Why should I be?'

'Because we thought you'd been kidnapped.'

'Why? What possessed you to think that?'

'We had our reasons.' Rocha was looking at his watch. 'Is there somewhere else you want to be, man?'

'No sir, I was just… '

'Don't lie to my face, Rocha.'

'Sorry, sir.'

'Just go and get to your precious match. The rest of you can go too.'

The men trooped out under the fierce disapproval of Oliveira. Lopes knew that as soon as they'd gone, the focus of his ire would switch.

It did.

'So, if you haven't been kidnapped where have you been?'

'With one of his fancy women, that's where.' Lopes' wife had come down the stairs and was standing at the bottom. Her face was streaked with tears and twisted with anger. 'That's where he always is when he can't be found. Humiliating me again.'

Lopes stepped towards her. 'Maria Sofia, please. I wasn't…'

'Get away from me!' she shrieked. 'Don't you dare touch me? Not with the same hands that touched that whore you fathered that bastard with.'

Lopes stopped. 'Maria Sofia, please,' he repeated. 'I wasn't with her. I haven't seen her since she came here.'

'So who were you with?' Lopes started to speak but then hesitated, his mind a blank. 'Well? Don't you dare lie to me?'

'I'd be interested to hear that too,' said Oliveira. 'You've created quite a stir and ruined my day off, so I think we're owed an explanation.'

Lopes swallowed. He cursed himself for not thinking things through and preparing a proper excuse.

'I was conducting investigations,' he said.

'All night? I told you not to lie to me, Dinis,' said Maria Sofia. 'And I know you. I can tell if you are, and you are now, aren't you?'

He hesitated only briefly before he said; 'Yes.'

'You were with a woman, weren't you?'

He nodded.

Maria Sofia stepped towards him and slapped him once across the cheek. By the time he'd recovered from the smart, she was upstairs in her bedroom, sobbing loudly. Lopes closed his eyes briefly; her crying, as usual, had the effect a crying baby has on a parent, a trigger for a strong emotional reaction. With an infant it was the need to provide succour; this sound triggered immense guilt, felt even though, for once, he hadn't betrayed her.

Then he remembered Elena's lingering touch and knew he had just lied to himself.

He opened his eyes. He had to face reality.

Oliveira looked at Lopes and sighed. 'Good God, man, you're an idiot, aren't you? Especially if there's a pretty face involved.' He looked upstairs as Isobel, the maid, tapped on her mistress' bedroom door.

'Madam? Can I help?'

This only increased the sound of wailing.

'What a noise,' said Oliveira. 'Is there somewhere quiet we can go?'

Lopes nodded and guided them to his study. He knew from experience that the solid oak door and thick wall gave some respite.

'Can I get you something to drink, sir?' Lopes indicated the decanter and bottles on the table in the corner.

Oliveira scowled. 'A bit early for me. I hope it is for you too.'

'Yes, of course.'

Oliveira looked at the spines of some of the books on the bookshelves but gave no sign of approval before taking his seat behind Lopes' desk. Had he taken the position of power deliberately? Lopes decided he probably had but couldn't protest. Meekly he sat in front.

'I know you're a grown man, Lopes but, under the current circumstances you really should be more careful.'

'Careful?'

'Yes, for goodness sake, just think — with your head for once.'

'Yes, sir.'

'You know the gangs are after you. They tried to kill you last week, remember that?'

'Yes.'

'So, when you just up and vanish, just think how it looks – especially when we've had a report of someone matching your description being bundled into a car near here.'

Lopes swallowed. It had been a risk in a society like Salazar's Portugal with informers and snoopers as a way of life.

'Well, that wasn't me,' he said, hoping that his lies weren't as obvious to Oliveira as they were to his wife.

'No, clearly, but it doesn't mean that the gangs weren't after you. They probably just got the wrong poor sap in your stead.'

Lopes nodded.

'So no more gallivanting off with strange women, alright?' Oliveira frowned. 'I hope she wasn't that Jewish girl you ran off with in May?'

'No sir, it wasn't.'

'Good, because that would be particularly stupid, wouldn't it? She's hardly a friend of the state.'

'No, sir.'

Oliveira looked at his watch and sighed. 'If I don't get home soon, you won't be the only one with marital difficulties. Right, on Monday morning I understand your assistant will be back at work. I want you to look into the bombing and kidnapping. We can't have this lawlessness on the streets of Lisbon.'

'No, sir. Er, about my other tasks…'

'Not so fast, Lopes. You're not getting out of those so easily. We still want that refugee organisation closed down and I'd like that female spy caught.' Oliveira got to his feet. He looked upstairs where the sobbing, muffled but still audible, was still going on. 'Use your Sunday wisely, Lopes. The professor does not like marriage difficulties. I'll show myself out.'

Once he was gone, Lopes filled his pipe and tried to resist the lure of the decanters. Things were getting harder rather than easier. He turned to the paperwork on his desk; he'd never been good at keeping up to date with it and often only did so when, like now, he needed a distraction from other things.

Even now though, he couldn't muster the concentration for it. There was one letter from his bank that he needed to deal with. He'd been trying to set up a regular payment from his account into a trust fund with Joao as its beneficiary to give him a lump sum on his 21st birthday. Some of the letters were there, but not all. He wondered if the PVDE, maybe even Oliveira himself, had been rifling through his papers and taken some but then dismissed this.

No, it was just him being sloppy and careless.

Once again.

He put away the paperwork and succumbed to the lure of the decanters.

CHAPTER 25

27th OCTOBER 1941 - 0830 HRS

After a difficult Sunday spent getting back on Maria Sofia's civil list, there was a welcoming sight facing Lopes when he reached their basement office on Monday morning.

Costa was back.

'Alvares, so good to see you!' Lopes grasped his assistant's hand and shook it warmly. 'How are you?'

'Still a bit deaf, sir, but otherwise fine. And I'm glad to be back.'

'I'm very glad you're back too.' He filled in what had happened whilst he'd been off. When Lopes had finished, Costa nodded. 'I'm glad they've started to take the danger to us seriously at last. What's the first step?'

'I believe the international section examined the remains of the car and the bomb. I presume they have a report. We could do with seeing that. You know what they think of me up there. They're more likely to give it to you than me.'

Costa wrote this down in his notebook. 'I'll go up and see them. What about the police? Would you like me to go down to headquarters and pull any files they have on bombings and any other assassinations that might be gang-related?'

'I'll do that.'

Costa looked surprised. 'Haven't you got enough to do already, sir?'

'Yes, but there's some other inquiries I'd like to make at the same time.'

'Oh, right.' Costa got up.

If Lopes was going to ask, now was the right time.

'One moment, Alvares.'

'Sir?' Costa sat down again.

'I need you to look at another group whilst you're in the international section.'

Costa frowned. 'Is this to do with the bombing?'

'Yes, possibly.' Lopes swallowed away the distaste about lying to Costa. 'I want you to look into the possible involvement of a Communist cell.'

Now Costa looked surprised. 'A Communist cell? I thought the PCP was dead, or at least kept under such a tight rein that they were no threat.'

'The locals probably are, but I'd like you to see what they have upstairs on cells with Spanish connections.'

Costa nodded thoughtfully as he wrote in his notebook. 'Ones who came over after '39? When it got too hot under Franco?'

'Exactly, yes.'

Costa thoughtfully tapped his lips with his pencil. 'I'm surprised there'd be any. It would be falling from the frying pan into the coals. If there's one thing the Doctor hates, it's them.'

'Still, I'd like you to look, especially any connected with an Italian who goes by the name of Pietro.'

Costa looked up in surprise. 'So, you've heard something concrete? Where from?' Costa then looked a bit embarrassed. 'Sorry, sir, I didn't mean that to come out like a cross-examination.'

'That's alright. Yes, I got this from a reliable source.' He swallowed. The source was, of course, himself. Was he that reliable?

'Alright,' Costa agreed, shrugging. 'But it doesn't make a lot of sense that the Communists should come for us. Most of our wolfram seizures are intended for the Nazis, but fair enough, if you've got a lead, I'll look into it.'

Costa was as sharp as ever. He was right, it didn't make sense. Lopes breathed a sigh of relief when Costa just nodded and wrote down the name. 'Right, then, I'd better go and do some grovelling in the hope that they'll let me see the files.'

'Yes. Some cooperation would be nice for once.' Lopes wondered if he should tell Costa about the message about the bomb that hadn't been passed on from upstairs but decided against it.

After Costa had left, Lopes closed his eyes and shook his head. Not yet nine o'clock and already he'd lied to and suppressed the truth about important things to a man he cared about. Such was the influence of Elena.

She was bad for him.

But avoiding things that were bad for him was not in his nature.

He sighed, opened his eyes and rose. Time to go and lie to someone else.

CHAPTER 26

27th OCTOBER 1941 - 1033 HRS

Lopes put his PVDE badge away. It had had the usual effect of acting like a magic wand that, once waved, removed obstructions and placed the subject under his control.

It was useful but still disgusted him.

It had worked its magic on the records officer at the police headquarters who had initially tried to resist Lopes' enquiry.

'Yes, sir, of course. Records we have on contract killings. Going back how far?'

'I'm looking for people who are active now, so just the last two or three years.'

'Right, inspector.'

'Oh, and anything you have on bombings or attempted bombings.'

The man frowned.

'Other than the one up at your place last week, I can't remember having any since the one that God saved the professor from. Anyone who's been thinking of something like that has ended up in Tarrafal sharpish.'

Lopes suppressed a shudder at the mention of the so-called prison in Cape Verde. It was a horrible place.

'I know, but that proves that terrorists are still active. If there haven't been arrests then finds of bomb-making equipment.'

The records officer noted all this down. 'This could take a while,' he muttered. 'Are you going to be waiting?'

'No, I've got to meet someone first. I can come back this afternoon.'

'That will be fine. I'll put them aside for you.'

'Good. I'll see you then.'

*

Twenty minutes later, Lopes was in a little café. He checked his watch. His visitor was late. That was understandable. It would be hard for him to slip away.

He had to wait another ten minutes before they arrived.

Pedro Cruz came into the cafe, took his hat off, nodded at Lopes and came over to sit down.

'Hello, sir, how are you? Why this cloak-and-dagger stuff?'

'I'm fine, Pedro and I trust you're the same. Sorry about all this secrecy.'

'I'm sure you have your reasons.'

Lopes winced at this.

'I'm sorry, Pedro. I know you have your career and a family to think about, and, as you've probably guessed, I'm going to be asking a favour from you.'

'One that will require me to go behind my boss' back, I'm guessing.'

Cruz didn't look any happier.

'Yes, it will.'

Cruz sighed and beckoned over the waiter. 'I might as well have a good strong coffee whilst you tell me.' He looked at Lopes. 'Right, what's all this about?'

In response, Lopes took out his notebook and pushed it across the table to Cruz.

*

Twenty minutes later both men's coffees remained untouched.

Cruz handed the notebook back to Lopes.

'Good God, I knew the murders were going on, but this many? Do you think there's been nine of them? What you've summarised in there is accurate?'

'I've seen the evidence and, yes, it is.'

Cruz looked up and straight at Lopes, frowning.

'How have you seen it? This must have come from our files. We haven't been told about our records being requested by the PVDE.'

'They haven't been.'

'Then how has it all been brought together?'

Lopes now reached for his coffee and took a sip. It was unpleasantly tepid. 'I can't tell you that. All I can say is that it exists and it's not been examined as a whole before.'

'But why not? I mean the killings are making the papers, but there's no great clamour either inside or outside Homicide. Why isn't more of a fuss being made?'

'It's because of who the victims are. Or what they're not.'

'What? Oh, I see.'

Cruz now deep in thought picked up his coffee. He shuddered as he tried it.

'Can I get you a fresh one?' Lopes asked.

'No, I've gone off the idea,' muttered Cruz. 'So you're implying that because these women are not good Portuguese housewives and mothers they are allowed to be slaughtered and we, in the police, are letting it happen?'

'I don't think it's a conscious decision, but that's the result. I'm sure Ribeiro would be quite happy to make an arrest if someone stumbled into his grasp, but he's not going to put much effort into it if no one's pushing him.'

Cruz bit his lip, his brow furrowed.

Despite Lopes' low opinion of Ribeiro, criticising a colleague, especially in front of the man's assistant didn't sit well and he was about to say just that when Cruz nodded.

'What do you want from me?' he asked. 'Though I'm not going to shop the boss, you know I can't do that.'

Lopes sighed with relief. 'I know that and I wouldn't ask. No, all I need is someone inside Homicide that I can feed information to, and perhaps get some back if needs be when it's fresh and not out for people to gossip about or hacks to write about.'

'You want me to be your spy?'

'No, no, not at all, I wouldn't ask that. We're just building up the full picture of the way our man operates, so if God forbid he strikes again, we can see any new information that's found. It could be vital.'

Cruz nodded. 'Alright. Anything else?'

'Any suspects who might be picked up, or people who've been pulled in for any extreme violence towards a woman. I'd like to have a look at them, if possible.'

Cruz stared at the floor. At last, he nodded. 'I'd better make a note of what you want.' He patted his pockets. 'Damn, I've left my notebook in the office,' he said, looking at Lopes guiltily.

Lopes laughed. 'You're right to look embarrassed. Ribeiro's a bad influence on you.' He passed over his notebook.

'That, and losing sleep with a teething baby.' Cruz took the notebook, flipped the page over and scribbled down a few lines. 'So this is it. That's all you want from me?'

'Yes, it is. What I'm hoping is that the most useful tips will flow the other way, that we can give you pointers that will lead to an arrest.'

Cruz looked at Lopes and gave a grim smile. 'I hope so too.' Then the smile vanished. 'Dare I ask who the 'we' are, sir?'

Lopes shook his head. 'It's best if you don't know,' he said.

Cruz's look after he'd torn out the page from the notebook and handed it back said more than words ever could.

CHAPTER 27

27th OCTOBER 1941 - 1209 HRS

Lopes queued at the tram stop, deep in thought. The tram was just coming towards him when he remembered that he was supposed to go back to the Central Police Station to review the files.

'Sorry, please,' he murmured, as he pushed past the other people waiting behind him.

'Make your mind up,' muttered one.

Lopes cursed himself. He was distracted, he knew that, and now he was making mistakes. That would have to stop; he was already playing a dangerous game. And for what? What level of protection could Pietro's men give? It may well be an illusion, it had to be. And Oliveira had given instructions to investigate the threat, which suggested that his and Costa's safety were now being taken more seriously. He should break off contact and stop this madness.

But he was involved now. He'd gone along with it. And he knew why; yes, it was partly due to wanting justice for the slain women, but there was another reason why he was doing it.

Lots of reasons in fact; guilt, lust, sorrow, loss.

He had to keep going.

He had reached the police station.

'Bloody fool,' he muttered to himself before going inside.

*

His stomach rumbled as he pulled the last of files over. It had been a longer job than he'd expected, made worse by being out of practice; he'd moved on from this sort of task, it took him back to his early days in the force, days spent in dark rooms like this one wading through a veritable sea of paper. He'd been glad to pass on these tasks to his juniors as he'd risen in rank; now he was back here. Life had come full circle.

Even so, in his junior days, he wouldn't have been as sloppy as young Cruz had been. When Lopes had settled down to work through the files, he'd been irritated to find that the notebook page that the young detective had written on and torn out, had on the other side the last of Lopes' notes on the killings. From the first days of his training it had been drummed into Lopes that his notebook was sacrosanct; its contents were to be the contemporaneous record of a policeman's observations and experiences, they were and could be used as evidence. That record had to be both accurate and complete. Granted, these notes could not fall into this evidential category, but they still represented principle and procedure, and now noting the gap in them he almost felt physically ill.

Cruz should have checked before writing and certainly before tearing out the sheet. It was disrespectful and sloppy.

But then Lopes shook himself. How sloppy had he, himself been? He'd almost forgotten to come and do this work, something that he'd taken on himself. At least Cruz had the excuse of having his brain fogged by a child-induced lack of sleep. What excuse did Lopes have? Unrequited love and jealousy.

Pathetic.

He stopped his musing and went back to work, trying to push the fact that he'd thought of love and not lust out of the place where he'd need to address the difference.

The files had told a consistent tale. This was the apparatus of state security that had been very effective against state terrorism and violence. On the criminal side, certainly, gangs were operating. These centred around certain families, but their extreme acts of violence were topped off. Hit men had operated, but where they appeared and, particularly where the targets had been members of the establishment - businessmen, judges, politicians and police - a concerted effort had been made to find and eliminate them, either by imprisonment or judicial killing. In this, the extensive network of informers had proved invaluable. Lopes detested the idea, the way the state had turned a large part of the population into snoopers and gossips, spies on their neighbours and work colleagues, the oppressive nature of it, the duplicity, but he had to admit it had worked. The number of assassinations was low and there were only a couple of open case files, both of which seemed to involve foreign shooters brought in for a specific job. Both of these were killings of senior members of rival crime families, a fact that spoke for itself.

The bombing files were different. For one thing, there were fewer of them, Yes, this represented a rarer thing, but also the fact that bombings were mainly a political act targeting the state. That meant the police were less involved; most of the investigations and crackdown would be left to the PVDE. Hopefully, Costa would be able to find something within their own organisation's files - if he was allowed access to them, of course.

This last file was a bombing case, or at least a suspicion of a bombing campaign. A house had been raided but no arrests made. A substantial amount of bomb-making equipment had been found as well as lists of potential targets - mainly government departments and ministers, as well as some of the more conservative judges. Lopes didn't need to read the notes on some of the propaganda found to know that this was a left-wing group, the targets made it obvious. He almost skipped over this section entirely when something caught his eye.

'Bloody hell,' he muttered and read the section on the seized propaganda again but more thoroughly this time.

When he'd read it, he quickly made notes on the rest of the file and then went to the records officer to tell him he'd finished. Lopes walked out of the police station and into the street, hardly noticing that he was being dazzled by the Autumn sunshine slanting in low and cutting into his eyes. He was too caught up in his thoughts to do more than automatically keep his head down.

It was a coincidence, he told himself. He was seeing connections that weren't there. He was allowing his personal feelings to create suspicion.

However much he told himself otherwise, the facts remained: the raid, carried out in March of this year, indicated that the group - whoever they were - had been recently active, if not still active today, had uncovered considerable quantities of Republican Spanish propaganda material.

Before the case had been passed onto the international section of the PVDE as the police were bound to do, the investigating officer had made speculative notes, backed up by interviewing the neighbours, that the group had come over fleeing Franco after the end of the civil war and that they were a multi-national communist terrorist cell.

A cell just like the one Lopes suspected that Pietro was a part of and that Elena was sheltering.

It was just a copper's instinct, he knew that. He also knew his instincts were more often right than wrong.

'Damn, damn, damn,' he muttered. 'Why didn't you look into them like you said you should?'

He noticed that a couple passing by had looked at him oddly. He realised why; he'd been talking to himself. They must have thought he was crazy.

He smiled. Perhaps he was.

'Lopes!'

The shout came from behind him. He turned, expecting to see an old friend or colleague but, instead, found himself gazing at a masked man holding a revolver.

Amidst screams from other pedestrians and people throwing themselves to the ground, Lopes stood, transfixed facing the gunman.

'This is from the boss,' he said and fired.

CHAPTER 28

27th OCTOBER 1941 - 1620 HRS

'Keep still.'

The first aider treating Lopes had the non-existent bedside politeness of the medics from the trenches; he was no-nonsense to the point of brusque rudeness. Still, despite his cheek stinging, Lopes meekly tried to keep as still as possible.

'You should have gone to the hospital.'

Lopes looked past the hands cleaning his wound across at Oliveira.

'It's nothing. It's just a stone chip from the wall by my head where the bullet hit. The guy was a lousy shot.'

Oliveira scowled. 'This is no joking matter. This hoodlum shot at an Officer of the State. One of my officers too.'

The first aider, having finished cleaning the wound, now applied some antiseptic. Lopes jerked his head away as the stinging cream was applied. The man looked like he was going to admonish him, but Lopes, tired of being prodded and probed, pushed him away.

'A few days ago, one of your officers was nearly killed by a bomb. You didn't make such a fuss then, did you?'

'That was different,' muttered Oliveira.

'Different? How?'

'He was more junior.'

Lopes gave a grunt of laughter. 'Oh yes, of course, that was the reason.'

'And, this time, they had the effrontery to attack in broad daylight and in public. People witnessed it. That was the state being attacked.'

Lopes fell silent. For all Oliveira's annoying bluster, he knew he was right on this point.

The first aider was packing up his things. 'Thank you, please hurry up and leave,' snapped Oliveira. 'I need to speak to the inspector in private.'

'Sir.' He quickly scooped the last of his bandages and potions into his bag and hurried out. Oliveira waited until the door was shut.

'This is unacceptable. They've gone too far this time.'

Lopes came over and took the chair in front of Oliveira's desk.

'Who have, sir?'

Oliveira, who'd been staring at his blotter, snapped upright and stared at Lopes.

'What do you mean, who? The crime gangs of course. The ones involved with wolfram smuggling.'

Lopes shrugged. 'But which one? There's so much money to be made I wouldn't be surprised if the pickpockets left Rossio Square for the mines to pick up a few lumps because they'd make more cash. There are just so many petty criminals involved in smuggling now in one way or another.'

Oliveira's gaze was steady. 'It doesn't matter.'

Lopes frowned. 'What do you mean?'

'Which are the biggest gangs involved?'

Lopes pulled a face, though this was mainly at Oliveira answering a question with one of his own rather than being forced to give names. 'There's the Galicians. They've come across the border because of Franco cracking down on them. Oh, and the Santos family. We've taken a couple of their shipments.'

'Good. And you've got information about them. Members, houses, warehouses, things like that?'

'Yes, but no direct evidence against them. We're still building a case.'

'So?'

Lopes frowned. 'What do you mean, so?'

Oliveira smiled. 'Lopes, who are we?'

'We?'

'Us here. The organisation you work for.'

Lopes swallowed. 'The PVDE.'

'Exactly. Do you think you're still back in the police? We don't need evidence.' He sat back in his chair and put his hands behind his head. 'We'll strike. Raid them all at the same time. Lock them up and throw away the key. That's the way to send a message.' Oliveira continued to stare at Lopes, a look of amusement on his face. 'I can see your displeasure, Dinis. I'm surprised at you. What has following procedure, and the letter of law got you? Attempts on your life and that of your assistant. You need to toughen up. What's the point of power if you don't use it?'

'If you say so, sir.'

'I do say so. Pray supply the information to this office and I will pass it on to the Domestic group. That way you won't soil your own hands.'

'Right,' said Lopes, getting up. 'Will that be all, sir?'

'Not quite,' said Oliveira, opening a desk drawer and thoughtfully pulling out a card. He looked at it for a few moments. Lopes sank back into his chair. 'How are things at home, Lopes?'

'At home?'

'With your wife, man. You know, the woman you are married to. Remember her?'

'Yes sir. Of course.' Oliveira was looking at him expectantly. There was no avoiding this. 'Still difficult. She's not speaking to me.'

Oliveira shook his head. 'Lopes, you know what the Doctor thinks about marriage. How it is the central plank of society, vital to church and state.'

'Yes, sir.'

'You say that but with no conviction, Lopes. Don't you believe it?'

Lopes remained silent.

'Lopes, I have been asked to pass on the disquiet of Capito Lourenco and powers higher than that about this situation.'

Lopes swallowed. 'You have, sir?'

'Yes, I have. You need to take steps to repair the situation otherwise there will be consequences.'

'Consequences? You mean I'll be fired again?'

Oliveira's eyes bored into Lopes.

'You take this too lightly. Yes, you would be fired, but there would be no safety net this time. You'd never work again, for anyone. You'd live the life of a pauper. Understand?'

Lopes swallowed. 'Yes, sir.'

Oliveira took one last look at the card in his hands and then passed it over. 'This is an invitation to a reception at the US Embassy tomorrow night. It was for me, but I think you should go instead. And take your wife, Lopes, your wife, not anyone else, understand?'

'Yes sir.'

'That should, at least, go some way to repair your standing with her.' Oliveira looked up. 'Off you go,' he said waving his hand. Lopes was halfway to the door when his superior called after him. 'I'll expect the names of your suspects to be with me before you leave tonight. We need to strike now and send a message. Understood?'

'Yes, understood,' Lopes muttered.

CHAPTER 29

27th OCTOBER 1941 - 1750 HRS

'Are you alright, sir? I heard what happened.'

'Yes, I'm fine. Whoever they were, they were a terrible shot.' Lopes sat down at his desk. 'How did you get on at the records office? Did you get the report on the car bomb?'

'Eventually, sir' Costa put a manila folder in front of Lopes. 'I'm not sure it will help all that much. It's very technical.'

'I'll have a look through it, there may be something.'

'Yes, sir. Is your face alright? It looks sore.'

Lopes brought his fingers up to the wound on his face. 'It's nothing, I've had worse. It was just from a stone chip. To be honest, I don't know how they missed.'

'Do you think they missed on purpose? That it was just a warning?'

Lopes nodded. Costa's thinking was often similar to his own, and he was not afraid to give voice to his opinion now that he had gained confidence that his opinions were not going to be slapped down. This made working with him productive. It helped Lopes shape his ideas.

'It certainly crossed my mind. Whatever, the attack's certainly got Oliveira jumping. After doing nothing after the bombing, he's now going all out after the gangs.'

Lopes told Costa about Oliveira's request.

'Well, I suppose it may make our job easier if we have a few fewer gang members around,' he replied.

'It might make it harder if removing the gang leaders causes an all-out war.'

'Sir? Oh, you mean there'll be a struggle for power amongst the ones that are left?' Costa pulled a face. 'That's a good point. You think that would happen?'

'I've seen it happen before, so yes, absolutely.' Lopes sighed. 'The thing is I'm surprised that the gangs would have done it at all. Normally they try and avoid moving against the police or the State. It's not in their interests to stir things up. Fight with other gangs, yes. Fight amongst themselves, absolutely, but take a pop at us?' He shook his head. 'It doesn't make sense.'

'Maybe it's just the price of wolfram that's done it. There's an awful lot of money to be made. That can twist peoples' minds.'

'Yes, but even so…' He sighed. 'Even if we disagree with what he wants, we can't not give him the names. His instruction has come from on high.'

'Right, sir. When does he want the list?'

'Now, I'm afraid. Sorry, Alvares. I'd hoped I could get you home on time today.'

'That's alright, sir. My youngest is teething, so work is the only place where I can get some peace.'

'Doesn't your wife deserve some peace too?'

'Yes, sir, but you know what mothers are like, they'd do anything for their children.'

Lopes gave a ghost of a smile. Would his wife have been willing to do that if they had had a family? Somehow he doubted it. Maria Sofia had never shown signs of having strong maternal instincts, quite the reverse in fact, she had told him at first that she wanted to wait before having children but later it became clear that she didn't want them at all. How this fitted with her religion Lopes couldn't see, and certainly wasn't going to ask her. He would, of course, have to speak to her tonight, on Oliveira's instructions. Maybe Oliveira was right, perhaps this could be a good start for a reconciliation.

He was so caught up in his thoughts that he almost missed what Costa was saying.

'I don't know where you got the information about him but it was spot on. He sounds like a real thug and a clever one too.'

Lopes frowned. 'Who is?'

'That communist, Pietro. Nasty piece of work, all told. Wanted for all sorts in Spain and is suspected of killing a couple of cops in Porto.'

Lopes swallowed. 'What did the files say about him?'

'Quite a lot. He was in a specialist unit in the Spanish war that went around bumping off nationalist officers and politicians. Strangely enough, that didn't make him too popular with Franco. They thought he'd head off back to Russia after the republicans lost so it was a shock when he ended up here. Anyway, I'll type up my notes for you. I guess I should sort out the names for the boss first.'

'Yes, you should. Yes, sure, I'd appreciate you typing them up but may I read through your notes before you do?'

Costa smiled. 'As long as you can read my writing, sir.' He handed over his notebook and then went over to the boxes where they kept their files.

'I'm sure it's no worse than mine,' said Lopes, flicking to the pages.

He skipped through them, conscious that he was due to meet Elena shortly. Reaching the end of Costa's notes, he then read through them again. The facts in them did not improve in their second reading.

The conversation with Elena now looked as if it was going to be as difficult as the one he faced with his wife.

CHAPTER 30

27th OCTOBER 1941 - 1910 HRS

'You're late.'

She was sitting at the same table as she had the day he'd found her here with Connolly. Despite the admonishment, Elena looked more pleased than annoyed.

'I'm sorry. It's been a busy day.'

He saw her frown when she saw his face. He'd looked in the mirror of the toilets before leaving the PVDE. The wound itself was drying, but his cheek was starting to swell from the bruise.

'What happened?'

He shrugged, 'I got lucky,' he said and told her about the assassination attempt.

His frown deepened. 'You were supposed to be being watched, kept safe. How the hell did they let this happen?'

'I don't know. I'd been in the Central Station for hours. They may have missed me when I left. You said yourself it was difficult to guard me.'

Elena pursed her lips. 'Maybe so, but I'll still be having words with Pietro when I get back.'

Pietro. He should tell her now, grasp the nettle, get it over with.

But she'd likely get angry, and leave.

He didn't want her to go just yet.

'Well, it probably doesn't matter now. Oliveira is taking action. He's going to crack down on the crime gangs. The raids go in at dawn.'

Elena gave a little laugh, 'One advantage of being a Fascist state, I suppose.'

'The Estado Novo isn't Fascist.'

'It may lack the uniforms and the goose-stepping and seem dull and relatively benign, but it's still a one-party state with a secret police force that makes people disappear.' She smiled. 'A rose by any other name and all that.'

He nodded. 'Indeed. Shall we order and go over what you've got?'

'Yes, but let's eat first. I'm famished.'

Lopes raised his hand to attract the waiter's attention.

*

The kick onto his shins was light, might have been accidental but, then again, somehow he doubted it, Lopes glanced up and found that Elena was staring at him. Her light blue eyes sparkled in the light of the candle on the table.

'What?' he said.

'I was checking you were still alive.'

He frowned. 'Pardon?'

'You've not said a word for ten minutes,' she said. 'I was getting bored.'

'Sorry, but you've done quite a job with this.' He tapped his fingers on the neatly typed pages that she'd passed over when they'd finished eating.

'Too much detail?'

'Hardly, you can't have too much in cases like this. Somewhere in the lives of these women, the places they went and the people they know, there may be a clue to who the killer is and how they came to meet.'

'Really?'

'Yes. I wish the policemen I've worked with were half as diligent as you've been. The level of detail is amazing.'

'Perhaps you need more women in the police.'

'Perhaps.'

'Are there any? Detectives. I mean, rather than secretaries and filing clerks?'

He shook his head. 'No. It wouldn't...' his voice trailed off.

'It wouldn't work? Too many distractions for you poor men?'

'No,' he said, though he knew that he would be distracted every day by Elena. 'The man at the top wouldn't allow it.'

'As I said, a Fascist state in everything but name. Salazar just lacks the silly uniform and the gold braid.'

Lopes couldn't help but glance around, Talk like that could be reported. 'Whatever, this will help.'

She took a sip of wine. 'I hope so. The more I looked at them, the more important it became to flesh out their lives, to make them more than a typed few words in a file.'

Lopes flipped back to the section covering the first victim, Sarah. It was indeed, thorough and detailed, describing who she'd travelled with on her journey to Lisbon, where she'd lived, the friends and acquaintances she'd made, even down to the fact she'd been laid up with the measles for five weeks whilst she'd stayed in Elena's safe house. The truth was that there was probably too much detail to be fully effective, but he wasn't going to tell Elena that. There was certainly enough about the crucial last few days that an investigator like Cruz working on the case could use and follow up on.

'I'll have another read of all this and then pass it on to someone who can use it to best effect.'

Elena smiled and nodded. 'Fingers-crossed that it will help catch the bastard.'

'Indeed.'

There was an awkward few moments of silence. Eventually, Elena broke it. 'I suppose we'd better get the bill.'

'Yes, I suppose so.'

So the evening was ending without him raising the issue which had been troubling him all night. Perhaps that was for the best.

She started to look around for a waiter but then stopped. Lopes realised that she was staring at him. His face had betrayed him.

'What is it?' she said. 'Is there a problem?'

Still, he hesitated. Was it any of his business?

The answer was simple; he was a policeman still so the answer was yes, it was his business.

'Yes, I think there is a problem.'

Elena settled back down in her seat. 'I thought so. I could see it in your eyes. You've had that look all night.' She crossed her arms. 'Go on, then. What is it?'

There was no going back now.

'How much do you know about Pietro?'

Elena gave a snort of derision. 'Pietro? Really? I thought so. You're pathetic, Lopes.'

'Elena, this is not about jealousy. This is far more serious.'

'Yeah, right. Of course it is.'

'Where did you meet him? Let me guess, he came looking for you.'

'That's none of your business.'

'It is my business.'

'Only because you're jealous that he's with me.'

'No, as a policeman. Did you know Pietro is wanted both in Spain and here?'

'That's no surprise, is it? He fought against Franco, and your country's regime is hardly tolerant of foreigners.' She got to her feet. 'I'm not staying to hear any more of this rubbish.'

Lopes rose too. 'Elena, please listen. He did more than fight in Spain, he ran an assassination team in Madrid. He also killed two uniformed cops in Porto. He's a killer, Elena, he's dangerous.'

He could see that his words had struck home, that she hadn't known. But then she shook her head.

'No, I don't believe it. You're making all this up to make me doubt him. Well, it won't work.' She started to leave, then swung around to face him again. 'Another thing that won't work is our meeting. It was a mistake on my part, Carole was right about that, I shouldn't have run to you for help. Well, this is the end of it, Lopes. You'll never see me again.' She nodded towards the file. 'Please make good use of that.'

And then she was gone.

Lopes sighed and took his seat. There was some wine left in the bottle. He filled his glass and picked it up, looking at the empty chair on the other side of the table where she had been sitting. .

He sighed and raised his glass in a toast.

'Goodbye, Elena,' he whispered and then signalled the waiter to bring the bill.

CHAPTER 31

28th OCTOBER 1941 - 0712 HRS

Lopes's wife looked up in surprise as he walked into the breakfast room.

'I thought we'd agreed that you'd take breakfast in your room when I'm at home,' she said.

'Good morning, Maria Sofia,' said Lopes. 'I'll take some coffee, Isobel,' he said to the maid before taking his paper and sitting down at the table.

'Didn't you hear me, Dinis?'

'I did, my dear, but I think this has gone on long enough, don't you?'

'What do you mean?'

'This marriage. As it is it's just a sham, one that's doing both of us more harm than good.'

Maria Sofia's mouth tightened. 'I've told you. Divorce is out of the…'

'I'm not talking about a divorce. I'm suggesting that we make an effort to make what we have work. Or at least bearable for both of us.'

Her expression changed from astonishment to fury. 'You dare say that when you…' She stopped mid-sentence as Isobel brought a pot of coffee and a cup and put it on the table in front of Lopes. Maria Sofia waited until she'd left the room before continuing in a low hiss. 'You dare say that when you go gallivanting off with every floozy you meet?'

'You may not believe me, but there was nothing untoward about who I was with the other day.' He mentally corrected himself with the adjustment "not of a sexual nature, anyway" before continuing. 'It was in connection with a case I'm investigating without Primeiro-tenente Oliveira's knowledge, which was why I told him what I did.'

She gave a snort that clearly expressed disbelief.

'I may be many things, Maria Sofia, but I am not a liar, you know that. Yes, the person I was with was a woman but nothing of any intimate nature took place. I needed to speak with her about this case, a case of murder, more than one murder in fact.'

'More than…? You're investigating the 'Hemline Killer?'

Despite the circumstances, Maria Sofia was intrigued. Lopes knew she took a somewhat prurient interest in murder cases, both real and fictional and that she clipped articles from the newspaper that interested her.

'Of course, I cannot confirm that, but it's a reasonable supposition.'

'But why are you working on that case? You are not in the Homicide police anymore?'

'No, I'm not but I believe that the person who is in charge is inept, as does his assistant. He will not find the killer. I'm working with this assistant on leads that wouldn't be considered by the Head.'

Maria Sofia's mouth dropped open. 'Do you think you can catch him? This fiend?'

He nodded. 'Yes, I do. Obviously, as this is no longer my job I must work quietly and with some, unfortunate as it's turned out, secrecy.'

She nodded. 'You would be famous if you brought him in. It might put your career back on track.'

'It might.'

He could see her anticipating the reflected glory. But then the glow faded. 'But still, you expect me to forget your constant dalliances?'

'No, I don't, but I assure you they're over. The relationship that produced my son actually ended several years ago. I kept them both secret because she was blackmailing me to support them. I bitterly regret it and I apologise to you profusely.'

'And since then? Since I moved out? What about then? Are you telling me you haven't been with anyone over that time?'

'I swear on the name of our Saviour, Jesus Christ, that I have not,' he said though he prayed that she wouldn't press the point about the period just before they started living separate lives. The vision of the naked Elena rising from the Tagus like a dark-haired Venus immediately came to mind and totally refused to leave. As usual, he tried to ignore her. 'You know that I would not take the name of our Lord in vain.'

Maria Sofia crossed herself.

'No, even you would not,' she said. 'So what do you propose? Go back to how things were. Surely you're not proposing that? I am not ready for that.'

'No, neither am I, but neither is this life we are living good for either of us. I suggest we try to spend some time together again.'

Maria Sofia nodded. 'Yes, we could try that. Like we are now, at breakfast and mealtimes.'

'And we could be seen out together,' Lopes added.

She frowned. 'Out? Where. Not that awful Fado, it's so common.'

'No, I was thinking of something a bit grander.'

He passed over the invitation. He saw her eyes widen as she read it.

'A reception? At the United States Embassy.'

'Indeed. Would you accompany me?'

'Yes, but… Oh, good heavens, Dinis, it's tonight! I have nothing to wear.'

'Then it looks like you'll need to spend your time at the shops.'

She puffed out her cheeks. 'Typical man, it's not that easy. I'd better get ready now. I know you mean well, but you've made a lot of work for me. ' Despite her protestations, Lopes could tell she was pleased. She rose. 'Isobel,' she called. 'I'll take more coffee in my room and I'll need your help dressing. Then I'll need a taxi to take me into town..'

'Yes, ma'am.'

Maria Sofia started to leave but then came back and kissed Lopes on the top of the head. 'At least your current position pays better than your old one. That will help me get something nice.'

Lopes looked at her in some surprise. He barely paid any attention to the salary he received from the PVDE. It felt too much like blood money.

'Is it?'

'Oh, you are hopeless at times, Dinis. Yes, if you'd bothered to read the correspondence from the bank you'd know. Our balance at the bank is very healthy.'

'That's good. Well, it's there for you to use.'

'I always knew that. Perhaps I could start to redecorate the house?'

'Of course, whatever you want.'

She smiled broadly. 'I will, thank you. Now, I really must go.'

Lopes was left with mixed feelings. On one hand, he'd taken the steps his employers had demanded and they'd be pleased. On the other hand, the steps he'd taken would act to renew the bindings that he'd nearly escaped from. Unlike Caesar who'd crossed the Rubicon, Lopes had dipped his toes in the water and then retreated.

'You've done the right thing,' he muttered.

He didn't believe himself.

He picked up the newspaper. The headlines proclaimed

Russia 'effectively destroyed': Hitler.

And;

The final assault on Moscow begins.

He thought about the communists who were working with, or through, Elena. Defeat for Russia would be a disaster for them. Maybe they would leave her alone.

He dismissed that thought. They were none of his business and Elena, after today, was most certainly none of his concern.

Personally at least.

CHAPTER 32

28th OCTOBER 1941 - 0914 HRS

'That makes 37 I've counted, Costa.'

'I think there were quite a lot brought in pre-dawn, sir. It's probably a lot more.'

Lopes pulled a face. 'Indeed, Costa, indeed.'

They were in the rear compound of the PVDE building where they'd been told they were picking up the new car that Oliveira had supplied to replace the one lost in the bombing. There had been the now customary institutional obstruction from the quartermasters, who first denied knowing anything about the car at all, then claiming that, yes there was a car but that Costa and Lopes had been mistaken about the time to collect it and that it would be there "in a few days." When this was protested, an old Ford was produced that failed to even start. It was only when Lopes threatened to go to the very top was progress finally made and a Traction Avant identified. It was now being checked over by the mechanics.

Whatever, they'd had a grandstand view of the arrivals, the results of the crackdown on the wolfram gangs.

'They are criminals, sir,' murmured Costa.

'Only when and if proved in a court of law, which requires evidence, Alvares.'

'Yes, sir...but they did try and kill both of us.'

'These men, Alvares?' Lopes pointed at a newly arrived prison van which was disgorging its cargo. 'Or the ones that arrived before? Or those that will come later?'

'Well, they might be.'

'Or they might not. They are as likely not to be.'

'Right, car's ready. Here's your keys.' The quartermaster tossed them over to Costa who caught them. 'Try to bring this one back in one piece, eh?'

'Thank you so much,' muttered Lopes. 'You've been *so* helpful. Come on, Costa.'

They walked over to the Citroen in silence. Costa started the engine and drove it out of the compound, having to wait as yet another prison van came in. When they parked, Lopes decided he had to say something.

'Costa, I apologise, I didn't mean to snap at you. Yes, these men are involved in organised crime, either directly or indirectly, but taking them in without evidence or charge? It's against the principles I was taught in the police.'

'That's alright, sir. Though,' he added, 'we're not in the police now, are we?'

Costa got out the car, leaving Lopes alone with his thoughts.

'No,' he sighed. 'We're not.'

A few minutes later they were back in the office. Almost immediately the phone rang. Costa answered it.

'It's for you, sir,' he said, passing over the receiver, 'Sargento Mendes.'

Lopes took it.

'Alex, how are you?'

'Hello, Dinis. Sorry to bother you but I've got a bit of a problem here. I thought I'd come to you first.'

Lopes sighed. What now?

When Alex explained, Lopes swore. 'I'll be right over,' he said.

CHAPTER 33

28th OCTOBER 1941 - 1105 HRS

'He's in here,' said Alex, leading Lopes towards the cells.

Lopes flicked aside the cover to the observation window and peered inside. Then he let it fall away and stepped back.

'Have you charged him with anything?' he said quietly.

'No, we haven't. We could have though. He threw a few punches and did have a knife on him.'

'So why didn't you?'

Alex pulled a face. 'I suppose we should have. But after last time…well, you told me about what happened to him, so…'

'So he gets a second chance?'

Alex smiled. 'Make that a third chance, I suppose.'

Lopes sighed and shook his head. 'Alright, open up. I'll have a word with him.'

Alex nodded and moved toward the door. He, too, flicked the cover aside and took a look inside; all experienced custody staff did that by instinct, the last thing anyone wanted was to be surprised by a burly thug lying in wait on the other side.

But there was no burly thug back there.

Alex opened the door and then stood aside for Lopes.

Edward was already on his feet, swaying unsteadily and with his eyes bleary from drink. Lopes looked at him for a few moments then waved his hand at the bed. 'Take a seat.'

'But…'

'Do it!' barked Lopes.

Obediently Edward did as he was told. Lopes was about to ask Alex for a chair but the sergeant was already bringing one in. Lopes sat on it.

'What the hell did you think you were doing, Mr Jenkins?' he said.

'What do you mean?'

'Oh come on, going to a brothel on Pink Street?'

'What do you mean? Is it a crime to go to one o'them places?'

'No, it's not, but it is when you get drunk and go there to cause trouble.'

Edward raised his chin in defiance. 'What do you mean? What trouble was I causing? I just wanted one o'the girls.'

'You wanted one particular girl, Edward. You were looking for Ana Maria, weren't you?'

Edward shrugged. 'What if I was?'

'Because, young man, haven't you learnt your lesson? Do you remember what happened last time? What happened to your ship and crew?'

'Fuck you, Lopes!' Edward leapt off the bed and launched himself at Lopes. Luckily, Lopes was ready for it and was able to rise enough to deflect the attack and use Edward's momentum to ensure he ended up on his back on the floor with himself on top. Edward fought briefly to escape. but Lopes was in the ideal position to put the struggles to an end. He slammed the boy's head against the tiled floor of the cell several times.

'Alright, alright, stop!'

'Are you alright, Dinis?' Alex was at their side. 'You, Jenkins? What's wrong with you? Wait, I'll get the cuffs.'

'No, Alex, I think Mr Jenkins and I have come to an understanding, yes?' Edward didn't answer so Lopes repeated the head slam, 'Yes?'

'Yes, for God's sake get off me.'

'Only if you've finished being an idiot and are willing to listen. Well, are you?'

'Ow, yes, get off.'

Lopes got to his feet. His chair had been sent flying in the struggle so he righted it and sat again. as Alex pulled Edward up and slung him down on the bed again.

'Right, listen, Edward, and listen well. This is the second time you've ended up in a police cell in a few days, and the second time you've got away with something that should, rightly, have ended up with you going before a judge. You haven't because of your age and what happened to you and your ship. Understand?'

Edward nodded.

'Good. But understand this; this is the end of your credit. This is it. Any more and you will be the guest of the state for a long time. You won't be going home to see your mum for months, and then, when you do leave, you'd never be allowed back in Lisbon.'

'Don't want to come back here anyway,' Edward muttered sullenly.

'Do you want to go to prison? I can assure you, that the Estabelecimento Prisional de Lisboa is not a nice place, overcrowded, dirty. Do you want to go there?'

'No.'

'Good. Then this stops. Your search for her stops, understand?'

To Lopes' shock, tears had started to course down Edward's cheeks. 'But she killed them. She killed my mates. Swanny, the rest of them, all of them on the 'Gibson.' He turned and buried his face in the blanket. Lopes got up and knelt against the bed, putting his arm over the boy.

'I know, son, I know,' he murmured. 'I know what it's like to lose friends in war.'

'But it was my fault.'

'It wasn't, it really wasn't. She used you, she tricked you to give the information.'

Edward raised his head, his face was red, his eyes brimming. 'That's why I need to get her. He said that's how I could make it right.'

'No, you don't need to get her. That's our job. Leave it to us.'

'But…'

'Wait,' Lopes interrupted him. 'He said?'

'What?'

'You said "he said." Who were you talking about?'

Edward dropped his head. 'No one. I didn't mean nothing.'

'It didn't sound...' Lopes got to his feet. 'It's alright. You've no need to tell me, I know.' He turned to Alex. 'You alright to keep him here until he sobers up?'

'I'm not drunk.'

'Yes, you are, boy. Alex?'

'Yes, no problem. No charges?'

'No. But Edward, this stops. Any more trouble, and I mean anything, from swearing to spitting in the street, and we throw the book at you. Understand?'

Edward looked sullen. 'Yes.'

'Right, thanks, Alex. Now if you'll excuse me I have to make a visit.'

'Where to?'

Lopes gave a grim smile. 'The British Embassy.'

CHAPTER 34

28th OCTOBER 1941 - 1220 HRS

Lopes sat on the tram deep in thought.

His anger had subsided somewhat and so he was able to think rationally again. Yes, it was clear that someone in the British Embassy had set the boy on a mission to find Ana Maria/Angel and that this was likely to have been Armstrong, but so what? The boy could have been acting on what he thought the diplomat had said to him but, even if it had been an unequivocal instruction, Lopes had no jurisdiction or power over Armstrong. He might not even see Lopes.

He was on a fool's errand.

The tram had reached the Rossio. Lopes ended his foolishness by getting off.

Rather than cross the tracks to catch a tram back, he set off walking. It was a warm day, dry and sunny, more like summer than autumn. A walk would help him clear his head. There was just too much happening, too many things all at once. His life and work had been a confused jumble over the last week. He didn't like it like that; he preferred to concentrate on one thing — one case, ideally — at a time. Clearly, he had too many tasks at the moment to do that, but he needed to plot a clear course.

He needed thinking time.

He stepped past diners on the street enjoying lunch at one of the square's cafes. These places took advantage of their location and their attractiveness to tourists and recent arrivals in the city, spilling out of the station to charge a premium so Lopes normally shunned them. Today though, he was hungry and the food did look and smell excellent. He could sit and think as well as getting well-fed. There was a small, unoccupied table at the cafe he was passing. Getting the approval of the waiter, he sat at it.

Twenty minutes later he was finishing an excellent pork steak washed down by a carafe of the house red. Even if he hadn't plotted his course yet, he had, at least, had the most pleasant ten minutes of his last week, sitting in the sun, watching the world go by and listening to the gossip of his fellow diners.

But as he poured himself another glass, the sun went out, obscured by the bulk of a man who loomed over him.

'I hope you enjoyed your meal, inspector,' said the newcomer. 'May I sit?'

He took the seat opposite Lopes without waiting for an assent. Lopes made a quick appraisal of his table companion; a big man, tall and bulky, the bulk muscle rather than fat. His dark complexion suggested a colonial birth - Lopes would have guessed Brazil - and he was dressed in a tailored suit made of a fine-quality lightweight cloth ideal for the warmth of the day.

'Good afternoon,' said Lopes. 'Have we met?'

The man shook his head. 'No, inspector, we haven't, though I feel I know you very well. I have been watching your career for many years. You have had quite an impact on my business.'

'Then you have me at a disadvantage because I don't know who you are or what business you're in.'

The man laughed. 'You don't know how happy that makes me,' he said. Then his expression turned more serious. 'It underlines how grave this matter is that I feel the need to meet you face to face.' He held out his hand. 'I am Arthur Santos. You may not know me, but you certainly will have encountered my men.'

Lopes shook the proffered hand but frowned. 'Your men?'

'Yes. Only last week you arrested some of them and deprived me of one of my shipments.' Santos smiled. 'I've waited a long time to meet you, Lopes.'

CHAPTER 35

28th OCTOBER 1941 - 1312 HRS

Lopes looked in horror at Santos and then started to rise.

'Come on, inspector, there's no need to panic. If I had wanted to do you harm I could have done so at any time. And if I had wanted you dead, the assassin I sent would not have missed. Please sit.' Santos picked up the empty carafe and held it up to attract the waiter's attention. He nodded and went inside the cafe, presumably to get another one. Lopes resumed his seat.

'So, Mr Santos, what is it you want?'

'Want? Who says I want anything?'

The waiter brought a full carafe and set it down on the table, taking away the old one. Santos poured himself a glass and then topped up Lopes.'

'I presumed you do. Why else set up this charade?'

'It's not a charade. I thought we should get to know each other.'

'Why? We're on opposite sides of the law.'

Santos took a sip of his wine and nodded.

'I suppose so. But we have a common enemy.'

Lopes frowned. 'We do? Whom might that be?'

Santos looked surprised. 'I'd heard you were quick, inspector. I'd have thought you'd have got it by now.' He puffed out his cheeks. 'Very well, I'll make it simple for you. Yes, we're on opposite sides, but there's still a code that we both work to. You, for example, have a reputation for honesty. Unlike other members of your profession, you are known not to invent evidence. If a crime has been committed, then you investigate it properly. We all respect that, and by all, I mean that I do not only speak for members of my organisation but those from rivals ones.'

Lopes gave a mirthless laugh. 'I'm so glad Lisbon's crooks respect me. You suggested that you, too, had a code. What might that be?'

'It is a simple one. We do not kill cops. Nor do we try to kill them. We certainly do not set car bombs. We never have and we never will. We don't do this out of kindness or respect for the law, but for practical and selfish reasons; it would be counterproductive. There would be crackdowns, like the one we had today. We would simply not have the space to operate.' Santos drained his glass. 'Do you understand what I'm telling you, inspector?'

'Yes. You're saying the attempts on my assistant Costa and myself were not made by you, or, as I believe you've been asked to speak on others' behalf, nor by anyone else on your side of the fence.'

'That's right. Do you believe me?'

'As a matter of fact, I do. It didn't feel right that people like yourselves would be involved.' Now Lopes puffed out his cheeks. 'This common enemy? I presume it's the communists?'

Santos smiled and got to his feet. 'Don't forget we have another code; we do not inform on others. Although they have created huge problems for us, we still won't. All I will say is that it would be better if you focused your attention in that direction.' He reached into his jacket pocket and took out a card. He put it on the table and pushed it across to Lopes. 'That has a telephone number on it where I can be reached. It may be useful for us to talk from time to time. It would allow matters like this to be clarified to avoid confusion in the future.' Santos touched the brim of his hat. 'Good to meet you at last, Lopes. I'm sure our paths will cross again.'

Lopes watched as Santos walked across the square and vanished into the crowds.

He drank the last of his wine.

Yes, he was sure their paths would cross. But in the meantime, he had work to do.

He looked at the card with the number on it. After a few moments, he picked it up and put it in his wallet. Only then did he call for the bill.

CHAPTER 36

28th OCTOBER 1941 - 1406 HRS

'You really believe him?'

Costa had been on the phone when Lopes had got back to the office and the call seemed to have left him in a black mood. Nonetheless, Lopes had recounted the meeting with Santos, and Costa now looked at his boss with incredulity. Lopes shrugged.

'I've no reason not to believe him.'

'I can give you one; he's a crook. He's one of the people we've been going up against for the last five months.'

'Yes, yes, I know, Costa, but think about it. We both said it wasn't the gang's style to target us and, as for car bombs, that's just something they've never done before.'

Costa pulled a face. 'There's always a first time.'

Lopes nodded. 'I suppose so but… Well, what did he have to gain by telling me all this.'

In reply, Costa tapped the file in front of him on his desk. Lopes knew which one it was; the list of people arrested in the dawn raids. It ran to nearly 60 names. 'Isn't this enough reason? To stop this crackdown? It must be hurting them.'

'It will, but there's no big names on there. It's just foot soldiers.'

'Come on, sir. The gangs need manpower, especially to shift something as heavy as wolfram. You know that's why they recruited so many men in the last year. They needed them. This is going to stop the shipments until they can get more.'

Lopes sat back in his chair and inspected the ceiling. Costa was right. Of course, he was right. Was Santos just trying to mislead him? Of course, he might be - and yet, deep down in his bones, he didn't think that had been the gang leader's intention.

Lopes straightened up.

'He was being honest. I know it. As he said, if he'd wanted to kill me he could have done it there and then.'

Costa shook his head. 'I'm sorry, you're being naive. Remember what that thug we arrested last week said? He said, "You're a dead man, Lopes. We know who you are." Have you forgotten that?'

'No, but…'

'And whose shipment was it we took?' Costa stared at him. 'I'll tell you, it was Santos'. For God's sake, you need to get a grip on yourself.'

Lopes was taken aback. Costa had never spoken to him like this before. 'Alvares, what's the matter? I've never seen you like this.'

'Because I've never been as angry as this before.'

'Angry? What, with me? What have I done?'

Costa shook his head. 'You know very well what.'

'No, I don't. Tell me, Alvares.'

'I trusted you, sir. I always did. But now…'

'Pardon? What do you mean?' Lopes was genuinely bewildered. 'Come on, Alvares, we've always worked well together. We've always talked openly and I respect your views. Just tell me, what is it you think I've done?'

'It's what I *know* you've done.' Costa folded his arms. 'Alright, Santos implied the bombing and the shooting were down to the communists, right?'

'Yes, he did.'

'So, The PVDE has a section to deal with the threat from Communists, don't they?'

'Yes.' Lopes had a sinking feeling where this was going.

'So go to them. Tell them all about it. They'd be more than interested, wouldn't they?'

'Yes, they would.'

'So go to them with what Santos says about Pietro. That's who you think is the bomber, yes?'

Lopes nodded. 'Yes. I think it's him.'

'So what's stopping you from beating a path to their door? Tell me that, boss? Why aren't you doing it?'

Lopes sagged in his chair. 'I have my reasons,' he muttered.

Costa nodded. 'Yes. Let me guess what those reasons are. A small, pretty, Jewish woman by the name of Elena - how am I doing?'

Lopes shook his head. 'She's not the reason.'

'Isn't she? You've seen her though, haven't you? Recently? Last night, in fact?'

Lopes took a deep breath and then exhaled slowly. 'Does Oliveira know? Did he have me followed? Did he ask me to spy on you again?'

Costa slapped his fists down on his desk. 'No, he didn't. Of course he told me to, but I turned him down, out of loyalty to you. Pah! Why was I so stupid? Why was I loyal to you when you've shown none to me.' Costa was on his feet. 'I thought, given the assassination attempt, I thought I'd better pull in a few favours and ask some of our old colleagues to keep an eye on you, just in case. They were following you last night. I just spoke to them on the telephone. Thet told me all about your meeting, described who you met.'

Lopes swallowed. 'Costa. It's not how it looks.'

'Don't lie to me! It's exactly how it looks. And I put two-and-two together. The fact that you'd been seeing that woman again and you're coming up with the name Pietro seemingly from nowhere. Well, it didn't take me long to do my own digging. She's in cahoots with them, isn't she, Pietro and his Communists? They are her protectors.'

'Yes, but I don't think she knows who they are or what they've done.'

'Rubbish! Whatever, shopping Pietro and his men is a no-go area, isn't it, because it would lead the PVDE to her, wouldn't it? And you can't let that happen can you? Because her working with the Communists would be enough to have her locked up and you wouldn't let that happen to her. would you?'

'No.'

'But it's deeper than that, isn't it? She runs that women's refugee organisation, doesn't she? The very one you're supposed to be shutting down.'

Lopes closed his eyes. 'Yes.' He opened them again. 'I'm sorry Costa.'

Costa shook his head. 'It's alright being sorry. Once I had her name it didn't take me long to find the connection. It won't take the others long to do the same. How bloody stupid are you?'

Lopes nodded.

Costa was breathing heavily. 'In case you're wondering, no I haven't told anyone but it's only a matter of time that Oliveira or the big boss finds out. And when they do, what will happen then? You'll be out of a job and so will I. I need this job. I don't have a rich wife, remember?'

'Costa, that won't…'

'How do you know? Actually, I may not live to see it happen. If I get killed, that will be down to you too. Either because of this bloody Pietro who you won't hand in or because of you taking your eye off the ball with the gangs. All because, Lopes, you're thinking with your privates and not your head.' Costa puffed out his cheeks. 'I can't let that happen, sir. I'm getting out before you get me sacked or killed.'

'Costa, I…'

His assistant got to his feet. 'I'm going, sir. I've already asked for a transfer.'

'Costa, please, wait.'

But Costa had already slammed the office door behind him.

CHAPTER 37

28th OCTOBER 1941 - 2016 HRS

Maria Sofia took hold of Lopes' arm.

'Isn't this wonderful?' she enthused.

'Yes,' he replied, running his finger around the collar of his over-starched dress shirt. It was already chafing. His wife frowned at him.

'What's wrong with you?' she hissed. 'You've looked miserable all evening. You could at least make an effort for me. Try to show that you want to be here with me.'

He forced a smile. 'I do want to be here with you, my dear.'

'No, you don't. I can tell by just looking at you.'

'It's not you. It's something at work.'

But he said these last words to her back. Maria Sofia had left him behind and plunged into the throng of the great and good - and not-so-good too. Lopes had recognised a couple of familiar faces who he had had in interview rooms over the years — and had vanished from sight.

He sighed; he should have made more of an effort, but it was difficult. Costa was one of the few bright spots from his time at the PVDE. And now he had gone, or at least, threatened to go. Perhaps he would change his mind when he calmed down. But then again, why should he? Lopes had hidden his meetings with Elena from him. Costa had no idea about the protection deal, how could he?

Protection? Hah, so much for the protection that Pietro had offered! From what Santos had told him, what he offered wasn't protection at all. There was a good chance that the bombing and the 'attempt' on Lopes' own life were carried out by Pietro or some of his men.

But why? Why do it?

He felt he had the answer, but it wasn't yet ready to reveal itself. It was somewhere in the fog of his mind, like a forgotten name on the tip of his tongue that just wouldn't come to mind.

'You look troubled, inspector. Penny for them.'

It was Armstrong. He had a glass of champagne in hand Unlike Lopes, the British diplomat suited evening dress. Although Lopes hadn't seen him in formal attire before, he did not look odd or out of place dressed this way. It appeared more like his natural plumage. What was odd was that he was not on his own, he was with a woman who had peroxide-bleached permed hair. This was not the only odd thing; it was that she had turned and was trying to walk away.

'Carole? Where are you going?' Armstrong called after her. 'Carole!'

She stopped, turned and, briefly Lopes saw her give Armstrong a withering look, but then it was replaced by a smile and she came back. 'Sorry, honey, I was heading to the powder room.' Whoever Carole was, she was certainly a striking woman, with high cheekbones and full lips.

'Oh, I'm sorry,' said Armstrong. 'Most remiss of me to stop you. But, please, let me introduce you to Inspector Dinis Lopes of the PVDE. Lopes, this is Carole Young.'

Lopes took Carole's hand and kissed it. 'Pleased to meet you, Miss Young.'

'Carole, please, inspector.'

Her accent was American, Lopes gauged it to be East Coast, possibly Boston.

'Carole. Please call me Dinis.'

'Of course. Now if you will please excuse me, I really must make that visit.' She smiled. 'See you, honey,' she added to Armstrong.

'She seems familiar,' said Lopes. 'I was trying to work out whether I'd met her before.'

'She's quite a lady,' Armstrong murmured as she walked away. 'And you could have, she's been in Lisbon a few months. Oh, and beware what you say in her presence.'

'Why?'

'She's a correspondent for her father's papers. You could find yourself famous for the wrong reasons.'

'Her father? He's Hiram Young? The newspaper king?'

'The very same and it's not just newspapers - radio and films too.' Armstrong drained his glass and exchanged it for another from a passing waiter. 'I'll say something for our American cousins; they know how to throw a party.'

'I'm surprised they invited you.'

'Why do you say that, inspector?'

'After you helped foil Connelly's plans back in May.'

Armstrong smiled. 'Come, come, inspector, that was far more your doing than mine.'

'But the result was what you wanted, in the end at least.'

'It was. But it doesn't matter. It's ancient history now. There's been a change in attitude, both in America and in this embassy. Connelly has long gone, along with his isolationist cronies. Things are changing.'

Lopes took the opportunity to quietly appraise the diplomat. There had been a change in him. There was a confidence there.

'You think America will join the war?'

Armstrong nodded. 'It's inevitable, only a matter of time. Who's to say what will trigger it, perhaps it will be the U-boats again, who knows? Whatever, Roosevelt has been gearing up for it ever since it became clear that Britain was not going to be knocked out of it. Perhaps even before.'

'Surely Britain could still be forced out of the war. The U-boats are sinking a lot of your merchantmen, are they not?'

'They are, but we still have the empire and we have a co-combatant now that means that Hitler can't invade us.' He raised his glass. 'Here's to Uncle Jo and his Red Army.'

Lopes didn't join in the toast. Even before Pietro, it was not a wise thing to do in Salazar's Portugal to toast a communist, even in jest. You never knew who might be watching. 'I thought the Nazis were at the gates of Moscow.'

'They are, but the Russian's greatest defender is about to enter the fray. Surely you've heard of General Winter. It's true, yes, that there have been setbacks but with the manpower and resources that Stalin has, Hitler cannot win. It might take a while but he's lost, in the long term, he's lost. And, whatever, my country and the US will not let Russia lose. We'll do everything in our power to make sure it doesn't happen.' He drained his glass again. 'And I mean anything.'

Lopes frowned. What did he mean by that? The man looked a little tipsy. Had he said something he didn't mean to say.

Before he could bring his thoughts together, Armstrong seemed to shake himself. 'Actually, Lopes, I'm surprised to see *you* here.'

Lopes frowned. 'Because of Connelly? I thought you said…'

'No, not Connelly. I'm talking about your extracurricular activities.'

'Extra?' Lopes immediately thought of Elena. 'I'm not…'

'I'm not talking about your dalliances, though it would not surprise me if you were straying again. No, I mean your investigations. The 'Hemline Killer?' Oliveira told me you'd get involved and told you to stop, but now I've heard you haven't. I didn't think you'd have time.'

'The 'Hemline'…? How did you know?'

Armstrong smiled and took another glass from a passing tray. 'I have my sources, Lopes. Let's say a little bird told me.' He touched his forehead in a mock salute. 'Have a good evening, Lopes. Your wife's over there in case you've forgotten who she is.'

Armstrong drifted away into the crowd.

A little bird? So who knew about the investigation? Elena obviously but she wouldn't. So that left, who? Not Costa. Costa didn't know what he'd been doing.

Then he got it; Cruz. It had to be him. He was the only person outside Elena's safe house whom he'd confided in. He thought he was straight, and the last person to become an informer, but it made sense. Cruz didn't come from money. That was one of the reasons that Lopes had taken to him, he came from a similar background to Lopes' own. Now he was married with children and his salary from the police was not generous.

Hell, Cruz even had a piece of Lopes' notebook with the case details on it.

'Pedro, how could you?' he muttered. 'For 30 pieces of silver. Or British pounds.'

He shook his head and drained his glass. He'd alienated and betrayed his wife, and then Costa and now Cruz.

He sighed. He was alone in a crowded room.

Again.

CHAPTER 38

29th OCTOBER 1941 - 0910 HRS

The office was silent, empty and depressing. Lopes had hoped that Costa might have calmed down overnight and had a change of heart, but his absence showed that this was not the case. He sat down at his desk, looked at the files piled up on the left-hand side and then those over on Costa's desk. He couldn't raise any enthusiasm to open any of them.

He made a decision. He would resign. Damn the consequences, he'd do it anyway. He took some paper out of his desk drawer and started to write.

Halfway through, he paused. His eyes were drawn to the still-open drawer. Inside was his Walther. He reached in and took it out, passing it from his left hand to his right and then back again. For the life of him, he couldn't remember if it was loaded or not. Normally he would unload it before putting it away but he couldn't be sure whether he had last time.

He'd let fate decide.

He flicked off the safety, raised the gun to his temple and willed himself to pull the trigger.

The telephone rang.

He scowled at it. It was interrupting his concentration. But then, he did say he'd let fate decide and this was definitely fate.

He put the pistol back in the drawer and went over to Costa's desk where the phone was and picked it up.

'Lopes,' he said.

'Outside line. Sergento Cruz.'

Lopes swallowed. He wasn't sure he wanted to talk with him. But was too late.

'Hello, sir.'

'Hello, Pedro. What can I do for you?'

'We've had another woman murdered overnight.'

Lopes glanced at his desk. Elena's file was still there. He hadn't passed the information on. He swallowed, had his neglect led to this? 'Is it him? The 'Hemline Killer?'

'I'm not sure, sir. You seem to know the cases better than anyone, would you mind coming over and taking a look? She's in the morgue.'

'What about Ribeiro? Does he know about this?'

'He's not here. He's off sick.'

Lopes gave a little grim smile. Fate, it had to be.

'I'll be right over, Pedro.'

CHAPTER 39

29th OCTOBER 1941 - 1023 HRS

'Thanks for coming, sir,' said Cruz. 'This is puzzling. I felt I needed a fresh pair of eyes on it.'

'That's alright, Pedro. Our past relationship means that I'm always willing to help. It's a matter of loyalty.' Lopes searched Cruz' face for signs of guilt but only saw some slight puzzlement.

'Er, yes, quite. She's in here.' He looked at the mortuary attendant. 'Is she ready?'

'Yes, she's waiting for you.'

'The autopsy hasn't been done yet?' Lopes asked.

'No sir. The Sergento here said we should wait until you'd seen her.'

'Good. Lead on then.'

The attendant led them into the autopsy room. The body was on a slab, covered by a white sheet. One thing struck Lopes straightaway. Whoever the woman was, she was tiny.

'Let's have a look at her.'

The attendant nodded. walked over to the slab and pulled back the sheet.

'Mary, mother of Christ!' Lopes stared at the body in disbelief.

'What is it, sir?'

'I know her - or rather I've met her, just once.'

He shook his head.

The body on the slab was Ana-Maria. also known as Angel.

It took about 30 seconds for him to recover sufficiently to become a professional investigator again.

'Where was she found?'

'In the Bairro Alto.'

Lopes nodded to himself. Yes, that fitted. As did the wound, a single cut across the throat.

So why was a second opinion needed? He'd long since stopped holding Cruz' hand. Had he lost so much confidence that he couldn't investigate this on his own?

Lopes stepped away from the body. Sod Cruz, sod the murderer, sod everything. He was beyond caring.

He was about to tell Cruz that, but something about the woman's body caught his attention. Yes, she had had her throat cut, and from left to right but the slice looked deeper than the ones he'd seen on the police photos, and from what he remembered from the actual crime scene he'd seen with his own eyes.

Beatrice.

Her name was Beatrice. Like his mother's name.

He had to remember that. These were real women, with lives and hopes and fears. He hadn't met Beatrice but he had this woman, whatever her real name was. He recalled how she felt sitting on his knee; live, lithe, vital. Okay, she had secrets, who didn't, maybe she was a spy, maybe she had the blood of sailors on her hands, but she had a right to her life. That had been taken.

He had been wallowing in his troubles for too long. He was an investigator. He could help bring the killer to justice by knuckling down and just doing his job.

'Pull yourself together,' he muttered.

'Sorry, sir? What was that?' said Cruz.

'Nothing, Pedro, I was talking to myself.' He walked up to the body and looked closer at the wound. It was deeper and, unlike the ones he'd seen in the photographs, it was slightly higher on the left side. The woman also had a black eye. The bruise had occurred shortly before death as it had time to colour. She also had marks on both upper arms. She'd been held. Tiny details, but enough.

'Were there any photographs taken of the crime scene?'

Cruz pulled a face. 'I'm afraid not. Inspector Ribeiro wanted her removed.' He pulled out his notebook. 'I took notes though.' As he flicked through the pages, one dropped out. Cruz picked it up and looked at it. 'Oh, sorry, yes, this is the sheet from your book. I hadn't realised I'd used a page which had your notes on the back, I'm sorry about that, sir. I felt awful about it, as you always told me a policeman's notebook is sacrosanct. It's evidence and should be complete.' He held out the page. 'You should have this back, sir.'

Lopes took it. He quickly read his notes. It was a summary of how the murder scenes looked.

At the same time, Cruz was reading out his notes. 'The body was lying with her back propped up against the wall. The hands have been pressed together as if in prayer and the clothing arranged neatly and modestly, given the shortness of the hemline.'

Lopes waited. Nothing more came.

'What about the bead?'

'There wasn't one, sir. That's why I called you.'

Lopes looked again at the body. 'It might have dropped out of her hand. Was a search carried out?'

Cruz nodded. 'Inspector Ribeiro called me an idiot for scrabbling about in the dark searching. I might have missed it but I don't think so.'

They both looked at the body again as if willing it to reveal its secrets.

'It's not him, is it, sir?' said Cruz at last.

'No, I don't think so. It's been made to look like the killer's work though.'

'Why? And how did anyone know how to make it look that way?'

Lopes looked at Cruz. Not only did he look genuinely perplexed but he knew the details of the murderer's modus operandi - all the details. If he'd been Armstrong's informer he'd surely have included everything, especially the bead.

Cruz wasn't the source.

Lopes could trust him.

He turned back to the body.

'I think I know why someone wanted her dead,' he said. 'And probably who would want it too.'

'What? But how do you know that?'

Lopes went closer to the body and stared down at it for a few seconds before pulling the sheet up over her face. 'I came across her during another investigation. One into a suspected

Nazi agent operating in the city. I think it's almost certain that she was the agent.'

Cruz's mouth dropped open. 'A Nazi? Then it would be…'

'The British, yes.'

Cruz stared at the sheet-covered body then opened his notebook again. 'She had a scrap of paper in her pocket. It was an address in a British city. It's here somewhere. Ah yes.'

'Is it a Liverpool address?'

'Yes, sir, how did you know?'

Lopes sighed deeply. 'We need to get down to the Sailors' Mission, and quickly.'

CHAPTER 40

29th OCTOBER 1941 - 1132 HRS

The Sailors' Mission, on the 1st floor of the building on the Rua Du Moeda, was teeming with sailors playing darts and reading newspapers whilst they waited for a hot meal to be served by the volunteers. Judging by the languages being spoken, many nationalities were represented but, predominantly, the clientèle were British.

'Hello, I'm Mr. Perkins, the superintendent. How can I help you, gentlemen?'

They had asked for a manager as most of the staff were volunteers drawn from the ex-pat community and were likely to have little idea of detailed comings and goings. It had taken a few minutes for the superintendent to appear. They showed Perkins their badges.

'The police and the PVDE? This looks serious,' said Perkins. 'I hope you're not here to upset our boys. Some of them are quite shaky, they've been through a lot.'

'That's certainly not our intention, Mr Perkins,' said Lopes. 'We're looking for one particular man. Well, a boy. Edward Jenkins. Do you know him?'

'Yes, indeed. Poor lad. His ship was sunk.'

'I know. He stayed with me for a while. We're trying to find him again.'

'Is he in trouble? He's been through a lot. If it's just some fight or something he's got himself into, then I'm sure… '

'It's not a fight, I'm afraid. We're investigating a murder.'

Perkins looked shocked. 'Oh right, I see.'

'So if you could tell us where he's staying?'

'I can do better than that. He's here.'

'Here?'

'Yes, I believe he's in the Billiard Room. Come with me, gentlemen.'

Lopes exchanged glances with Cruz who looked as surprised as he felt, and followed Perkins into the Billiard Room. The room was dark, illuminated only by the lights over the table. A game of snooker was in progress, a pairs game by the look of it, with others watching on from the sides. The atmosphere was close as most of the players and spectators were smoking and Lopes felt his chest tighten.

Edward was taking a shot as they entered. He missed, then looked up in surprise.

'Inspector? What are you doing here?'

'I'm sorry, Edward, we need to talk to you.'

'But I'm playin.' I've got half a crown on this.'

'Someone else will have to take over from you.'

'But...'

Cruz walked over to him and took hold of his arm. 'Come on,' he said. He took the cue from Edward's hand and handed it to one of the spectators.

'What is this? What have I done?' Edward protested but didn't struggle as they took him away. 'I ain't done nothing, I swear.'

'In that case, you'll be fine.'

'Hey, leave the lad alone.' A sailor stepped in front of Lopes. Another joined him.

'Now, now, Jones, and you, Griffiths,' said Perkins. 'Let these gentlemen do their job.'

'Why can't they leave him alone? The lad's been through a lot. '

'Please Jones, they are investigating a murder. I'm sure they'll sort it out, they just need to talk to young Jenkins, isn't that right, inspector?'

Before Lopes could answer, Edward got there first; 'Murder? What murder? Who's dead?'

CHAPTER 41

29th October 1941 - 1240 HRS

Lopes finished his coffee just as Alex Mendes came into the ready room.

'Alright, we've got a room free now,' he said.

'Thanks, Alex,' said Lopes getting to his feet. 'I appreciate you doing this.'

'Glad to help, Dinis. Given you're not supposed to be involved, I guess you wouldn't be welcome in Homicide.'

'No, he wouldn't,' smiled Cruz. 'My boss would go nuts, first at the inspector and then at me.'

'You think it's him?' Alex frowned. 'This lad, Jenkins? I mean he's a scrapper but a killer? The 'Hemline Killer?'

Lopes shook his head. 'The 'Hemline Killer,' no. He wasn't here for most of them. But this one, well, I don't know. It's possible. He was so wound up about her.'

'And he did have a knife when he was arrested last time.'

'He did. But let's see what he has to say. Come on, Pedro.'

The three policemen went into the interview room, Lopes and Cruz sitting at the desk, Alex sitting at the back in one corner. Edward was brought into the room, in cuffs, and sat on the far side from Lopes. He looked at the three men, bewilderment written on his face.

'What's this about? What 'ave I done? Who's dead?'

Lopes saw Cruz glance at him. He understood what the look meant; if he'd done this, then he's a great actor.

Lopes agreed but he knew he couldn't reveal his feelings yet.

'Mr Jenkins…Edward, we'll conduct this interview in English. I believe my colleagues…' he paused to check with

Cruz and Alex, 'understand enough of the language to be able to follow.' Both men nodded. 'However, there may be times when we clarify points in Portuguese. This is not something we will be doing to try and trap you.'

'Whatever. Get on with it. I'm supposed to be flying home tonight. I need to do some shoppin' for me mum.'

Lopes was making notes and looked up in surprise. 'Flying? Tonight? Who arranged that? Actually, don't bother, I can guess. The British Embassy?'

'Yeah, that's right. Mr Armstrong thought it was best if I got 'ome to mum as quick as. Save her worrying, like.'

'I bet he did,' muttered Cruz in Portuguese. 'Who is this Armstrong? A spy?'

'Probably,' murmured Lopes. 'Haven't you met him?'

'Never had the pleasure, thank God.'

Interesting, thought Lopes.

'So what is this? Who's been killed? Whoever it was, it weren't me.'

'Could you tell me what your movements were last night, Edward,' said Lopes.

'I was at my digs. You told me to keep out of trouble.'

'Where are they?'

Edward gave them the address. Cruz nodded and whispered to Lopes that this was a well-known lodging house for British and other allied sailors.

'You weren't there all night, were you?'

Edward looked awkward.

'No.'

'Where did you go?'

'Somewhere, I dunno,' Edward mumbled.

'You went to see Ana-Maria, didn't you?'

Edward looked surprised. 'Yeah, how did you know?'

'Just a lucky guess. How did you find her?'

'I didn't. Some bloke that the embassy knew did. He took me to her.'

Lopes raised his eyebrows in surprise. He wrote this down all the time thinking about the next question.

'How did that meeting go? She wasn't exactly happy to see you last time, was she?'

'No, she weren't this time either. At first, at least.' Edward smiled. 'I had to give her a bit of a slap and then she came round.'

'You gave her more than a slap, didn't you?' Cruz interjected.

'What do you mean by that? Wait, summats 'appened to her?' Edward jumped to his feet. 'Where is she? Is she alright?'

'Of course she's not. You know that.'

Lopes put his hand on Cruz's arm to stop him.

'Edward. Please. Sit down.'

'No, I want to know. What's 'appened?'

'Sit!'

Obediently, Edward sank back into his chair.

'She's dead?' he said, tears on his cheeks.

'Yes, I'm afraid so.'

'No, no, no!' Tears sprang from Edward's eyes. 'No. Not her, not Ana. They did her, didn't they? The bastards!'

'Who Edward, who?'

'Are you saying someone else killed her, lad?' said Alex from the back of the room.

Edward swung his gaze over to him. 'Of course, I didn't do it. She were fine when I left her.'

'But you had a knife, didn't you?'

'Yeah, but… '

'Armstrong gave it to you, didn't he?' said Lopes. 'When he told you what she'd done, what you'd done by telling you about your ship.'

Edward now stared at Lopes. 'Yeah, but how did you know?'

'He told you that you had to find her, to put things right, didn't he?'

Edward nodded.

Lopes bit his lip. He'd have to handle this next bit very carefully. 'Is that all he asked you to do, just to find her? Or was it more?'

Edward nodded again.

'What did he tell you to do?' asked Lopes. Edward opened his mouth but then closed it and shook his head.

'No. You're tryin to trick me.'

'Edward, we're not. You said you didn't kill her, didn't you?'

'Yes! I didn't!'

'I believe you.' Lopes saw Cruz look at him in surprise. 'So tell us what happened so we can find out who did.' He reached out, put his hand on Edward's arm and gave it a comforting squeeze. 'Come on, you know me. I've never lied to you, have I?'

'No. You've been kind.' Edward forced a smile but the tears still ran down his cheeks. 'Alright. That Armstrong, he said I had to find her. He said I had to bring her in, that it was my duty.'

'Was that all? If you couldn't bring her in, what then?'

'I was to use the knife on her,' whispered Edward. 'To stick her, stop her killin' any other British lads like me. He said she were a Nazi, that she were a liar. She weren't. She told me that when I found her. She had a kid, with a German sailor. He took her from Brazil back home, then snuffed it. They took her kid, made her do it.'

Lopes watched as Cruz scribbled all this down.

'So you found her?'

Edward nodded.

'Yesterday?'

He nodded again.

'Tell me about it.'

'I saw her on Pink Street. I followed her. She went to the room she had. We just talked, that's all, I swear.'

'You hit her though,' said Cruz.

'Yeah, but just a little slap. It weren't nothin....' She calmed down.'

'And you gave her your address? Asked her to write?'

Edward nodded.

'Where was this? Where was her room?'

'It was in some wreck of a place, somewhere up by that big castle thing.'

Lopes looked up in surprise. 'St Georges? That's Alfama, not the Barrio Alta.'

'I dunno. I don't know names, do I?'

'No, of course not. Go on then, Edward. What did you do?'

'I weren't going to do anything, but the guy I was with said I had to go and deal with her.'

Lopes stared at him. 'You were with someone? Who was it? Someone from the embassy?'

Edward pulled a face. 'Sort of. He just appeared after I got arrested the other day. Said that Mr Armstrong had sent him. Said he was there just to keep an eye on me.'

'What was his name?'

Edward shrugged. 'He never said.'

'What did he look like?'

'Little guy but built like a boxer. Sounded like an Eyetie. Got a burn mark or summat on his cheek.'

Lopes swore and thumped the table, much to the surprise of Cruz and Edward.

'Pietro! Damn him!'

CHAPTER 42

29th OCTOBER 1941 - 1350 HRS

'I take it you know this Pietro?' said Cruz.

'I do, yes, unfortunately.' Lopes filled his pipe and looked across at his former assistant. He could see that Cruz was waiting to hear more. How much could he say? Then he thought of Costa. Keeping things back had led to where he was now. Still, he also did not want to get other people in as deep.

He lit his pipe and puffed on it for a few moments.

'Pietro, if that is his real name, is an Italian communist and terrorist,' he said. 'My assistant, Costa, found evidence that he ran a Republican assassination team in Spain, often operating behind the lines.'

'Nem fodendo!' Cruz shook his head. 'So what is he doing here? The same?'

Lopes shrugged. 'I don't know for sure, but it's possible. I know he's already wanted for murder up in Porto, a couple of cops got in his way.'

'So we can put out a wanted bulletin? That's the least we can do?'

Elena's face came into Lopes' mind. He dismissed her; the needs of the state had to come first.

'Absolutely,' he said.

'But how does this murder fit in? Is this Pietro the 'Hemline Killer?' He doesn't fit the profile of the suspects that have been picked up so far.'

'I'd forgotten, the last time we met you were about to start looking at them, weren't you? Did you get anywhere?'

Cruz pulled a face. 'Not really. Oh, don't get me wrong, there's been plenty of thugs and weirdos picked up over the last few months, most of whom need to be locked up if you ask me, but they aren't strong suspects.'

'Why not?'

'Because, as much as I hate to say anything good about our killer, he respects women. He kills as quickly as possible and then doesn't humiliate them after death. All the suspects I've looked at are pretty much bastards, quite happy to beat women and girls who cross their paths. They are usually inadequates.'

'Who want to humiliate.'

'Exactly, sir. Inspector Ribeiro was keen on pinning the killings on a couple of them but they had alibis.'

Lopes gave a humourless cough of laughter. 'I bet he was delighted by that. Did he ask you to burn the alibi evidence? No, don't answer that.'

Cruz gave a little smile which was all the confirmation Lopes needed. It was also reassuring; his protege had not yet been corrupted by negligence.

'As to whether Pietro is the 'Hemline Killer,' Pedro, I think the answer is no. That he did this one, I've little doubt. It's a good facsimile of the murders but it's not our man.'

Cruz nodded. 'The lack of the bead and the wound being different, I see. But it's otherwise so similar. Where did he get that from? The newspapers?'

Lopes had a nasty feeling that he hadn't, but said, 'It's possible.'

Cruz frowned. 'You don't think so, do you? So, where do you think he got it from?'

Lopes bit his lip. In his mind's eye, he pictured the table in the study at Elena's house, all of the photos laid out on it, neatly sorted, victim-by-victim. A cursory glance before Elena locked it all away from prying eyes would show the broad brush of the killer's modus operandi, but the fine detail, like the bead and the neatness of the cut, could easily have been missed.

'You know, don't you, sir?' Cruz stared at him. 'I can see it in your eyes. Why don't you want to tell me?'

Yes, why don't you, you old idiot? Lopes sighed.

'Because I'm a fool. I've allowed myself to be used because of an emotional attachment. And it's not the first time.'

There. He'd said it. He felt better having got this off his chest. And now he had, there seemed to be no reason to stop.

'I'd better tell you everything, Pedro,' he said. 'If you've got time.'

Cruz nodded. 'I'll make time, sir. Go on.'

*

By the time he'd finished telling Cruz the story - the full story - his former assistant was looking both shocked and exasperated.

'Eu não entendo essa sua vontade de fazer merda!' he muttered. 'Sorry, sir, but really. How the hell do you manage to get into such situations?'

Lopes puffed out his cheeks. 'I know. I can be an idiot.'

'That's an understatement.' Cruz shook his head. 'So what do you want me to do? Find this house where this Katz woman is living?'

'No. And, no, not for the reasons that that look suggests.'

'Sorry, sir.'

'I won't let my feelings get in the way of matters of national security, not any more. We should stick to the roles our jobs are most suited to. Pietro and his group are most definitely a threat, but this is a job for the PVDE, the organisation I work for. You are in Homicide, and we still have a killer to catch, the *real* killer. I think you should concentrate on that.'

'Yes, sir.'

'I have the file on the victims that Miss Katz prepared in my office. I'll send it over. It's an impressive piece of work, I think you'll find it useful.'

Cruz nodded. 'Yes, sir, But still, from what you've told me about the PVDE, you could end up working alone. I don't like the thought of that.'

Lopes gave Cruz a grim smile. 'Neither do I. That's why I intend to do something about that.'

CHAPTER 43

29th OCTOBER 1941 - 1539 HRS

Lopes laboured his way up the last flight of stairs and took a few moments to recover his breath before knocking on the door.

A young, dark-skinned woman opened the door, a child held on her hip. She looked tired but she gave Lopes a little smile.

'I hoped you would come,' she said.

'I was afraid to, Luisa.'

'Why, he adores you.'

Lopes nodded. 'And I, him. How is he?'

'Miserable. Moody. Difficult,' she said. 'It's like having another child in the house, to be honest.' She stepped back. 'Come in. I'll make coffee. He's through there.' She nodded at the door behind her.

Lopes steeled himself and then opened the door.

Costa was on his feet in an instant.

'Oh, it's you. What do you want?'

'Alvares, I've come to apologise - and to explain.'

'It's too late for that.'

'Alvares, don't be such a fool,' Luisa pushed past Lopes and waved her finger at him. 'You know this is what you wanted, so stop being stubborn. Sit down and listen to the inspector.'

Costa did as he was told. Lopes picked up some wooden blocks and passed them down to the toddler playing on the floor before sitting down next to him.

'Alvares, I came to apologise and I mean it. I thought I was right keeping things from you. I thought it best for your safety for you not to know. I was wrong, we are… were a team, a partnership. For that to work we must be honest with each other. I wasn't, I am ashamed that I wasn't, and I'm deeply sorry for it.'

Costa was quiet for a few seconds.

'Alright,' he said at last. 'But I need to know everything and I need to know it now.'

Lopes sighed. For the second time today, he started his confession.

*

'So, you see, I thought I was doing right, I thought I was protecting us.'

Costa nodded. 'I see,' he said. 'And I believe you.'

'But you're still angry?'

'Yes, I am. You withheld so much from me. I needed to know what you were doing.'

'Yes, because it affected you and your family. I know, and I'm sorry. I quite understand if you don't want to work with me again. But I hope you do, Alvares. I need you.'

Costa closed his eyes and leaned back in his seat. The seconds past by slowly.

At last, Costa opened his eyes and straightened up. He held out his hand.

'It's good to be back, sir,' he said.

Lopes took it and shook the hand warmly.

CHAPTER 44

30th OCTOBER 1941 - 0840 HRS

Surprisingly, Lopes's wife was all smiles at breakfast.

'You look pleased with yourself,' he remarked.

'Because I have the architect coming in today.'

'The architect?'

'For the remodelling of the house. You agreed. Don't tell me that you've changed your mind. I've already paid a deposit for his services.'

'No, of course. I'm sorry, my mind is elsewhere.' He saw a suspicious look start to form and reflected quickly on his words. 'On the case.'

Her face brightened. 'The 'Hemline Killer?' You think you know who the killer is?'

He thought of Pietro. 'Actually, yes, I think I do.'

It was a lie but only a partial one.

Maria Sofia was satisfied. 'I can't wait to see your name in the paper. Perhaps Dr Salazar will invite you over to congratulate you. '

Lopes doubted it but smiled as he helped himself to coffee from the pot on the table.

*

Costa was in the office when Lopes arrived.

'Morning, sir.'

Lopes wondered if he should reference yesterday's conversations but decided that a line should be drawn under it. Costa was back and that was all that mattered.

'Good morning, Alvares,' seemed to be sufficient.

He took his seat behind his desk.

'So we need to address the issue we have with Pietro and his colleagues,' he said.

'Yes, sir.' Costa looked thoughtful. 'Of course, you realise this would mean also investigating the AMR. It would lead to problems for Miss Katz.'

'I know that, Costa. So be it.'

Costa nodded. He turned to his desk and picked up his notebook. 'I don't know if you are interested, sir, but I've been giving some thought to the case. I'd started before yesterday but after you filled me in on some of the things you found out I carried on last night.'

'Of course, I'm interested, Costa. I think that would be helpful.'

'It doesn't lead to any conclusion. All it does is raise more questions.'

'Questions are useful, especially if we combine our efforts to answer them. Carry on, please.'

Costa nodded and opened his notebook.

'It seems that this man Pietro was behind all the attacks on us. This includes the bombing and the attempted shooting. There is no direct evidence for this but the circumstantial evidence is strong. Pietro was a known bomb maker, he used bombs to assassinate Fascist opponents in Madrid and he was linked to the bomb factory found earlier in the year. He is a violent killer who co-ordinated other killers, including gunmen. He is likely doing the same here, and he instructed the man that attacked you.'

Lopes nodded. 'Yes, I believe that to be correct.'

'But this raises several questions. Firstly, did those attacks intend to kill us? In this, the warning is important.'

'Yes, I agree.'

'Let's deal with the bomb first. If the bomb had come from the crime gangs, the warning could have come from someone within the organisation who felt it was foolhardy to do something like this. You know I have doubts about a gangster like Santos telling the truth but, in this case, given the strong circumstantial evidence of Pietro's involvement and the fact that it's out of keeping for the gangs to act this way, I believe, this time, he was.'

'I'm sure you're right about that.'

'So, as the gangs did not know about the bomb, the warning had to come from either the bombers themselves.' Costa looked up pointedly from his notes and looked across at Lopes. 'Or someone close to them.'

'By someone close, you mean Elena? That she knew about it and intervened?' Lopes said. 'That's what you're asking, isn't it?'

'Yes, sir. I'm sorry but I have to ask.'

'Of course you do. I don't know for sure but, from what I know about her, it would be out of character for her to be involved in anything like a bomb plot. It's just not her, she's not a radical.'

'But if she found out about it, she might have taken it on herself to give the warning.'

'Elena is so blunt she'd have told me directly. That's her way.'

Costa nodded slowly. 'I'll have to take that at face value. You know her better than I do.' He turned back to his notes and crossed out something, presumably the question about Elena. 'So the warning must have come from the bombers.'

'Yes, it must have.' Lopes filled his pipe. 'So it means that they didn't want to kill us.'

Again Costa nodded. 'Which leads to more questions. Why stage the attacks and why keep us alive?'

Lopes tamped down the tobacco in the bowl of his pipe whilst he thought. 'Well, let's look at the results. What did it provoke?'

'The clampdown. The rounding up of gang members,' said Costa.

'Exactly. And who did that benefit? Or rather, whose interests did it damage?'

'The gangs?' said Costa. 'Oh, no, you mean wider than that, don't you?'

'Yes. Most of the gangs smuggling unlicenced wolfram did so on behalf of German interests. Taking the gang members off the streets favours the allies, including, now, the Soviet Union.'

'And Pietro and his gang are communists, of course!' exclaimed Costa. He scribbled some more notes in his book but then frowned. 'It would have had the same effect, though, if we'd been dead, wouldn't it?'

Lopes lit his pipe, puffing it to life and filling the office with smoke. 'Yes. That's where the logic breaks down. Either that or there's something we don't know yet.'

Costa nodded and tapped his pencil on his notebook. Neither man spoke for the next few minutes. Lopes' pipe went out and he started to clean out the ash.

'Let's leave that for now,' he said. 'What other questions do you have in there?' Lopes pointed the stem of his pipe at Costa's notebook.

His assistant flicked forward a few pages. 'I'm not sure if this is important or not, but I think you mentioned that this Pietro referred to a boss whose orders he was following. You also mentioned a woman, possibly an American?'

Lopes nodded. 'Yes, this mysterious Rosa. Yes, I think she is important. We need to know who she is and what role she plays in all of this.'

Costa tapped his notebook again. 'Particularly if she's giving the orders that this Pietro follows. Other than looking to get Pietro behind bars we should investigate her. I wish we had more than the name "Rosa." That's likely to just be fake, isn't it?'

'It is yes, but I think I might have met a possible candidate for her.'

Lopes told Costa about the reception at the US Embassy and about meeting Carole Young.

'So you've no reason to suspect her other than her accent was similar to the voice you heard?'

'I know, it's a tenuous link, but it might be worth following up on her. I have a feeling.' He opened his tobacco pouch to start refilling his pipe. 'Anything else?'

Costa flicked to the end of his notes. 'The murder of this German agent — or supposed agent.'

'She was an agent. She was well-trained.'

'Alright, she was an agent. But why did Pietro kill her?'

'Well, again, looking at the result of what her actions led to; sinking wolfram destined for the British war effort. Britain and the communists are now on the same side.' Lopes paused.

Something had just struck him, something about what he'd just said.

'Yes, but how did Pietro know about her? There was no connection between them as far as we know.'

Lopes frowned, thinking hard. Costa was right. But then, suddenly like a flash of lightning on a dark night, it all slotted into place and he could see everything.

'Damn it,' Lopes slapped the table.

'What is it, sir?'

'There is a connection. In fact, I just said what it was! Britain and the communists are on the same side!'

Costa looked puzzled for a moment, but then he too got it. 'They're working together. That Mr Armstrong and Pietro.' He shook his head in wonder. 'They are strange bedfellows if they are, the diplomat and the terrorist.'

'But they are, that's the only thing that makes sense, a common enemy and a common cause. Still, I didn't think Armstrong would stoop so low. but he's got blood on his hands now. Except he can deny it and blame his communist allies.'

'Or that young sailor,' said Costa.

Lopes stared at him for a moment and then nodded. 'You're right. Armstrong had set Jenkins out on a mission and given him a knife. They'd quite happily throw him to the wolves to cover their tracks.' He closed his eyes. 'I hate their world.'

Costa flicked back through his notes. 'This Carole Young. She was with Armstrong when you met her?'

'She was, yes. She seemed surprised to see me there and couldn't wait, which is even more interesting. Pietro is wanted, he'd have to be careful about showing his face. If Carole is 'Rosa' then she would be the one to liaise with the British.'

'I take it we need to track her down and talk to her?'

'Yes, we should. As a priority.'

Lopes frowned, deep in thought.

'Of course, you know what this means?' he said. 'Armstrong and Oliveira work closely together. He's not going to like this.'

Costa nodded. 'The boss will try and shut down any investigations that involve Armstrong and the British. Even with the communists being involved?'

'Indeed. Certainly, I'm sure the Tenente didn't know anything about the assassination attempts on us, I can't believe he would sanction anything like that but the whole reason we were set up in the first place was to counter the Nazi sympathisers within the PVDE. He's not going to approve of us going against Armstrong's activities.'

Costa looked glum. 'Does that mean we do nothing? We let them get away with murder?'

'That's up to us, and I mean us rather than just me this time.' Lopes looked straight at Costa. 'It's a risk. We can go on, but it would mean both going behind the boss' back and also working with some unpalatable people, some of whom work here at the PVDE. There's a risk to us both, we could lose our jobs. We could also lose more than that. These are some dangerous people we're going up against.'

'And working with by the sound of it.' Costa smiled. 'But we can't let them get away with this, not in our country. What's our next step?'

'Good man.' Lopes put his pipe down and stared at it as he marshalled his thoughts. 'We need to come up with a plan of action to get Pietro and his thugs off the streets.'

Costa tapped his notebook thoughtfully. 'We've got more than we had before. We can take these names to International, see if they've got anything specific on them.'

Lopes thought back to his encounter with the PVDE's international section a few days previously. 'Good luck with that. You're going to need it.'

Costa smiled. 'Yes, sir. What about you? What's your first step?'

'I need to arrange a meeting.'

'Who with?'

'Someone from the German Embassy.'

CHAPTER 45

30th OCTOBER 1941 - 1205 HRS

Lopes rose to greet his guest as he came into the bar.

'Thank you for coming. Can I get you something, Herr Von Wernsdorf?'

The German shook Lopes' hand. 'Otto, please,' he said, sitting. 'I have a feeling what I take rather depends on what you have asked me to come for.'

The diplomat wore a warm smile.

Lopes laughed. 'Indeed,' he replied.

'You do have a habit of landing huge problems on my lap, especially when you ask to meet me here.'

Lopes looked around. This used to be one of his favourite Fado bars but he'd not been able to face coming here since the last time he'd been in the company of the diplomat back in May. Then he'd done his, Germany's and Britain's interests a favour by dealing with something that could have embarrassed them all but had, in doing so, betrayed Elena.

'I do, I admit. This one is less of a bombshell…'

'That wouldn't be hard.'

'It's more of a humanitarian request but it is, I admit, potentially embarrassing for your embassy. Though it needn't be.'

Von Wernsdorf frowned. 'Now I'm confused. It sounds like a double brandy sort of problem.'

Lopes signalled the waiter and placed the order. They made small talk until it arrived.

The diplomat took a sip. 'Now I am sufficiently fortified, I can face whatever problem you are about to drop into my lap.'

Lopes took a sip of his brandy and began.

*

When Lopes had finished, Von Wernsdorf stared thoughtfully into his glass.

'There is no concrete link between the agencies of my country and this woman, is there?' he said at last.

'No. It's just circumstantial.'

'But doing what you propose could be construed as admitting such a link exists.'

Lopes sipped his brandy. 'It could, but it depends on how it was done.' He grimaced. 'Look, Otto, I realise the way this world works. It's one of the things I dislike about politics and espionage and all the other activities which involve obscuration, dissembling and down-right lying. I'm a simple cop, I prefer things to be as black and white as possible.'

Von Wernsdorf gave a grunt of laughter. 'You must be enjoying life in Lisbon at the moment then.'

'Indeed. But you and I and the embassies of your country and the British the truth. Whether or not any of us choose to admit it, it doesn't matter.'

'So what does matter, Dinis? Why are you doing this?'

Lopes thought for a few moments, framing his answer. 'I'm not entirely certain other than to admit I'd rather lost my way over the last few months. I lost sight of the things I'd always found important, the things which fired me up, and gave me the values I lived and worked by. Maybe you're right, maybe it is what Lisbon is like now that caused me to lose my focus.' He sipped his brandy. 'Maybe I'm just getting old and maudlin, but this seems to be one of those important things I've neglected.'

The diplomat shook his head and then drained his brandy. 'No, I don't think you are getting maudlin. You're just remembering who you are. Perhaps we should all do that.' He stood. 'You don't like injustice, you don't like little people being used then discarded like they were rubbish when their usefulness ended. That mustn't happen.' He smiled and held out his hand. 'Perhaps we will all get back to thinking that way when this madness is over. Though I doubt it.'

Lopes shook his hand. 'So do I.'

'Whatever, leave it with me. I will see what I can do.'

'Thank you.'

Once Von Wernsdorf had gone, Lopes spent a few moments looking around. He sighed. There were too many endings associated with this place. He could not bear to stay any longer.

He put some money down on the table, put his hat on and went out into the street.

CHAPTER 46

30th OCTOBER 1941 - 1420 HRS

Costa was back in the office when Lopes arrived. He looked glum.

'How did you get on with our colleagues, Alvares?' Lopes asked, although he could guess what the answer was.

Costa sighed and shook his head. 'It took me half an hour just to get anyone to see me and, even then, it wasn't anyone high up. They did at least take down what I said and told me they'd look into Pietro and his gang, but whether they will or not...' Costa puffed out his cheeks and shrugged. 'And, of course, nothing was flowing our way, information-wise. It was like I was some informer.'

Lopes nodded. 'We tried at least, I think this is going to be down to us. Us and the police.'

'Is that where I should try next?'

'Yes, Alvares. What about the woman, Miss Young? Did they have any records on her?'

'None that they were willing to share with me, well not officially.' Costa looked sheepish. 'There's a typist who's taken a bit of a shine to me. I can rely on her to help me out from time to time.'

Lopes looked in surprise at Costa. 'Be careful, Alvares, don't get into the kind of mess I have. You've got a lovely wife.'

'Don't worry, sir, I wouldn't let anything happen. It's her chasing me, not the other way around. Whatever, she's useful to know. She does filing for the international section so I can get her to give me the odd titbit.' He opened his notebook and flicked to the last written page. 'Carole Young is a long-term resident at an old favourite of ours, the Avineda Palace

Hotel. This is her suite number.' He passed it over to Lopes who noted it in his book.

'Thanks,' he said.

'I did give them a call, asking whether she was there or not,' said Costa, taking his notebook back. 'She wasn't when I called, although they were their usual unhelpful selves.'

'I hope you impressed on them how important it was to assist the PVDE?'

Costa smiled. 'I did, sir.'

'So they'll call us when she returns?'

'They will, sir.' Costa looked at the clock. 'I should head over to the central station to have a look at their records.'

'Perhaps I should do that, Alvares. I can talk to the more senior ranks. You know what they're like.'

'Yes, sir, I do. Perhaps we should both go? That means I can look at the records and put some feelers out amongst the lower ranks that I know. Sometimes the cops on the streets see and know a lot more than the higher-ups do. No disrespect, sir.'

'None taken, Alvares. That's a good…'

He was interrupted by the ringing of the telephone.

Costa answered it. 'Yes? Ah, that's good, thanks.' He put down the receiver, 'That was the switchboard. Carole Young is at the Avienda. Should we go there first?'

Lopes thought about this for a few moments. 'Perhaps we should split our time. The Avienda don't like too many cops sullying their marble at once. You go to the central police station as we originally planned whilst I go and have a word with Miss Young.'

Costa nodded.

'Yes, sir.' He smiled. 'It's good to be back working with you, sir.'

'It is, Costa, it is.'

CHAPTER 47

30th OCTOBER 1941 - 1530 HRS

Lopes went straight up to the desk of the Avenida Palace and showed his badge. The concierge was well-trained, showing only the briefest flicker of alarm before reverting to smooth servitude.

'Yes, sir, how can we be of service?'

'You have a guest, an American woman by the name of Carole Young?'

'We do, sir? I will have to check.'

'Of course, please do.'

The concierge started to leaf through the register. 'Ah, yes, we do.' He looked back over his shoulder at the numbered pigeonholes where some keys were hanging. 'The key isn't there, so Miss Young must be in residence.' Lopes was relieved; he had been concerned that she might have been and gone in the time it had taken to cross the city. 'Would you like me to ring her room?'

The concierge reached for the telephone.

'No. I'll go up. Could you tell me the number?'

The concierge frowned. 'I don't think the management would… '

'I don't care what the management thinks,' snapped Lopes. 'That's what's happening. Now, her room number.'

The concierge's mouth tightened. '410.'

'Thank you. Oh, and please don't ring her to warn her of my coming.'

'I wasn't going to, sir.'

'Good.' Lopes smiled at him and headed to the lift.

Arriving at the fourth floor, he made his way along the corridor to room 410. The lack of doors surrounding it told Lopes that this was a suite, hardly surprising for a wealthy guest, which, given her father, she must have been. He knocked on the door.

'Who is it?'

That confirmed it for Lopes. He had been fairly certain before, but now he was sure. The voice, muffled by the door, sounded just like it had in Elena's house. This was 'Rosa.'

'PVDE. I need to talk with you.'

Now Lopes could hear a murmured conversation. She was not alone.

A moment later the door was opened. A rather delicate young man looked down at Lopes.

'I am Miss Young's secretary. Who should I say is calling for her?'

Lopes showed him his badge. 'My name's Lopes.'

'It's alright, Charles, the inspector and I have met. Let him in.'

Charles stood to one side allowing Lopes to see into the room. Carole Young was sitting at a table, papers out in front of her.

'Good afternoon, Miss Young, I'm sorry to disturb you.'

She smiled. 'I'm sure that's not true, inspector, though I am working to a deadline to submit my story, which I'm likely to miss given your visit.'

'I'm sure, given who you are, your father would give you some leeway.'

'Obviously, you don't know him.' The smile had disappeared. 'Charles, we can complete this later. Go to your room and I'll call you when I need you.'

'Yes, madam.'

Charles stepped out of the room and closed the door behind him.

'So, inspector, what brings you here? How can I help you?'

'May I sit?'

'Of course.'

Lopes took a seat and looked around him. He had not been in one of the Avenida Palace's suites before but it was as opulent as he'd expected. Now he had doubts. Could this wealthy American, slick and chic, really be Rosa, the communist agitator and organiser? If so, she disguised it well.

'Inspector? Is there something troubling you? Have you started to have doubts?'

Lopes brought his attention back to Carole. She was acting differently to how she had been at the reception. Then she had done everything to get away from him, but now…'

'Well, I…'

'Oh come on, inspector. This isn't at all what I expected from you. This isn't the man that Elena told me about.'

The fog of doubt evaporated.

'So, you *are* Rosa,' he said.

She smiled. 'Of course I am. I'm surprised it's taken you this long to find me. I thought you were the master detective. '

'You didn't exactly help me, did you? Staying hidden at Elena's house and doing everything you could to avoid me at the reception.'

She shrugged. 'Given your country's attitude to my politics, what choice did I have? I needed to play this role to be able to act and move around as I wish.'

'The role of the rich heiress playing at being a reporter.'

For the first time, a flash of anger crossed Carole's face. 'I don't play. I am a reporter and a damned good one. I'm good at what I do. Or don't you consider women capable of such things?'

'That is not how I think. Surely Elena has told you that?'

'What? Her? Why would I care what she thinks?'

Lopes was puzzled by her reaction and, by the look of awkwardness, this seemed like an unguarded comment. Perhaps it would be useful to provoke her further. He looked around the room. 'Do your comrades know this is how you live? It doesn't exactly fit in with the communist ethos.'

Carole shrugged. 'It is what it is. None of us can help where we come from, can we? From what Elena told me, both of us detested our starts and wanted something different. You, yourself came from humble beginnings and clawed your way up the slippery pole. I came from a place of wealth and privilege. I want a better world and am willing to use all resources at my disposal to get it.'

'And if you enjoy the trappings whilst they last, so much the better?'

'Enough of this,' she snapped. 'How I conduct my life is none of your business, inspector.'

'I think you'll find it *IS* my business, Miss Young. I'm a member of the security services of this country whose task is to keep Portugal free of dangerous enemy aliens and foreign interference. By your admission, you fall into those categories.'

Carole stared at him with defiant confidence. 'Yes, I do. What are you going to do about it?'

'I could arrest you and have you deported.'

'You could. But you haven't. Yet.'

'No, I haven't. Yet.'

'Why not?'

'Because I prefer not to be so heavy-handed. You are intelligent. It would be better for you if you simply left Portugal of your own accord.'

Carole gave a little tilt of her head as if she were thinking this over but the look of amusement on her face told a different story. 'Leave? I don't think so.'

'Then I'll have to arrest you.'

Carole shook her head and rose from her desk. She went over to the bedside dresser and retrieved some photographs from the drawer. She brought them over to Lopes and gave them to him.

'No, you won't.'

They were of Lopes and Elena outside the study door in Elena's house, he holding the two cups of coffee whilst facing her. He remembered that moment, the feeling of longing he felt for her, and the photograph perfectly caught that expression on his face.

'It would be awkward for you, wouldn't it, to have that image of apparent domestic bliss passed to your superiors? You with her, the head of an organisation you're supposed to be investigating to close down.'

Lopes stared at the images. Then shrugged and handed them back.

'It could cause some embarrassment, I suppose. But it could have been taken at any time. Miss Katz and I have met before, as you know.'

'I did know that, which is why, on the original negatives - which are not here in case you start looking for them - are photos of the newspaper for that day, clearly showing the date.'

He stared at her for a moment, then shrugged again. 'My superiors know that I use unconventional methods. They will just take this as one of them.' He nodded towards the photograph. 'That means nothing.'

'On its own, I agree it doesn't.' Carole rose once again and went back to the nightstand. This time she extracted an envelope and again brought it over to Lopes. 'This tells a different story.' She held out the envelope. He took it. There were two photographs inside this time, rather smaller than the one of him and Elena. They were not of people, but of a handwritten ledger. They were records of a bank account.

His bank account.

But a bank account containing deposits that he didn't recognise. Regular and large deposits, made in cash.

And there had been a large withdrawal, made by a personal cheque signed by Maria Sofia the previous day.

The deposit for the house remodelling.

He looked up into the smiling face of Carole Young.

'You've set me up,' he muttered.

'Well done, inspector,' she said.

CHAPTER 48

30th OCTOBER 1941 - 1605 HRS

Lopes stared at the photographed documents in disbelief.

'How did you get these?'

'We have sympathisers to our cause everywhere.'

'But how did you get my account details? They're private and…' he began, then remembered. The correspondence from the bank, the one about Joao's trust fund that he'd thought he'd lost. 'You burgled my study. You took my account details.'

'Well done,' she said. 'If only you'd been as diligent about your financial and personal affairs as you are in investigating crime, perhaps you could have avoided this. As it is, you didn't and you are now in a rather awkward position. Not only consorting with someone you were told to investigate but also, given this evidence, in their pay. And now you are shown to be in cahoots with your wife to spend your ill-gotten funds. Now that would be embarrassing for you in so many ways, wouldn't it? More than embarrassing, fatal.'

Lopes stared at her for a long few seconds.

'This is why you hid from me until now,' he said. 'You needed to set the trap and have my wife walk into it.'

Carole nodded. 'Of course.'

Lopes forced himself to think more. 'Was this always what you intended? I assumed that if your group was using Elena, it was for her wealth and property. But you've got access to that yourself.' He waved his hand around the room. 'So now I'm not so sure.'

Carole raised her eyebrows in surprise. 'You really can be astute when you want to be, can't you, inspector? It's a shame you can be so slow in other areas. And so easily swayed by a pretty face. Miss Katz's wealth is handy, it saves me having to use so much of my father's, though I'm happy to relieve the old man of the burden of his sins. Whatever, it's a bonus. She deserves to lose it anyway, since it came from one man's exploitation of others. No, it was always you we wanted. Though we didn't want you living in her house. That was awkward but she was so set on you coming in to investigate the death of her precious women I couldn't persuade her not to.' Carole wrinkled her nose in disgust. 'She's a fool.'

'Elena is no fool.'

Carole looked surprised. 'You still defend her? I thought you two had finally fallen out. Whatever, it doesn't matter. Her main usefulness was in her links to you, which I heard rumours about on the grapevine when I was reporting on another story.'

Now it was Lopes' turn to be surprised. 'Links to me? Why me?'

Carole gave him a smug smile. 'Oh, for many reasons. First, you're vulnerable. You've far too many, secrets, inspector.'

'Most of which have come out.'

'Maybe so, but it's established a pattern of weakness that makes your corruption believable by your superiors.'

Lopes didn't rise to this.

'The second reason is where you work. It's appealing to have someone we can control in the PVDE, the organisation that wants to eradicate us from Portugal. And we need to be here.'

'You won't control me, you never will.'

'We'll see about that. Do you think you could survive this scandal? Another one? Clear evidence of corruption involving your wife?'

'I'd rather not survive it. Not if it means I have to do your bidding. I'll confess to my boss.'

'And risk losing everything? I don't think so. It would destroy your wife, wouldn't it? She's put up with so much already thanks to you, hasn't she?'

Lopes swallowed.

'I don't care. Perhaps it all should end.'

'I still don't believe you'd do that. But it doesn't matter because we know other things; things that you don't.'

'What things?'

Carole's smile was now positively vicious. 'The whereabouts of two people you care about most; your son Joao and Elena.'

Lopes stared in disbelief.

'You wouldn't. He's just a child. And Elena, I don't… '

'Rubbish, Lopes. Remember, I've seen you with her, but as I said before, you've too many secrets, Lopes. Too much to hide and too many points of weakness. I'm surprised you're in the position you're in, you're so vulnerable.' She leaned towards him. 'But you are in the position you're in and I'm using that vulnerability.'

Lopes closed his eyes and tried to bring his breathing under control. How had it come to this? Having steadied himself he opened them again.

'I don't understand. What do you want from me? What can I bring that's so valuable to you rather than just vague help at the PVDE?'

'Finally, we get there,' said Carole. 'The real reason we targeted you in the first place. Why you are so important.'

Suddenly it came to Lopes.

'Wolfram,' he said. 'It's about wolfram, isn't it?'

Carole just smiled.

CHAPTER 49

31st OCTOBER 1941 - 0423 HRS

Lopes gave up the battle between his racing mind and his need for sleep and swung his legs out of the bed. He put the bedside light on and reached for his pipe. He found as much comfort in the familiar routine of cleaning, filling, tamping and lighting as he did from the tobacco smoke itself.

How had he got into this situation again? How had he become so vulnerable?

Did he believe the American woman? Did she and her thugs know where Joao was? His mother had moved since he'd been kidnapped in May. In fact, she'd left the city. He'd heard rumours she was in Porto. That made sense. Margarida made her living from Fado singing, so she'd need a big venue. If they could find her, they'd be able to find Joao.

But how did they know about him in the first place? Certainly, the remaining members of Da Souza's team, the ones who hadn't died at Lopes' hand on the raid on his mother's house that had led to her death, knew about him. But Da Souza's men were Nazi sympathisers, they certainly wouldn't have willingly passed any information onto Carole Young's communists.

No, there was only one possible source; Elena. Elena knew.

Was she really at risk? Or was she working with Young? She might have been. He'd wronged her, and she'd initially wanted to kill him for it. She still wanted revenge — didn't she? Lopes thought back to the time when they had worked together on the murder, sifting through the evidence. She'd been cautious at first but the warmth and vitality he'd first seen at his mother's house all those months ago had started to show through again.

Yes, they'd fallen out over Pietro, but nothing he'd seen had suggested she was playing a duplicitous game.

No, she'd been fooled too, fooled and used.

Which meant she was at risk.

Which brought him back to his problem and what he'd been told to do.

Obey his new masters or lose what he loved.

He couldn't lose them, but he couldn't do what they instructed. It was betraying his country.

It was betraying Costa.

Costa. Costa with a loving wife and a young family of his own. Loyal to a fault.

He'd deceived him before, he'd hidden things from him.

He'd have to hide things from him again.

There had to be another way.

CHAPTER 50

31st OCTOBER 1941 - 0810 HRS

Costa stared incredulously at Lopes, and then shook his head.

'Oh my God, sir. That's a nightmare.'

'I know, Alvares, I know,' said Lopes, glumly. 'And I'm sorry you've got mixed up in it all too.'

'We're in this together, sir, and I appreciate your telling me. It would have been easy to keep it to yourself.'

'I did think I should, at first. I have to admit that. Sorry Alvares.'

'Thanks for being honest about that, sir.'

'It's the least I could do. Keeping things to myself is what's got us into this position in the first place.'

'So what is it she wants us to do?'

'She wants us… Well, me, to feed her information on the wolfram smuggling gangs and, in particular, when they are moving a shipment. And it will be me, I'm not having you getting mixed up with anything like that.'

'Look, sir, I already am.'

'Costa, you can't.'

'Sir, I'm not going to back down. Anyway, why does she want to know?'

Lopes sighed. He'd run into stubbornness almost as bad as his own. 'She wants to make sure none of it gets through to the Nazis. It's her contribution to the Soviet war effort, and I don't think it's being done independently. I think her instructions come straight from Moscow.'

Costa nodded thoughtfully. 'It's us who are tapping into the informers. It's us who get to know about the smuggling first. Clever.'

'Yes, it is. It's why we were targeted in the first place. Not to stop us intervening in the smuggling, but to keep us doing it.'

Costa nodded to himself again. 'The arrests that followed the attacks on us. It would have weakened the gangs. Taken away their experienced men.'

'Yes, and now they've done that they've moved onto the next stage. Giving them our intelligence allows Pietro and his thugs to make plans for an ambush, ambushes that are a lot easier now some of the firepower has gone.'

Costa looked thoughtful. 'Perhaps it's not such a bad thing. It achieves the same result as our efforts without the risk to us and our men.'

'It does, in part. Don't forget the British smuggle illicit wolfram too. She wants us to let that through. The ore that Pietro takes off the smuggling gangs would likely go to the British too but at a price, I'm guessing. That money would go to buying more weapons and recruiting sympathisers. Effectively we'd be puppets, unable to act except at their bidding, sanctioning murder and funding the growth of communism in Portugal.'

Costa puffed out his cheeks. 'Dr Salazar would not be pleased.'

'No, he wouldn't.'

'But what do we do? If we take this to the boss, your career would be over.'

'And my son dead, most likely,' added Lopes glumly. 'I know.'

'So we go along with them? Is that our only choice?'

'No,' said Lopes, taking a deep breath. Once he'd proposed this option, there would be no going back. But he had to do it. 'There is another way. The trouble is it's a hell of a gamble. Fail and we lose everything. It's also almost as unpalatable as working as puppets for the communists.'

Costa smiled. 'Only almost as unpalatable? It sounds like it might be our best option then. What is it?'

Lopes started to explain the plan he'd formulated during the early hours.

Costa's eyes widened as he did.

CHAPTER 51

4th NOVEMBER 1941 - 0220 HRS

Lopes pulled his coat tighter around himself. In the early hours, the temperature had dipped before the cold front had swept in. Now the rain was beating down and dripping off the brim of his hat.

He peered around the side of the ruined farmhouse into the darkness of the countryside. There was no sign of life.

'They're late, sir.'

Even Costa sounded doubtful. That didn't bode well; he was usually the optimistic one of the pair.

'They'll come,' said Lopes. 'They said they would and I'm sure they will. It's in their interests too, long-term.'

'Yes, but...' Costa began.

Lopes waited. There was no need. He knew what Costa wanted to say. The truth was he felt the same.

'We'll just have to,,, '

'There's a truck, sir,' whispered Costa. 'I can hear it coming.'

Lopes couldn't as yet, but, as always, he trusted Costa's younger ears.

'Right. It's all in play.'

He peered around the farmhouse wall. Now he could see the headlights of the truck wending its way down the track. They were still a good ten kilometres from the sea. They wouldn't be expecting anything yet.

At least supposedly.

He found himself feeling sorry for the men in the truck. He knew what they were about to go through.

And then it was happening. The truck lights abruptly slewed to one side. One went out, then the other. Red streaks flashed away into the night, ricochets from rounds fired at the smuggler's truck. Now the sound of the gunfire could be heard, soft like firecrackers but Lopes knew how deadly they were.

And those firing were not men Lopes trusted, they were not the army or the police, those were Pietro's men. This was his ambush.

This was the first of the betrayals of his beliefs and his country's goals that he'd fed to Carole Young.

And he wanted them to succeed. They had to.

'I think it's over, sir,' said Costa, who was watching the distant scene through binoculars. 'Bar them loading the wolfram and taking it away.'

Lopes nodded in the darkness.

'So now we wait,' he said. He looked at his watch. 'Hopefully nothing will happen before 11 am.'

'What happens then?'

'I'm going to a funeral,' said Lopes.

CHAPTER 52

4th NOVEMBER 1941 - 1122 HRS

'In manus tuas, Domine, famulum tuum dilectam sororem tuam, tanquam in manus fidelis Creatoris et misericordissimi Salvatoris, commendamus, deprecantes ut ipsa pretiosa sit in conspectu tuo.'

The priest standing over the grave and who was intoning the familiar Latin words of the funeral rite was bare headed despite the rain, as were the three mourners who stood, hats in hand, heads bowed as the coffin was lowered into the ground. The weather, grim, cold and wet, seemed appropriate for the occasion.

Lopes, standing alongside Cruz, allowed his mind to wander. He wondered what this woman's childhood had been like, wherever she came from. Somehow he pictured her on a tropical beach, possibly the ones near Rio de Janeiro he'd seen in the guidebooks and films, happily playing in the sand, with friends and family all around, whilst the restless South Atlantic waves hissed and crashed in the background soundtrack.

He hoped that this was the truth or close to it. The truth was he didn't know. He had a hunch she was Brazilian, but he was going on no more evidence than her looks. He didn't know her name, which was why the priest had just referred to her as 'dear sister' in the rite rather than giving her the dignity of her identity. Lopes didn't know it and neither Cruz nor the third mourner had, officially at least, been able to find out what it was.

As the service drew to a close, Lopes glanced at the third man. Although no official acknowledgement had been made by the German Embassy that the young woman who was being buried today was their agent, the fact that Von Wernsdorf had arranged the service and had acquired the plot in the German cemetery at Alemao de Lisbon told its tale. The fact that this was attached to a Protestant church, yet the diplomat had brought in a Catholic priest to conduct the ceremony was the final confirmation; this was one of their own and they knew exactly who she was.

The service ended. The priest stepped away from the grave as the mourners, Lopes included, reached into the rain-drenched soil and tossed a handful of mud onto the coffin. The gravediggers stood respectfully to one side, spades at the ready, sheltering from the rain. One stepped forward, an old, ragged towel in hand, and offered it to Lopes who took it gratefully, nodding his appreciation. After he had cleaned his hands he passed it to Von Wernsdorf, who did the same and then passed the towel to Cruz to complete the ritual.

'Thank you for doing this,' murmured Lopes.

Von Wernsdorf shrugged. 'Sometimes you have to do the right things, even if they are awkward.'

'That is very true.'

Cruz had finished with the towel and handed it back to the gravediggers who were now moving to do their job. Lopes, Cruz and the German diplomat shook hands with the priest, thanking him for the service and then they strolled together towards the exit.

'Are you any nearer catching the man that did this?' said Von Wernsdorf.

Lopes hesitated. What was safe to reveal? He did trust the diplomat but...

'It's alright, I understand it's difficult for you to comment,' Von Wernsdorf smiled. 'I will leave it in the capable hands of you two gentlemen.' He raised his hat. 'Good day to you both,' he said and then he was gone.

'He seems like a nice chap,' murmured Cruz. He looked back towards the grave. 'Good of him to organise this.'

Lopes followed his gaze. 'Yes, he didn't need to. It would have been nice to give her a name but that will have to wait until the madness the world finds itself in is over, I suppose.'

He was about to turn away when his attention was drawn to a woman kneeling by another grave. She had just placed fresh flowers on it and her head was bowed. Even from a distance, the woman's grief was obvious. She'd lost someone very important to her, that was obvious. At least she was able to mourn. Poor 'Angel' or 'Ana Maria' didn't have that, her relatives, if she had any, would have no idea.

It also reminded him that he had not visited his own mother's grave since the funeral. Even in death, Lopes had been an inattentive child.

Still watching the woman, Lopes realised Cruz was speaking.

'Sorry, I was miles away, Pedro. What were you saying?'

'That's alright, sir. I was just saying that the background file you gave to me is really useful. We've been able to trace some of the people the murder victims met in the days before they were killed. It's given us some leads to follow up on, but there's nothing concrete yet. It's a good start though. Compliments to the person who put it together for you.'

Lopes gave a little laugh. 'I'd pass them on, but she's not talking to me at the moment.'

'She? A woman did this?'

Lopes didn't reply because thinking of Elena had, somehow, also focused his attention back on the mourning woman. Suddenly she looked familiar.

And, as if she sensed the recognition, the woman looked over at him.

He did know her. It was Ines.

As soon as she saw Lopes she was on her feet and heading for the cemetery's exit.

'Someone's got a guilty conscience,' laughed Cruz. 'Or is that another woman you've had an effect on, sir?'

'Not in that way, Pedro.' Puzzled, he took a few steps towards the flower-strewn grave.

'Ah, here's your man, Costa,' said Cruz.

Lopes turned, the grave forgotten. This could only mean one thing. He looked questioningly towards Costa.

He smiled grimly and nodded.

Lopes knew his night - and potentially his future - was now mapped out for him.

CHAPTER 53

4th NOVEMBER 1941 - 2230 HRS

Lopes scanned the wharf with his binoculars. He caught the briefest flicker of light as a match flared and then went straight out. He focused his attention on that spot. The breeze off the water was strong and gusty and he guessed that the smoker was struggling to keep the flame alight. Sure enough, the process was repeated with the same outcome. Now, though, Lopes saw at least two figures in the brief illumination. He stayed watching and was rewarded. The figures had moved to the shelter of the warehouse wall and, with hands cupped round the flame, a cigarette was successfully lit. In the flickering yellow light, Lopes could now see three men. Two of them had rifles slung over their shoulders. Once the match went out, the red glowing end of the lit cigarette was passed from hand to hand until three fireflies danced in the darkness.

He lowered the glasses.

'Damn,' he said. 'Rifles. We could have done without that.'

Next to him, Costa also lowered his binoculars.

'We always knew there were going to have set guards, sir.'

'Yes, but carrying weapons so openly? This was meant to be a coup rather than a gun battle.'

'Yes, but…'

He couldn't see much of Costa in the gloom but he made out a shrug. He understood why; there were Pietro's men out there, politically motivated thugs and killers, It was natural that he'd be indifferent to their fate.

'I'd still rather not have some poor bloody cops turn up here to investigate and get caught up in the middle of all this.'

'No, sir, but we're a long way from anywhere. By the time they get here, it will all be over.'

Lopes nodded to himself. Costa was right. They were on the docks but away from the busy area in a part where there were half a dozen small old warehouse buildings. It was a run-down part; in time, with the new-found wealth brought from the wolfram riches, it was likely that it would be redeveloped but, as yet, it was remote and relatively quiet. They had used the cover of darkness to sneak into the building furthest from that occupied by Pietro's men and had taken up a watching brief in the office, set high up on one gable wall so the one window was securely high above the wharf, making it harder for thieves to use it as a weak spot to get in, whilst affording the owners views of the Tagus and the wharf below.

Costa and Lopes were now taking advantage of this view for a quite different reason.

The creak of someone's body weight on the stairs up to the office caused Lopes and Costa to both turn away from the window. Lopes kept his hand off his gun but Costa had drawn his. Lopes held his breath as the office door was opened.

It was a man who Lopes didn't recognise. Still, he placed his hand on Costa's outstretched arm. 'Easy, Alvares,' he murmured. 'Put the gun away, we don't want to make our visitors nervous.'

Costa did as he was asked.

The man at the door glared at the two men then said, over his shoulder, 'It's clear, boss,' then stepped to one side.

Arthur Santos climbed the final part of the stairs and stepped into the room.

'Hello, gentlemen,' he said.

CHAPTER 54

4th NOVEMBER 1941 - 2255 HRS

Lopes moved away from the window and held out his hand. Santos took it.

Costa, rather pointedly, stayed where he was and, although his arm was lowered, still held onto his gun.

Santos didn't seem to notice.

'Everything's ready,' he said. 'Pietro's just arrived. As expected, they've not been slow to find a buyer. At a guess, they are here to meet him. Whatever, we can move in now.'

Lopes glanced back at the window. 'They've got armed guards on the wharf. They've got rifles.'

Santos shrugged. 'My men have got Tommy Guns.'

'You can't do that,' said Costa. 'We can't sanction a massacre.'

'Really? How are you going to stop us?'

Lopes frowned. 'Mr Santos, that wasn't our agreement. We agreed to minimise…'

'That was before those bastards executed two of my men the other night,' said Santos. 'That means the agreement we had is void. Anyway, don't forget it's not just my men who are here tonight, because of these sods all the crime families are short of manpower. We don't like working together. We've just got a temporary truce. This all has to end tonight.'

'This is what happens when we do deals with gangsters,' muttered Costa. 'Fucking scum and murderers.'

Santos strode over to Costa. 'Watch what you say,' he said. 'I've dealt with scarier young pups than you. You should learn to hold your tongue. As for murderers, it wasn't us who tried to blow you to kingdom come, it was those bastards out there. The same bastards who slaughtered my men.'

Lopes stepped between them. 'Santos, Costa, please. Let's not fight amongst ourselves.'

Costa and Santos continued to bristle at each other.

'Costa,' said Lopes sharply. 'Step away.' To his relief, Costa did. He went back over to the window and raised his binoculars. 'Mr Santos, I'm sorry about your men. I thought the idea was that you'd only send one man with the shipment of wolfram and that he'd run for cover as soon as he ran into the roadblock.'

Santos gave a wry smile. 'That was the idea. Unfortunately, I have men who make the mistake of thinking for themselves when they don't have the brains for it. They decided that they needed to add more security, that they'd look better in my eyes that way.' He looked pointedly at Costa. 'Second guessing your boss' orders usually ends up with those doing it, looking stupid.'

'Or dead, as in this case,' added Lopes.

'Yes. Whatever, my men are out for revenge. They'll do what they need to do.' Santos shrugged. 'I'm sorry, Lopes, this is out of your hands now. Anyway, Salazar is hardly likely to object to a few less communist thugs in his country, is he?'

Lopes puffed out his cheeks. 'No. He's not.' He glanced across at Costa. Even in the darkness, he could see the disapproval in his assistant. 'Do what you need to, but if the police come, you stop shooting and get the hell out of there. I don't want any poor cop's blood on my hands.'

'But if we haven't got the wolfram… '

'Then you leave it behind. I doubt it's got much value. I can't see you risking the best ore anyway. Am I right?'

Santos smiled. 'Of course not, it's low-grade scrapings. I'm still a businessman. So yes, if and when the cops arrive we'll make ourselves scarce. Now, can we get on with this?'

Santos turned to leave.

'Wait.'

'What is it now, Lopes?'

'Remember our deal. We're here to arrest Pietro. We want him alive. I want to see him in the dock. He's got crimes to answer for.'

'We'll do our best. But when the blood is up and the bullets are flying…' Santos nodded to his assistant. 'Jorge here will stay with you and try and get you to the Italian. We also need to make sure you don't become targets. Jorge…'

Jorge held out some strips of white cloth. 'Tie these around one arm,' he said.

Lopes took both and handed one to Costa. He stared at it in disbelief.

'Are you serious? Pietro's men will be able to pick us off.'

'The Italian has half the men we've brought,' said Santos. 'The odds are in your favour if our men can tell who you are. All our men are wearing them so they can tell each other apart.'

Lopes could see that Jorge did, indeed, wear one. He tied the cloth around his upper left arm. 'He has a point, Alvares.'

Costa reluctantly did the same.

Santos raised his hat. 'Gentlemen. Tonight ends our brief arrangement, but I'm sure our paths will cross again.'

And with that, he was gone.

Lopes went and stood by Costa by the window.

'I know, Alvares, I know,' he said. 'It'll be worth it though, if we can get Pietro.'

He heard Costa sigh deeply.

'I hope so, sir,' he said. 'It's starting.'

Out of the window, Lopes could see Santos' men moving towards the warehouse.

Within moments the first shot rang out.

'Come on, Costa,' said Lopes, taking the gun out of his holster. 'Let's try and not get shot.' He looked at Jorge. 'We're ready.'

Jorge nodded and led the pair down the stairs out of the office.

CHAPTER 55

4th NOVEMBER 1941 - 2330 HRS

As soon as they were outside they were greeted by a brief crack-crack of a pair of rifle shots followed by the gruff bark of a Tommy gun. A spent round ricocheted off into the darkness, painting a brief orange parabola against the night sky.

Lopes couldn't help but look towards the city.

'Let's hope to God there isn't a police patrol close,' he muttered. He made a silent prayer that they'd be slow to react and they'd have a few minutes for all this to be sorted out. His former colleagues would be seriously outgunned.

Jorge paused at the corner of the building they'd been watching from, holding up his hand as he peered around the corner. A few more shots rang out, quieter ones, probably from hand guns, but these were also responded to by the Thompson.

Then, after a few shouts, all fell quiet

'Come on,' said Jorge, who, head down, led them across the gap between the two buildings, a distance of some 50 metres.

They had only taken a few paces before a flash prefaced a sharp report that made the ground tremble. The shockwave from a blast peppered them with grit and splinters, as tiles lifted from the roof, came to earth around them. The three men covered their heads.

'What the hell?' said Costa.

'They've blown the doors off,' said Lopes in disbelief.

'Quickest way in,' said Jorge. 'Come on.'

Lopes could see that the blast had done more than just take the doors off; it had also set the building on fire.

They got perhaps another 20 metres when there were more shots and a scream of pain, this time from the right of the warehouse, the side furthest from the Tagus. Jorge stopped, holding his hand up as four figures emerged from that side, one turning back to fire his handgun down the passage between the warehouse and the neighbouring building.

'Fuck,' said Jorge and raised his gun.

'No!' muttered Lopes.

But it was too late. Jorge loosed off wild two shots that did nothing but draw the fire from the group onto him.

Lopes grabbed Costa alongside him and pulled him away from Jorge as a volley of shots was directed at him. The third or fourth smashed into the man's leg, spinning him around and leaving him screaming in pain, which only ceased after half a dozen more were loosed at him, at least three hitting his prone form.

Lopes had stopped paying attention to him, he was lying on the ground taking careful aim at one of the gunmen who was advancing towards the fallen figure of Jorge. Unlike Santos' man, he made his rounds count. Two rapid shots felled the man, but Lopes had already switched his aim to a second man, the one who had reacted quickest to Lopes' shots. He managed to get a shot off in Lopes' general direction before Costa, who had recovered from being manhandled, joined in. The concerted fire found its mark and the gunman crumpled.

The two remaining men had stepped away from the others, Lopes knew they were keeping out of the line of fire, which suggested that at least one of them was someone important that the other two had been trying to protect. Sure enough, as the flames breaking through the roof of the burning warehouse illuminated them, Lopes could see that one was Pietro.

He raised his gun to fire but then saw who was with him.

Looking terrified and struggling to get away from Pietro's grip was the British diplomat, Henry Armstrong.

CHAPTER 56

4th NOVEMBER 1941 - 2340 HRS

Lopes raised his pistol but hesitated; as good a marksman as he was he couldn't guarantee he'd not hit Armstrong. He was sure that Costa would be equally cautious, whatever the reason for the diplomat being there.

Pietro took advantage of their hesitation. He pulled Armstrong in front of him to shield his body further.

'Get off me!' Armstrong tried to twist away but Pietro pushed his gun, a Colt automatic, into the man's cheek.

'Keep still. And, you, Lopes, and him,' he nodded towards Costa. 'You keep back.'

Lopes had recovered from the surprise of seeing Armstrong at the ambush. He got to his feet and started advancing on the pair, his pistol raised.

'Why should we?' he said. 'That man is nothing to us.'

'Lopes,' gasped Armstrong. 'You can't.'

'I don't believe you,' Pietro spat. 'You'd have fired by now if that was true.'

'We're going to find out then, aren't we?' said Lopes continuing to walk towards them. Out of the corner of his eye, he could see Costa was on his feet and doing the same.

'Fuck you, Lopes.' Pietro suddenly pushed Armstrong away towards Lopes, turning the gun away from the diplomat and towards him and Costa, firing. Luckily, his aim was wild. Pietro moved towards the cover of the neighbouring building; Lopes took a bead on him and was about to fire when Armstrong blundered into his line of sight. He pushed the diplomat out of the way, re-aimed and fired a hurried shot just as Pietro disappeared behind the building's wall.

Had he hit him? Probably not.

'Blast!'

Lopes turned to Armstrong who had been sent sprawling by Lopes' push and was just getting back to his feet. He grabbed the Briton. 'What the hell are you doing here?' he asked, then heard a shout from behind him. He could make out uniformed figures making their way towards them.

The police had arrived.

'Costa, get your badge out,' he said. He pushed Armstrong towards his assistant. 'Look after him. Get him past them,' he pointed towards the police. 'Don't let them take him. But don't let him go.'

'You can't, I'm a diplomat,' said Armstrong.

'Right now, I and them,' said Lopes, gesticulating towards the uniformed men, 'don't give a toss who you are. Take him to HQ and lock him up.'

'But you can't,' protested Armstrong.

'With pleasure, sir,' said Costa. 'But what are you doing?'

'I'm going after Pietro,' answered Lopes.

He had reached the building behind which the Italian had vanished. with Costa's protests ringing in his ears.

CHAPTER 57

4th NOVEMBER 1941 - 2352 HRS

Lopes walked cautiously down the side of the warehouse where Pietro had last been seen. He was lucky; the clouds that had obscured the moon all night and helped to hide the advance of Santos' men, had started to clear. The moon was full and its silver light chased most of the shadows away. There was no sign of the Italian; at least he hadn't been waiting in ambush for Lopes — but where had he gone?

Lopes changed the magazine of his pistol as he walked. The little PPK didn't have much stopping power so he needed to ensure that the weapon had the full complement of seven. He only had one spare and, as he might need all he carried, put the part-used magazine back in his pocket. How many had he fired? He wasn't sure, probably five, but this was not the time to work it out. He needed to chase down Pietro.

The man was a murderer. Lopes wasn't going to let him get away.

Behind him he heard police whistles, the odd shout, and sirens could also be heard. This part of the docks, however, was quiet, so much so that Lopes wondered if Santos had enough influence in the police to ensure his escape route north was clear. He wouldn't put it past the man or, sadly, the force. Santos was resourceful and clever, the police were badly paid and, thus, vulnerable to bribes. Whatever, the way to the city streets and the Barro Alto was open.

He reached the outer wall of the docks. The gate here should have been watched and locked but, tonight, it was neither. Lopes walked through it.

Still, there was no sign of Pietro.

This was hopeless. Those few seconds whilst Lopes had handed Armstrong over to Costa and given instructions had been too long. Pietro had too much of a head start.

Lopes almost gave it up. Then he saw something, a few spots of darkness on the road which having been patched in concrete glowed white in the moonlight. He bent down and touched the spots. They were fresh. It was blood. It had to be Pietro's. Lopes' last desperate shot looked like it had found its mark.

Lopes crossed the road into the city proper, looking for more blood. He was now helped by both the moon and the artificial light from the streetlights. He soon found more, quite a lot more. It was probably a leg wound; that was the last image Lopes had of Pietro as he pulled the trigger. The man was running, his body passed behind the wall but his leg was still in sight as the PPK jumped in his hands at its discharge.

Yes, that was where he hit the man.

Now Lopes had a trail to follow, it was easy. Pietro had headed up into the Barro Alto keeping as much as possible on the side of the street shaded from the moon, probably to avoid drawing attention to his wound from the passing revellers, of which there were still many. There was still enough light to follow the trail.

Lopes hurried to catch up with his prey, moving as fast as his gas-damaged lungs would allow.

Abruptly, he lost the trail. There was no sign of the droplets on the cobbles. He cursed and looked around. Had the Italian gone into one of the houses? Or was he in a doorway ready to ambush him?

Lopes retraced his steps. He'd crossed over a side street about 20 metres back, he'd ignored it, it was little more than a narrow alleyway that descended steeply towards Rue de Misericordia. With relief, Lopes found a splash of blood on the steps a few metres down.

The chase was still on, The route also went a long way to confirming what Lopes had suspected from the start; Pietro was heading back to Carole Young at the Avenida Palace. He increased his pace. Damn the effect on his lungs, he was not going to let Pietro go to ground.

On the Misercordia itself the trail, as expected, showed that Pietro had turned left. There was little doubt now; he was heading to Carole's hotel, but how far was he ahead of Lopes?

Lopes reached a little square, the Largo Trindade Coelho if his memory was correct, dusty and dotted with trees. There was another narrow road down on the far corner that a late-night tram had just laboured up. That led down to the Rossio and then to the Avenida, which was almost certainly where Pietro would have gone. Lopes ran across the square but tripped on a loose cobble that sent him sprawling. Despite putting his hands out to break his fall, he hit the unforgiving ground hard, expelling the breath from his body. His pistol flew out of his hand and clattered away along the cobbles.

He tried to rise but couldn't. He couldn't get enough air.

He fought the panic. It was like the nightmare — the real nightmare — he'd endured 23 years previously when the gas shell had landed close by his platoon. He'd fought to breathe, fought to survive, writhing in the French dirt with his colleagues like landed fish.

He rolled on his back, forcing the air inside him.

And just as the pain in his chest started to subside, Lopes realised someone was standing over him.

It was Pietro and his gun was aimed at his head.

CHAPTER 58

5th NOVEMBER 1941 - 0006 HRS

Pietro sneered as he looked down the barrel of his automatic. Lopes' eyes were on the barrel, knowing that the slug that would end his life was a few centimetres away down the bore, but he could also see that the Italian's right leg was dark with blood.

'You pathetic little man,' Pietro spat on the ground. 'I told Rosa we didn't need you and that we could never trust you, but she said you were cunt-struck by that stupid Jewish bitch and that we could get you to do anything. Well, this is where it ends.'

Lopes hadn't the breath to say anything. But what was there to say anyway, other than a prayer to the maker he didn't truly believe in?

He closed his eyes.

The shot, when it came, was quieter than he'd expected.

He had often wondered what dying would feel like, but whatever it was he wasn't expecting it to be like a heavyweight landing on his chest.

A dead weight that was twitching and jerking.

Like a man in his death throes.

He opened his eyes and found himself looking into Pietro's sightless ones. The top of the man's skull was missing and blood was fountaining in pulses over the cobbles as the dead man's still-beating heart pumped its last.

'Get off him.'

Someone was trying to roll Pietro's corpse to one side. He knew that voice. Lopes came back to his senses and had recovered most of his strength, so half pushed the Italian away and did the rest by squirming to one side.

He got to his feet.

Then took Elena into his arms.

She felt so good.

At last, though, he was aware of a stifled scream and a curse.

Someone called; 'Call the police!'

Lopes let go of Elena and looked around. A handful of late-night revellers stood a little way away, obviously brought to the square by the shot. He took out his badge. 'Police,' he said, then corrected himself; 'PVDE. Keep back, please, let the police do their job.'

He saw the man closest to him was looking at Elena, not at her face but at her torso. Lopes followed his gaze and realised that she was holding his PPK in her hand. Quickly he put his hand on hers and took it off her. She didn't resist.

He put the gun back into his holster.

'Aren't you going to arrest her?' said one of the bystanders. 'She shot him in the back. I saw her do it.'

'Yeah, but he had a gun on that cop. He was chasing him,' said another.

The argument continued.

A police whistle sounded; someone had found a patrol who was calling in reinforcements. 'I'd better get you out of this,' Lopes murmured to her, then brandished his badge. 'Clear the way, I have to get this lady out of here.'

'But, shouldn't she stay for the cops? She shot him,' said the bystander who wanted

Elena arrested.

'No,' said Lopes firmly.

'Why not? She... '

Lopes took hold of the man's arm and led him out of the way. 'Listen, she can't stay here.'

'Why not?'

Lopes leaned closer conspiratorially. 'She's an undercover agent. She can't be seen, even by the police. It would blow her cover. I can see you're a good, upstanding citizen. I'm sure you understand and that you'd want to help your country?'

'Oh, yes. Yes, of course.'

'Good man. Tell the cops I was here but say nothing about her, alright?'

'Yes, I'll do that.'

Lopes smiled at him, then went back and took Elena by the arm and led her away from the square, moving in the opposite direction from where the police whistle had been heard. They were just in time.

'What did you say to him?' said Elena as they walked .

'I told him you were an undercover cop.'

'Hah, as if that would ever happen.' She stopped, 'I think we're far enough now. I need to be somewhere else.'

'Where else, Elena? The Avenida? To deal with Carole Young?'

She gave a grim smile.

'You know who she is then. That lying cow has been blackmailing you, hasn't she?'

'Yes,' Lopes sighed. 'I see you've worked it out.'

'Yes, I've been had. You see, sometimes I do listen to you.' She puffed out her cheeks. 'I already had some doubts. I looked at the books and saw what she'd done; the money being paid to you. That had to be a set-up, you're not corrupt. And if she'd betrayed me then I figured Pietro had done as well. So, tonight, I followed him. I saw him meet Armstrong, though why I don't know.'

'They were doing a deal for smuggled wolfram,' Lopes explained. 'That was why they were blackmailing me, to get information on when the gangs moved illicit ore for the Nazis.'

'Ah, that was the plan, eh? Anyway, seeing him meet Armstrong was the last straw. I was heading back to have it out with Carole when I heard the shots. I doubled back and almost blundered straight into Pietro,' she smiled. 'Then you arrived and fell flat on your face.'

'It was a good job you were there. You saved my life.'

'Don't mention it. But you got me out of there, so does that make us even? Hmm, maybe not. Can I borrow your gun again? I intend to put a bullet in Carole's smug face.'

'Elena, no! You can't.'

'Are you telling me what to do?'

'No, but I'm asking you to think. The last thing you need is to draw attention to yourself.'

'I don't care about that.'

'But you do care about your women though, don't you? They rely on you.'

'Yes but... '

'Carole could do you a lot of harm. She knows where your house is, she could take her revenge that way. I have a feeling she's ruthless enough.'

'But what's the alternative? Let her get away with everything?'

'No, I've no intention of doing that. Neither do I intend to let her carry on blackmailing me.'

'So what are you going to do?'

Lopes smiled. 'Leave her for now. Keep her wondering about what happened tonight and where Pietro is. Then I'm going to use someone who has conveniently fallen into our lap.'

Elena frowned, 'I don't follow.'

'Rather illegally I have a certain British diplomat locked up at PVDE headquarters. We rescued him from the shootout, so we've got clear enough proof of him dealing with Pietro and his communist chums. That's not going to go down too well with Dr Salazar - if he were to find out about it, of course. Armstrong will deal with Carole if he knows what's good for him. She's his partner in crime, after all.'

Elena grinned. 'Alright,' she agreed. 'Sometimes you can be quite clever.'

'Only quite clever?'

'Don't push it, Dinis. Right, I'd better get home then.'

She started to walk away and then turned back. 'Thank you,' she said.

'Why are you thanking me? It was you who saved my life.'

'Yes, but... thanks for not saying I told you so. About Pietro. You were right.'

Lopes shrugged. 'So were you,' he said. She looked puzzled. 'You said I was jealous. I was.'

Elena bit her lip, then nodded. 'Okay,' was all she said. Then she was gone.

CHAPTER 59

5th NOVEMBER 1941 - 0124 HRS

Lopes found Costa back in their office. To his surprise, Armstrong was there too, sitting behind Lopes' own desk, and by the look of the ashtray, chain smoking. The atmosphere in the basement was thick and barely breathable and Lopes felt his chest tighten. He acknowledged Armstrong and then indicated that he wanted to talk to Costa outside.

'Did you get him, sir?' Costa kept his voice to a whisper.

'Yes, he's dead.' Even with their new spirit of openness, he didn't feel the need to tell Costa about Elena's involvement. 'What happened at the docks? Was there any clash with the police?'

'Just a few shots from a distance. Santos kept his word.'

'Casualties?'

'Five bodies left on site. All communists by the look of it though Santos and his allies might have taken their casualties with them.'

Lopes nodded. 'Looks like we got away with that part of the plan. Shall we go and see if we can get a bit more from our unexpected visitor?'

'Yes, sir,' grinned Costa.

They went back inside.

'Mr Armstrong,' he said. 'Well, what are we going to do with you?'

Lopes expected resistance and protests by the Briton about his treatment but he seemed resigned to his fate and was quite mellow and self-deprecatingly apologetic.

'I don't know, Lopes. I admit it is rather embarrassing,' he said. 'At least your man here was decent and kept me down here,' muttered Armstrong. 'Which I appreciate. He could have locked me up.'

Costa pulled across a spare chair. Armstrong rose to take it but Lopes indicated that he should stay where he was and took it himself.

'Alvares here is a sensible man,' said Lopes. 'Unlike yourself. You have some unfortunate associates.'

'I know, I know,' sighed Armstrong. 'But it's war. We've got a common foe so we've ended up with some allies who we'd normally not go anywhere near. And, tonight, I wish we hadn't.' He looked straight at Lopes. 'Did you catch him? That double-crossing Italian bastard?'

'Yes, I did.'

'Has he said anything yet?'

Lopes kept his face expressionless. 'No, not yet.'

'It's only a matter of time, I suppose,' said Armstrong. 'Your colleagues here, whichever side they're on, hate communists more than anyone else. They'll not hold back in getting him to talk, will they?'

'You're right about that,' said Lopes. 'So you might as well tell us everything now.'

'There's no point in pointing out my diplomatic status, I guess?'

Lopes smiled. 'Given what you've been up to and the company you've kept, that status should be removed by our government.'

Armstrong nodded. 'Ah well, I suppose I'll be packing my bags when I get back. The ambassador will be furious.'

'It would go easier on him if you gave us a full confession,' said Lopes.

'How full? There are things...'

Lopes held his hands up to cut off the protests. 'I know, I'd just like enough on the plot with Carole Young and Pietro — yes, I know all about her. I'd like enough to have enough evidence for her to be expelled and the rest of the gang rounded up.'

'Evidence? As I said before...'

'I do things the right way. I'm still a policeman, deep down,' interrupted Lopes. 'I want evidence, PVDE or not.'

Armstrong bit his lip and nodded. 'Yes, I see. One thing I'd like to say is that I didn't know how far they'd go. I didn't know they'd try and kill you or your man here. I was horrified by that.'

Neither Costa nor Lopes tried to hide their scepticism.

'But you knew about the blackmail? You were quite happy to let them ruin my career.'

Armstrong opened his hands and spread them wide. 'As I said, it's war. If we can deprive Hitler of his precious wolfram, we'd do anything. It wasn't personal.'

'It felt personal when the bomb went off,' growled Costa.

'Quite. I'm sorry about that.'

Lopes rose, leaned over the desk and opened the drawer. He took out some paper and a pen and put them down in front of Armstrong. 'Please write your account here. Do as much as you like to deflect the blame to Young and Pietro. If we are happy then I'll do my best to ensure that your ambassador is not embarrassed and that your status can be dealt with as quietly as possible.'

Lopes still expected the diplomat to protest, but he picked up the pen and took the top off. 'You're a decent chap, Lopes,' he said. 'Salazar is lucky to have you,' he added and started to write.

'Could you see if there's any coffee, Alvares?' said Lopes. 'I think we could be here sometime.'

Costa nodded and left.

'Armstrong,' said Lopes. 'I need to ask you a favour. If you do it I'll see if I can do one in return.'

The Briton looked up. 'One you didn't want your assistant to know about?'

Lopes nodded. 'There are things I'd like you to leave out of your confession,' he said.

CHAPTER 60

5th NOVEMBER 1941 - 0935 HRS

Oliveira had already read the file that Lopes had presented to him once and now he was doing it again, more carefully this time. A couple of times he frowned. Finally, he finished and sat back in his chair, steepling his fingers and staring at the desk as if he were about to start interrogating it.

At last, he sighed and straightened up.

'This,' he said. 'Is disgraceful. I cannot believe that I've been put in this position.'

'It is awkward, sir.'

'It's more than awkward, Lopes, it's infuriating. The British know very well that the Estado Novo does not allow communists to operate in this country yet they did a deal with a cell. One that had murderers in it, bomb makers even. Bombs! Anyone operating in this country must know about the Santana plot and that it was only by God's grace the leader survived the Barbosa du Bocage blast. How could they even countenance talking to them?'

Lopes had never seen Oliveira this angry. The betrayal had cut deep. He found himself in an unusual position; defending Armstrong.

'I can understand it in a way. The war and the wolfram situation has twisted their thinking,' he said.

Oliveira looked incredulous. 'How does that justify dealing with a gang of thugs who tried to kill you and would quite happily overthrow the state?'

'It doesn't, but the loss of their ship, the smuggling of contraband ore to their enemy, all of this made them desperate. When Armstrong was offered this deal, one that would increase the British supply and reduce that to the Nazis, it was too good to turn down. He has now repented and given a full confession.'

Oliveira's stare was one of disbelief.

'Only because you caught him in the act buying that stolen shipment on the docks and rescued him from the gang fight to get it back. It would perhaps have been better for him to have got killed, to be honest.' Oliveira frowned and looked at the report on the desk in front of him. 'How did you and your man come to be there, by the way? Was it a coincidence? That seems unlikely.'

Lopes swallowed.

'We were acting on information from an informer.'

Strictly, that was true.

'What is the name of the informer?'

Santos, his name is Santos, thought Lopes.

'I can't tell you that, sir.'

'I am your superior.'

'Yes, sir, I'm aware of that.'

The silence in Oliveira's office was profound. At last, Oliveira accepted defeat. He picked up the file again.

'At least the main thug is dead. Well done for that. And Armstrong has given us this woman, Carole Young. She is the ringleader?'

'Yes, sir.'

'She organised the attempts on your and your man's life so we'd hit the crime gangs hard and reduce their manpower?'

'The ones smuggling for the Nazis, yes.'

'She got the information about them and the wolfram shipments by bribing and blackmailing people in this organisation?'

'Yes, sir.'

'Do we know who they are yet?'

This was where Lopes' prepared lie needed to be used. 'No, sir, not yet but I do know personally that an attempt was made to make it appear that I had taken a bribe. Money was paid into my account, ostensibly from one associated with the AMR, though I'm guessing it was from Carole Young's personal family fortune. Luckily, I picked it up before any harm was done, and Armstrong's evidence has now confirmed the source and intention.'

At least it does now thanks to Armstrong co-operating with the request to say that in his confession, thought Lopes.

Oliveira pulled an exasperated face. 'It's a good job you spotted it. Though, of course, some blame must fall on you.'

Now it was Lopes' turn to be astonished. 'Me sir?'

'Yes, you. You lay yourself open to be a target by your behaviour. I've warned you about that.'

'Yes, sir,' Lopes said through gritted teeth.

'How is your marriage now? Are you making an effort like we asked you to do?'

None of your damned business thought Lopes, and it's going to be worse when she finds out the AMR money has been returned.

'Yes,' was, however, all he said.

'Good. Right, has this Young woman been arrested yet?'

Time for his second lie.

'No, it seemed she had heard about what happened at the docks. Once Armstrong had given us her name and told us where she was staying we took a squad over to the Avenida to arrest her but she was gone. It was just after 5 am but we'd missed her by about an hour.'

Oliveira slammed his fist down onto his desk in frustration. 'Damn. Another leak?'

'Possibly, sir.'

'Is there anyone who can be trusted?' Oliveira muttered.

'She left some incriminating material in her haste to leave, we're looking at it now. We've also put out an arrest alert to the police to watch the stations, borders and ports, though I very much doubt she'd risk going through Spain.'

'Good? Any other arrests? And do we know where their base in the city was?'

'No more arrests. The smuggling gang who took their wolfram back on the docks did a thorough job. There were five bodies, all believed to be members of the Madrid Communist Death Squad. Their leader, who I killed, known as Pietro made it six. There may be a few more but without their leaders, I can't see them being much of a threat. As to their base, no, I'm afraid not.'

That part, at least, was true.

'Alright,' said Oliveira, tossing the report back on his desk. 'Good work, Lopes. Pass on the search for the American woman to the International Section. They'll use all their resources to catch her. I want her in the dock on murder and sedition charges.'

'Yes, sir.' Lopes bit his lip. 'Sir, about Armstrong.'

'What about him? I expect he'll be packing his bags right now.'

'About that. I wonder if it would be possible for him to stay in post?'

Oliveira frowned. 'You mean, not including him in my report? Why would you suggest that? The man has been compromised.'

'He has, sir, but isn't it a case of the devil we know? Armstrong owes us a favour. His replacement won't.'

Oliveira took a while to answer. He was pondering the problem. 'It's tempting,' he said at last. 'But we can't let behaviour like this pass. No, Armstrong has to face the music.'

Lopes nodded. He'd tried at least. He rose. 'If you'll excuse me, it's been a long night. I'd like to get home and get some sleep.'

'Of course.'

Lopes was almost at the door when Oliveira spoke again.

'By the way, Lopes, where's your report on the other matter?'

Lopes briefly closed his eyes, then turned back.

'The other matter, sir?' though he knew very well what Oliveira was talking about.

'Yes, the AMR. What progress have you made to close it down?'

'I've been too busy to…'

'Well, now this American woman's case has been passed on to someone else and with the German agent dead, you'll have more time, won't you?'

'Yes, sir,' said Lopes wearily.

'Good. I'll expect an update tomorrow afternoon.'

'Yes, sir.'

Lopes left the office as swiftly as he could before anything worse happened.

CHAPTER 61

5th NOVEMBER 1941 - 1020 HRS

Lopes did not go home. He had an important visit to make first.

At the police station in the Barrio Alto.

Alex Ribeiro was waiting for him and showed him into his office.

'You look shattered, Dinis,' he said. 'Coffee?'

'Please, Alex.' Whilst his friend had sent a young constable on an errand to get two strong mugs of coffee, Lopes settled into one of the chairs. 'It's been a long night.'

'It sounded like it.'

'How's your guest?'

Alex smiled. 'Loud and not at all happy.' He looked up. 'Ah, here's the coffee. Want to take it with us up to her?'

'Up? I take it you didn't put her in the cells?'

Alex shook his head. 'I thought it best that as few people as possible knew she was here. She's locked in a storeroom on the top floor.' He glanced up. 'Though she's making so much racket no one can miss her.'

'Well done, Alex. No, let her stew a little longer. She's not going anywhere. Not yet anyhow.' Lopes took a sip of his coffee. It was done in the classic Portuguese way, sweet and milky and, therefore, not to his normal taste but now it hit the spot. He needed the energy. 'How's the 'Hemline' case? Any more attacks?'

Alex drank some of his coffee. 'No, thank God. The one you and I looked at was the last so far. It's odd, he struck pretty regularly before, but now it's gone quiet. Don't get me wrong, I'm not complaining. In fact, I hope the guy has seen sense and thrown himself under a tram. He deserves to be roasting in hell.'

'He does that,' said Lopes. 'Still, I wonder. Has something changed?' He finished his coffee. 'Should we go and see her?'

'Yeah, let's do it,' said Alex.

He led Lopes out of his office and upstairs. Even before they were anywhere near, Lopes could hear the familiar voice shouting to be let out, alternating between English and Portuguese.

'Let me out, damn you. Deixe-me sair!' followed by banging.

'I hope the door's a stout one,' said Lopes.

'It is, thank God,' muttered Alex. 'Stronger than my patience, anyway.'

He took a key out of his pocket and unlocked the door. Immediately, it was pulled open and the blond-haired occupant dashed for freedom. Alex was too quick for her. He grabbed her and half carried, half pushed her back inside.

'Miss Young, Carole, stop it,' said Lopes. 'It won't do you any good.'

'Lopes, damn you, I might have known you were behind this. You'll pay for this, you know you will!'

She continued to fight, trying to free herself from Alex who held her in a bear hug.

'No, I won't. Carole, listen, it's all over. Pietro and most of his men are dead.'

'I don't believe you!'

'Carole, it's true. There was an ambush at the warehouse. The gangs took back their stolen wolfram. They weren't in the mood to take prisoners.'

Carole stopped struggling. She stared at Lopes. 'You? You did that?'

'I did, yes. You see, your blackmail didn't matter to me. You and Pietro had to be stopped. Too many people were dying.'

'Pietro? He's really…'

'Yes, he is.'

'Damn you, Lopes. Damn you to hell!' Tears started to flow down her face.

'I'm sorry. If it's any consolation I wanted him alive.'

'Yes, of course you did.'

The fight seemed to have gone out of her.

'Let her go, Alex. I don't think she's going anywhere.'

Alex released her, and Carole sank to the floor, her back against the wall. 'So what are you going to do with me? I'm here in secret, aren't I? So what is it going to be, a bullet in the back of the head and a shallow grave? That's the fascist way, isn't it?'

'No. We're not like that.'

'Of course, you're not. Why aren't I locked up in the cells, paraded in public?'

'We can do that if you choose.'

Carole looked up at him, clearly puzzled. 'If I choose?'

'Yes. My superiors want to charge you with sedition and inciting a revolution. You could spend the rest of your life in jail. Even worse you could end up in Tarrafal.'

He saw Alex's eyebrows shoot up at this. Lopes knew why; no woman, as far as he knew, had ever ended up in the Cape Verde hellhole. He was counting on the American woman not knowing.

'All right,' she said. 'But why wouldn't you want me locked up?'

Lopes smiled. 'I would like you locked up; it's what you would say beforehand that I'd rather escape. I know you would make things very awkward for me if you went on trial.'

'Of course I would.'

'And for other people too.'

Carole smiled and nodded 'I see. You still have a weakness for a certain somebody. That will be the death of you one day, inspector.' She got to her feet. 'But, of course, I'd prefer not to spend my life in one of your stinking jails and certainly not in Cape Verde. Even if my father did pull all the strings he could to get me out, I'd still spend longer there than I'd like. So what's the deal? You let me go on the proviso I'll be a good girl?'

'Sort of, but a little bit more than that. I'd rather not give you the chance to start again in Lisbon, or, in fact, anywhere else in Portugal. I would like you to leave the country. There's a

Boeing Clipper due in two days. You're going to be on it. I've secured you a ticket.'

Or rather a certain Mr Santos has, thought Lopes.

'Back to the States?' She shook her head. 'No, I don't think so.'

'That's the deal. Take it or leave it.' Lopes shrugged. 'Let's say you leave it. Yes, you could cause me and Elena a lot of problems but you still end up in prison. This way you don't. It's a good deal. Take it.'

Carole pursed her lips. 'Okay, inspector, I'll take it.' She looked around her. 'I take it I'm staying here until the Clipper flies?'

'I'm afraid so. Alex here will see that you're as comfortable as possible, won't you Alex?'

'I will, yes.'

Carole sighed. 'Right. It could be worse, I suppose.' She smiled at Lopes. 'You're a clever man, inspector. But one with so many weaknesses, you know that?'

Lopes returned her smile.

He knew only too well.

CHAPTER 62

5th NOVEMBER 1941 - 1241 HRS

Lopes walked slowly to the tram stop. His house and bed awaited him but only the latter was appealing and would give him any comfort. The house — or rather one person in it — would be cold, despite the warm breeze that brought the scent of the sea to the streets of the city.

The work of remodelling the house was supposed to be starting on the coming Monday. The architect would already have his fees to pay but materials would need to be bought if a start were to be made. He did not relish having to tell Maria Sofia that the funds that were in their account were a lot less than they had been, the money having been returned to the AMR account. If she wanted the work to go ahead she'd have to talk to her father again.

Lopes' brief springtime would abruptly end and he would be plunged into a deep winter of frozen contempt.

He would have no respite at work, Oliveira had made it clear that the AMR was not going to be forgotten. How could he be seen to be investigating Elena without actually succeeding? It was probably impossible and, even if he managed it, all that would happen was that the job would be given to someone else in the PVDE, somebody who was bound to be more ruthless than him. Elena was resilient and capable, but she now didn't have the backing of Carole Young and Pietro.

He now also had a way of finding out where the house was; Ines was the weak link. She was the one person who went to the house regularly and now he knew that she visited the German cemetery. By the brief look of the grave it was somewhere she regularly went to renew the flowers on it. By placing a watch on the cemetery it would be possible to find out where she lived - he didn't even know her surname so tracing her through normal means was closed off - and once he knew that she could be followed to work. Elena had, through her kind act of letting the woman stay on, created a weak link in her security which Lopes could exploit.

Betrayed for an act of kindness. What had he become?

Ines. Why was she there? To tend a grave obviously, but whose grave? Not her husband's. Elena said that he'd walked out. A parent then? Possibly, but then…

The tram he'd been waiting for drew up in front of him. He'd been so deep in thought that he'd not even heard its approach which, given the noise a typical Lisbon tram made with its iron wheels on steel rails, creaking wooden body and the bell, was quite an achievement. There weren't many others waiting but they got on in front of him. Lopes and the driver locked eyes for a moment. The latter gave Lopes a look that said quite clearly; "Well, are you getting on or what?" Lopes shook his head and turned away.

The tram seemed to sigh as it pulled away.

Lopes set off walking. The German cemetery at Alemao de Lisbon was perhaps a ten-minute walk away. He had to know, he had to find out why Ines gave him that look, why she was so frightened to see him. It made no sense if that were a parent's or sibling's grave. There was something else.

Something that she desperately wanted to keep secret.

CHAPTER 63

5th NOVEMBER 1941 - 1323 HRS

Lopes found the grave he was looking for with little difficulty. Although it had no headstone, the small mound of earth had fresh flowers in a vase which was set into the ground. The flowers were just starting to wilt, suggesting they were not fresh but perhaps a couple of days old. There was also a tiny statuette of the Virgin Mary placed at the head of the grave.

There was one thing that was immediately clear; this grave was tiny. This was a child's final resting place.

Lopes tried to swallow. It was difficult; he could have been in this position with his son if the gamble he'd made back in May had gone wrong. Looking back, he could not understand just how cavalier he had been.

He forced himself back to the here-and-now. He needed to know.

He looked around the cemetery. There were a couple of black-clad women tending a grave with an elaborate gravestone. He wondered about approaching them but decided against disturbing their afternoon. Instead, he went inside the pretty little, yellow-painted church, taking off his hat as he entered.

The interior felt comforting but austere compared to the sometimes garish insides of the churches Lopes was used to. It reminded him that this was a Protestant church and a German Protestant one at that. The influence of the Lutheran tradition and doctrine was quite clear.

'Guten tag, may I help you?'

Lopes turned. It was the priest, given he was dressed in a black cassock. The man was as lean and austere as his church but the smile on his face was welcoming.

'Good afternoon, Father.'

'Pastor. Pastor Landbeck. How may I help you, my son?'

'My name is Inspector Lopes, I work for the PVDE.'

A brief flicker of emotion crossed the pastor's face, the familiar mix of apprehension, alarm and distaste that Lopes was getting used to, but it passed and the smile returned though it seemed more forced and more wary now.

'Indeed. I hope that none of my congregation are in trouble?'

'I hope not too. I was wanting to know about a grave in your cemetery.'

'A grave?' Pastor Landbeck looked puzzled. 'Which grave?'

'It's probably easier if I show you if you've got a moment?'

'Of course.'

Lopes led the pastor out into the November sunlight and over to the child's grave.

'It's this one.'

Landbeck sighed and nodded. 'Ah yes, poor little Felipe. Such a tragedy. He was only five.'

'Felipe?'

'Felipe Fernandes. He died at the end of July.'

'And his mother is called Ines?'

'That's right, Ines Fernandes.'

Lopes wrote this down in his notebook and frowned. 'Fernandes is not a Germanic name, is it?'

'No, it's not but I believe that young Ines, or Ines Huebner as she was then, used to attend this church as a small girl. Her father was, I believe, a butcher but he died and her mother remarried. Her stepfather insisted that she followed his faith, and I believe she was married to a Catholic, hence that little idol.' He smiled and nodded at the statuette of the Virgin. 'We wouldn't normally allow it but, well, the poor woman needs as much comfort as she can find. Felipe was her world.'

Lopes nodded, his notebook open. Felipe died at the end of July. The first murder was early in August. It was slightly different from the rest.

Because it was the first. That was what he and Elena had decided.

It might even have been on the day of Pedro's interment.

The facts fitted. But why? Why kill? If she were the killer, it could just all be a coincidence. It was still hard to believe that a woman could do anything like this. Could she?

There was only one way to find out. He had to talk to her.

'Pastor, do you have an address for her?'

Landbeck frowned. 'I suppose we do somewhere,' he said. 'But why not ask her yourself? She's just arrived.'

The pastor pointed at the gate.

Ines was, indeed, there.

But she had stopped walking towards them. She stood, frozen to the spot. Lopes took a step towards her and that broke the spell. She dropped the small bunch of flowers she carried and turned and ran.

'Mrs Fernandes, wait!' the pastor called but she had already reached the gate.

Lopes ran after her but he knew it was too late. She had too much of a head start and he did not have the fitness for a pursuit. Sure enough, by the time he'd reached the street, there was no sign of her. He chose a direction to search in but knew it was hopeless; she'd got away.

For now. The pastor knew where she lived.

Lopes went back inside the church.

'Pastor Landbeck, I need Mrs Fernandes's address. Please, can you get it for me?'

The pastor looked troubled. 'I know you have the authority and I want to help the police but I'm not sure I feel comfortable. She's a grieving…'

'Pastor, this is not a minor matter. It's murder. Multiple murders. Lives are at stake.'

Landeck now showed puzzlement and astonishment but nodded. 'Of course, I'll go and see if I can find it.' He turned.

'Pastor Landbeck,' said Lopes. 'Before you do, how did her son die?'

Landeck turned back. 'It was tragic. He caught the measles. Such a shame.'

Lopes swallowed. 'I'll need a telephone too,' he said.

'We have one in the office. You'd better come with me.'

Lopes followed him. A cold dread was building inside him. He didn't want to believe this was true, but he was sure it was.

CHAPTER 64

5th NOVEMBER 1941 - 1420 HRS

Lopes and the pastor walked the short distance to Ines' apartment. It took them less than ten minutes and, as they arrived, so did Pedro Cruz in an unmarked police car.

Cruz got out. Lopes noted with satisfaction that he carried the dossier that Elena had put together. Cruz was frowning.

'Are you sure about this, sir? I mean, that a woman could have done all this?'

Lopes didn't answer at first. Instead, he took the dossier from Cruz and turned to the first few pages. And there it was.

'A suitably motivated and distraught woman, yes.' He showed Cruz the passage. 'Sarah, the first victim, had the measles. She was in a safe house in mid-July, a house where Ines works.'

'So?'

'So Ines' son, her only son, Felipe, caught the measles and died at the end of July. Sarah was murdered in the first few days of August.'

'Oh my God,' whispered Cruz. 'Sorry, father,' he then muttered to Pastor Landbeck.

'Understandable, my son.' He looked up at the apartment. 'I still cannot believe this. May I be the one to talk to her first?'

Lopes exchanged glances with Cruz and then nodded. 'We'll be right behind you though.'

The pastor led them into the building and upstairs. Ines rooms were, apparently, on the first floor. He knocked on the door which had "Fernandes" handwritten on a small piece of paper glued to the wall alongside it.

'Mrs Fernandes? Hello, can I speak with you? It's Pastor Landbeck.'

There was silence from within.

The pastor knocked again. 'Mrs Fernandes? Ines, please.'

Lopes had seen enough. He gently pulled the pastor away. 'I'm sorry, you tried. We need to do it our way now.' Before Landbeck could protest, he said to Cruz. 'Break it down.'

Cruz did not bother putting his shoulder against the door, instead, he started kicking it with the sole of his foot. It cracked at the second kick and broke completely at the fifth. Lopes was the first through the door.

The two rooms were neat, clean, austere but devoid of life and colour. The front room contained a small kitchen cabinet with a stove next to it, the flue running into the chimney breast. There was a small, cheap table and two chairs, plus a sofa. Off the front room, Lopes could see a bedroom. He strode over to it. On one side was a single bed, adult size, and, at its foot, was a smaller one, barely more than a cot. Above the cot there was something on the wall that Lopes couldn't make out in the gloom, the only window being the one in the front room.

He blinked, letting his eyes adjust. When they did he swore.

'Bloody hell,' he muttered.

He was aware of Cruz and the pastor joining him.

They too were stunned into shock.

The cot - obviously Filipes' - had a photo of the boy set on the pillow. On the wall above were newspaper cuttings. Each one was the report of a 'Hemline Killer' murder. They surrounded the words "The dirty bitches will pay" scrawled in red lipstick.

Even in the moment, Lopes recalled a line from Elena's dossier:

> *Sarah had a red lipstick by the American brand, Elizabeth Arden, that she treasured. It never left her purse. The purse was with her body but the lipstick was missing when her body was found.*

At the time Lopes had smiled at what he thought was unnecessary detail but now... His eyes were drawn to the floor, rough boards, no carpet. Next to the cot was a red stain, not liquid but greasy. Even though it had been cleaned up, the mark was still there, spread like a small explosion. Kneeling he peered under the cot. There, towards the wall, was what he'd hoped would be there, a flattened brass tube. He reached in and retrieved it. There could be no doubt now. Stamped on in anger, the words *Elizabeth Arden* could still be read on the side of the tube.

'She's the killer,' Lopes said quietly. 'This is a direct connection to the first victim.'

'But a woman... how could she have the strength? And to cut...'

'All the victims were slightly built. And she didn't have to overpower them, they all knew her, they'd all met her. They trusted her.'

'Oh my good God.'

This time Cruz did not apologise to the pastor. Landbeck had, in any case, gone white, clearly shocked.

'As for the knife, she was both a butcher's daughter and a cook. She's used to using them.'

The three men stood in shocked silence for a few moments.

Then Cruz said the words that were forming in Lopes' mind.

'Where is she now?'

Lopes knew. With an icy certainty, he knew.

'She's gone back to the safe house. She's going for Elena.'

'But...where's that?'

'I don't know, damn it,' said Lopes. 'But I know someone who does. Quickly, Cruz, we need to go to the Barrio Alto police station.'

CHAPTER 65

5th NOVEMBER 1941 - 1505 HRS

'Dinis, what are you doing back?'

Alex looked at him in surprise.

'I need to see her again. Carole Young,' Lopes said tersely.

Alex didn't ask why. He just took the key out of his desk drawer and passed it over. Lopes headed upstairs, followed by Cruz.

'Who is this woman?' Cruz asked. 'Why is she up here and not locked in the cells?'

'She's a troublemaker, a communist organiser but she holds some information that could be embarrassing,' said Lopes.

'To you or the State?' muttered Cruz. Lopes just stared at him briefly then unlocked the door.

'Inspector, you can't keep away, can you?' Carole had been given a chair and was reading a book.

'I need to know where Elena's house is, and I need to know now.'

Carole smiled. 'Oh, do you? Well, that's tough, isn't it? For all I dislike that stupid girl, don't think I'm going to help the secret police by giving her…'

'Miss Young, Carole, this is a matter of life and death. Elena is in danger. I need to find her.'

Carole's smile broadened. 'Ah, it's like that, is it? You need to rescue a damsel in distress - your damsel in fact. Interesting.'

'Carole, please. I'm not playing around. I need to get to the house.'

'What are you going to do, inspector, beat it out of me? I don't think you have it in you.' She looked at Cruz. 'Or is that why you've brought your handsome young companion? So he can whip me with his belt?'

'No, I would…' Cruz started.

'Forget it, honey,' said Carole. 'I was teasing you. Sure, inspector, I'll tell you where to go. In fact, I'll show you. But then you let me go. Deal?'

'You're in no position to do deals,' said Cruz.

'Deal,' said Lopes. 'Come on.'

Carole stayed where she was.

'I believe you're an honourable man, a man of his word,' she said.

'I am.'

'Then swear you will let me go free if I do what you ask.'

'I swear that I will let you go free if you take me to Elena's house.'

He held out his hand. Carole got up and took it. Lopes led her out of the room, trying not to look at Cruz's face, nor at Alex as they passed downstairs.

At the car, as Carole got in the back seat, she whispered in Lopes' ear. 'Are you serious? Are you going along with this?'

'I am. I promised.'

Cruz shook his head and got in the driver's seat. 'Alright. Where to?'

Lopes, now in the front passenger seat, looked back at Carole.

'Head for the Rue Don Pedro and turn north,' she said.

Cruz started the car and did as he was told.

*

'Yes, turn along here. There's the house. Behind the wall.'

They had turned down a rough cobbled street. Unlike the densely built-up centre of the city, they had reached a part of Lisbon where the houses became more sparse, where tumble-down shacks and larger detached villas existed side by side, separated by scrubby wasteland. They had passed building sites, suggesting that it would not be long before developers incorporated this suburb into the urban sprawl. Just the sort of place that Elena's late protector, Uwe, would have bought up with an eye to the future.

Lopes could tell, even from the outside, that this was where he'd been brought. The few glimpses of the skyline and the view of the house he'd had from behind the high wall matched.

'Thank you, Carole,' he said.

'Right, now let me go,' she replied.

'One more thing first,' said Lopes.

Carole frowned. 'I hope you're not reneging on our deal, inspector.'

'No, I just need to get through that door.' He pointed at the wall. The double door that he'd been driven through had a smaller door set in it. 'I presume you have a key?'

Carole didn't answer but, instead, reached up to her neck and pulled off the gold chain she was wearing. As she did, Lopes could see that at the end of the chain was a key that had been concealed beneath her clothes. She took the key off the chain and passed it to Lopes.

Lopes now got out of the car, a two-door model, and tilted the seat forward to let the American out.

'Thank you,' he said.

'Don't I get a lift to the station?' she said.

'Don't push your luck,' said Lopes. 'You're free. But you're on foot.'

Carole smiled and started walking. 'See ya, around, Lopes.'

Lopes watched her walk away. He didn't doubt that he'd see her again.

Lopes looked at Cruz. His younger colleague's expression clearly showed what he thought about all this.

'It had to be done,' said Lopes. 'We can find her again. This is more important right now.' He pointed at the house. 'There are women and children in there, vulnerable ones and there's likely a killer in there with them.'

Cruz nodded and looked at the house. 'Shouldn't we call for reinforcements now we know where it is?'

'There isn't time. Anyway, the nearest phone is inside, we can use it if we need to.' He looked at Cruz. 'Are you armed?'

Cruz nodded and pulled out his revolver.

'Good. Try not to scare the women inside if you can, they are terrified of the police. Come on, let's go.'

'I'll do my best, sir.'

Lopes led Cruz over to the door.

For all his experience, his heart was pounding. He was terrified about what he'd find inside.

CHAPTER 66

5th NOVEMBER 1941 - 1612 HRS

As soon as Lopes inserted the key, he knew there was a problem. It would not go in.

He bent down to peer through the keyhole. Yes, it was what he thought; there was a key in the other side of the lock. He tried the door; it didn't budge.

'Someone's locked the door from the other side,' he muttered. 'Then left the key in the door.'

'She didn't want disturbing,' said Cruz, bending down to see.

Lopes thanked him for not pointing out that having Carole's key made no difference; they were still locked out. Lopes looked at the lock for a few moments then up at the wall. It was high, too high even for a boost to get Cruz over, and the door itself far too solid to break down. They'd have to try and get the key out of the lock.

He took out his penknife, the one he used to clean his pipe out, and inserted the blade in the lock. If he could manipulate it round until the tangs lined up with the keyhole then, perhaps, he could push it out. He knew straight away that this wasn't going to be a quick job.

'I think I can get over,' said Cruz.

Lopes stopped and looked at him. 'How? The wall is, what, three metres? How are you going to get up there?'

Cruz pointed at the car. 'If I bring that up close to the wall, and we stand on the roof, then you should be able to boost me up high enough.'

Lopes could see Cruz was right.

'But, the drop…'

'I know, but we've got to do this.'

Cruz was already moving towards the car. Lopes knew he was right.

Moments later, the Ford was alongside the wall and Cruz was helping Lopes up onto the roof. The metal gave under their weight, denting it.

'This is going to be an interesting report to the car pool boss,' Cruz smiled. He looked up at the top of the wall, then down at the ground. The top of the wall was crazily high. He looked back at Lopes. 'Come on. Let's do it. Give me a boost.'

Lopes crouched and linked his hands. Cruz put his foot on them pushing upwards as Lopes also straightened up. The younger policeman was propelled upwards, too fast, Lopes realised but it was too late. Cruz made a fleeting effort to grab the parapet of the wall as he reached it but toppled straight over.

The thud was sickening, and Cruz gave a brief yell of anguish.

Then the swearing started.

'Fuck it. Oh shit. Damn, damn, damn.'

'Pedro, Pedro! Are you alright?

'The response was a gasp and another grunt of pain 'Yeah. Well, no…but…'

After more gasping, swearing and shuffling, Lopes heard the key turn in the lock then a heavy weight slump to the ground. He pushed the door open and went inside.

Cruz was leaning against the wall, his face white, beads of sweat on his brow. The reason was obvious; his right ankle was broken, and the foot was at an unnatural angle.

'What an idiot,' he muttered. 'Falling off a bloody wall, of all things.'

'I'll get help,' said Lopes.

'No, get inside first.' Cruz pointed towards the house. 'I'll live. Do the job we came here to do.'

Lopes nodded. 'Yes, I will.'

He started to move off, but Cruz stopped him.

'Sir,' he said. 'Take this. You may need it.'

He held out his revolver.

Lopes only hesitated a moment before taking it.

He stepped towards the house.

The side door, the one he'd been brought through when he'd been kidnapped was wide open.
Gun in hand he went inside.

CHAPTER 67

5th NOVEMBER 1941 - 1631 HRS

The house was eerily quiet.

'Elena! Elena, where are you?'

He kept his voice low, he didn't want to spook the women nor give Ines a target to attack.

There was no reply.

Lopes cautiously crossed the hallway, looking all around. There was no sign of Ines. The library door was shut. He knew the door could be locked - his thoughts went back to the photograph that Carole had taken - so it would be an obvious place to seek shelter. He tried the door; it opened. He edged into the room, half expecting a crazed attack. It didn't come, instead the room was empty, the table clear. Elena must have put the evidence away after she'd finished with it.

He hurried back into the hallway and headed into the dining room. He stopped in horror.

A small dark-haired woman was sitting at the table, her head resting on her arms as if she were sleeping. It was going to be a long sleep; her chair was like an island set in a pool of blood.

'Elena, no!'

He hurried to her. Taking a deep breath Lopes, lifted her head.

He breathed a sigh of relief; it wasn't Elena. But then guilt swept over him; this was - had been - someone's daughter, sister, cousin, aunt or friend. Her throat had been cut from ear to ear, from behind as she sat reading. The book lay in front of her, the pages spattered with the woman's blood as it sprayed from the incision.

Lopes gently lowered the woman's head back onto the table. He looked towards the adjoining kitchen. Kitchens had knives in them; it seemed unlikely that Ines had her usual weapon with her given that Lopes had frightened her in the cemetery. She probably wouldn't have risked going home, but instead, would have headed straight here for her ultimate revenge. She had a knife now; it would have had to come from the kitchen.

Ines had gone somewhere else, but Lopes had to know whether Elena was in there. With some trepidation, he went into the room.

Elena wasn't there, but the cook was. Her body was in the larder. She too had been attacked from behind and was sprawled across the vegetables. Lopes shook his head; she'd survived persecution and the passage through the Pyrenees as a refugee only to be murdered in what she thought was a place of safety.

It was sad beyond words.

He turned.

'No more,' he muttered to himself.

Ines had to be stopped, whether Elena was alive or not.

Lopes left the kitchen and dining room and went back out into the hallway. As he did so there was a scream from upstairs. A door banged.

'Let me in, you dirty bitch! Let me in.'

Ines. Lopes hurried to the stairs.

'Leave her alone! Elena, I'm here.'

'Lopes. What are you doing?'

He turned. Elena stood in the hallway behind him, coat on.

He turned back. He couldn't stop himself; he grabbed her, pulling her close to him.

'Lopes! What do you think—'

'Elena! I thought you were dead.' He kissed the top of her head.

'Dead? Why? Hey, come on, Lopes, you're crushing me.'

He realised what he was doing. He let her go. 'Where have you been?'

'Seeing my lawyers, sorting out the mess that Carole left me.' She pointed outside. 'What's going on? Your colleague is...'

Another scream came from upstairs.

'Forget Pedro. Ines is here. She's the 'Hemline Killer.'

'What? Ines? No, no, it can't...'

Lopes did not wait to hear. He dashed up the stairs. There was no sign of Ines on the first floor so he went up to the second. She was fighting to get into one of the rooms, pushing and kicking the door whilst whoever was inside was trying to force it shut. Despite being small and slim, Ines was both powerful and driven by a fury that gave her almost superhuman strength.

She was almost in.

Lopes had no choice. He levelled his pistol.

But, he hesitated. He couldn't do it.

'Ines!' he yelled. 'Stop or I fire.'

His words got through. Ines left the door which slammed shut behind her. She turned towards Lopes. In her hand was a kitchen knife, scarlet and dripping. She stood for a moment, breathing heavily.

'Lopes. Put that down, please.' Elena stood alongside Lopes.

'Elena, get back. She's...'

But Elena stepped past him. 'Ines, I'm sure we can sort this out. Put the knife down and...'

With a banshee-like scream, Ines sprinted towards Elena, knife held out in front of her like a jousting lance.

Lopes pulled the trigger without consciously thinking about doing it, once, twice. Both bullets hit home, Both in Ines' head. Both on their own were fatal, he knew that, but he also knew he couldn't stop the momentum of her body. It hit Elena, carrying them both to the floor at his feet.

He pushed Ines' body off Elena.

The knife was embedded in her chest.

Elena's eyes widened as her eyes focused on the handle. Then her eyes dulled and her head slumped to the side.

'Elena! No, no!'

His tears flowed into Elena's blood.

CHAPTER 68

7th NOVEMBER 1941 - 0833 HRS

Costa looked up as Lopes stepped into the office.

'Hello, sir. I didn't expect to see you in.'

Lopes shrugged. 'I work here, Alvares.'

Costa frowned. ' I know but you were given leave. Are you sure you're alright? Shouldn't you be resting? After what happened at the house?'

Lopes settled down behind his desk. 'It was awful, but we have to keep going, don't we? There'll be plenty of time to rest when I'm dead and gone, Alvares.' Costa frowned even more deeply and Lopes could understand why; what he'd just said was morbid. 'Anyway, I prefer the atmosphere here to that at home. My wife hasn't taken my giving the money back to the AMR well. She blames me for everything - which, to be fair, she's probably right about:

'That's a bit harsh, sir. Though, to be fair, so did I.' Costa smiled.

'Yes, you did,' Lopes sighed and looked at his watch. 'The truth is I've asked for a meeting with the boss. I'm seeing him in about 15 minutes.'

Costa's smile faded. 'The boss? Why? And you wanted to see me first?'

'I did, yes.'

Costa looked aghast. 'I was afraid of this. Please don't be hasty, sir. Think about things a bit longer.'

Lopes couldn't help but string Costa along a bit. 'What do you mean? Me? Hasty?'

'Well, you're going to resign, aren't you, sir?'

'No, I'm not. At least if this goes as I hope it will, I won't be.' He smiled. 'Don't look so worried, Alvares. I just wanted to check with you about what I propose first. If you say no, then I won't do it.'

Costa looked puzzled, so Lopes started to explain. When he'd finished, Costa was grinning.

*

Lopes was also grinning when, ten minutes later, he stood up to leave Oliveira's office.

Oliveira wasn't.

'You'll pay for this, Lopes. One day you'll pay for this disloyalty.'

Lopes couldn't resist. 'Disloyalty, sir?' he said, trying to look innocent. 'How have I been disloyal?'

'Don't give me that. You know exactly what you've done. One day you'll go too far and you won't have the protection you have now. Now get out of my sight.'

'Yes, sir,' adding, under his breath, 'With pleasure.'

Costa was waiting outside. He was still smiling. 'That sounded like fun, sir.'

'It was,' sighed Lopes. 'But he's right, I'm pushing my luck.'

'But you always do, sir,'

Lopes nodded. 'Yes, I do. Is the car ready?'

'Yes, sir, It's outside. And I've checked it for bombs.'

'I'm glad to hear that. Good, Let's go.'

*

'So, Pedro, how long have you got to stay here?'

The pair of them were sitting alongside Cruz's hospital bed. His leg was in plaster from his ankle to his mid-thigh.

He sighed, 'Not too long, hopefully, sir. The docs had to put a plate in. It still hurts like the devil and they were worried about an infection, but it seems okay. I'll be glad to get out of here. I hate these places.'

Costa laughed. 'So do I but I always seem to end up here. I wonder why?' He looked pointedly at Lopes.

Lopes ignored the barb and patted Cruz on the shoulder. 'Make the most of the rest. I'm sure your wife has her hands full at home.'

'She does, sir, that she does.' Cruz looked rueful and tapped his leg. 'I've got six weeks in this cast, so there's no going back to work until it's off. Unless I can persuade them to take me back for desk work.'

'Don't hurry, let your inspector do the legwork for once. Ribeiro could do with the reminder of how good you are.' He stood. 'We'll leave you to the nurses. Come on Costa.'

'Thanks, sir.'

Outside the ward, Lopes turned to his assistant.

'Right, our last visit of the day. Ready?'

Costa looked puzzled. 'You want me there, sir?'

'Yes, I do.'

'I thought you'd want to go on your own.'

'No, Costa. No secrets, Not any more. Come on.'

He led his assistant across the corridor and into the women's ward.

He smiled when he saw her. She looked so tiny and helpless in the bed. Elena's face was white and the top of her chest was heavily bandaged.

But she was alive, that was the important thing.

Her eyes were closed as they approached the bed but they opened as they reached it and stood over her.

She glanced from Lopes to Costa.

'So this is it, is it?' she said.

'This is what?' said Lopes.

'The point where you arrest me and deport me.'

Lopes pulled up a chair at one side of the bed and signalled for Costa to do the same. 'Deport you? What has she done, Costa?'

'Let me think. Oh yes, consorting with a communist death squad and running an organisation that the State objected to,' Costa nodded. 'That's quite a list.'

'Stop it,' said Elena. 'That's not fair. I suppose the AMR is no more.'

'I'm afraid so.'

'And my assets?'

'Seized by the State. In the main at least.'

'Bastards. That's not fair. But the important thing is the women. We were doing good work.'

'Yes, I know,' said Lopes.

'Where are the women now? Have they been arrested?'

Lopes glanced at Costa. 'Actually, no. I managed to get them out of the house before the ambulance and the police arrived. It was a hard job, believe me.'

'They must have been terrified,' said Elena. 'But thank you, I appreciate it. Even if they are on the streets again.'

'They aren't. Well, at least most of them aren't. I managed to find a Catholic charity to help them, and the pastor of the German church that Ines went to has also found some homes for those who aren't Catholic.'

'Thank you. And thanks for saving my life.'

'That was where the trenches helped. I knew not to take the knife out. You'd have bled to death otherwise. As it was you lost a lot of blood.'

Elena nodded. 'Ines...I can't believe it. Why did she do it?'

'Her son. He caught the measles and died.'

'The measles?' She closed her eyes and sighed. 'Oh, God, Sarah.'

'Yes, I'm afraid so.' Lopes reached over and squeezed her hand. 'We'd never have stopped her without you. Your report, your attention to detail, that was the difference.'

'But more people died; Inga the cook, and poor Lissy.'

'Yes, but it could have been more.'

Elena opened her eyes and nodded. 'I suppose so.' She seemed to notice Lopes' hand for the first time and tugged hers out of his grasp. 'Right, get it over with,' she said.

'What?'

'My deportation. Do you just take me away or do you serve papers on me or something?'

Lopes didn't answer. Instead, he reached into his jacket and took out an envelope. He held it for a moment then handed it over.

Elena just held it.

'Okay, so what happens now? Do I get better or do you take me to the border now?'

'If we let you get better and were deporting you, we'd have to handcuff you to the bed so we wouldn't have two fugitives to look for,' said Costa.

Elena frowned in puzzlement.

'For goodness sake, read the letter,' said Lopes.

Elena opened it and started to read. Her eyes widened and she scanned to the bottom of the page.

'This is a letter from Salazar,' she said.

'It is. As you can see it gives you a full pardon and leave to stay in Portugal indefinitely.'

Her mouth dropped open.

'But...how? How does he know about me?'

'Salazar knows everything,' muttered Costa. 'That's why the PVDE exists.'

Elena puffed out her cheeks. 'Alright, but...what do I do now? I presume the State has seized my houses?'

'They have, yes, but that's why Costa is here. He had to agree to this — as do you, of course.'

'Agree to what?'

Lopes looked at Costa.

'What the boss isn't telling you is that he went to see Salazar himself. It took him half a day to get an audience, and had to threaten to resign and go and work for the mob to get what he asked for.'

'That's a slight exaggeration, Alvares,' said Lopes.

'What?' Elena looked in confusion from one to the other.

In answer, Lopes pulled a second sheet of paper out and handed it to her.

'That's a job offer. Salazar has consented to you working for the PVDE.'

The End

---

[1] See Lisbon '41. Da Souza was the leader of a Nazi faction within the PVDE who kidnapped Lopes' son and was responsible for the murder of Lopes' mother.

AFTERWORD

I hope you enjoyed The Queen of Lisbon. Lopes, Costa and Elena will be back in the next instalment in 2025, life willing!

I would like to ask a favour; like all indie authors I don't have a massive marketing or production budget, we all rely on word-of-mouth and, above all, on ratings and reviews so that other readers can find them and also so I can get feedback about what you, as the reader, likes and where I can improve. So, pretty please, would you mind spending a few moments rating and reviewing The Queen of Lisbon?

Thank-you so much in advance.

Malcolm Havard
October 2024

THE ASSASSINATION OF A NOBODY

The Lisbon novels Book Three

Chapter One

LISBON, 27th NOVEMBER 1941 - evening

Lopes stood in the doorway of the terminal building watching as she walked across the tarmac to the waiting aircraft. Would she look back? He doubted it; that wasn't in her nature. She only ever looked ahead because the past was too painful.

He wished he was like that too. It would make living more bearable.

'Do you want me to come with you to the airfield?' Costa had asked.

'No, Alvares, there's no need,' Lopes had replied, then wondered if Costa himself needed to say farewell. But then he saw the look on his assistant's face and knew that he'd only asked out of kindness. Costa had recognized that this was something that Lopes needed to do alone.

She'd reached the steps now. She went up them, carrying her little suitcase, without, of course, looking back. One of the propellers was spinning, slowly, jerkily as the starter motors pushed against the compression in the cylinders. The exhaust coughed, smoked, the big radial ran for a few seconds then stopped again. Perhaps this was fate, perhaps a mechanical fault would keep her here? But no, the engine sprang back into life followed shortly after by its brother. There would be no reprieve. This was the end.

It was an odd bird to take her away. Not the usual BOAC DC3, modern and streamlined, it was unfamiliar, Lopes hadn't seen this type before. Strangely angular and awkward looking with immensely thick wings and twin tails, it looked like a throwback or a missing link between the biplanes of Lopes' youth and the modern monoplanes. It was in the same colours as the American aircraft, a hybrid of the drab greens and browns typical of a military machine with the civil markings emblazoned on the fuselage and wings, To Lopes' eyes this seemed to present mixed messages; was the machine meant to be seen and identified or not?

The oddness of the situation was increased by the aircraft stood a few dozen metres away; a silver trimotor with the black markings and German registration number, a Lufthansa JU52 due to depart a little later that night. The passengers had already started to arrive, overlapping earlier with those waiting to embark on the British machine. They had sat together in the waiting room in an uneasy peace until those bound for Britain were called to their machine.

'No photographs!'

'Who says?'

'It's against the rules.'

'Rules? What rules? I'm an American Citizen.'

An argument was taking place back in the waiting room. It dragged his attention away from the aircraft.

The airport manager was facing off against a photographer.

'Hey, get your hands off. Thats private property.'

The photographer was holding his camera up in the air whilst the manager was trying to grab at it. As the latter was short and the photographer tall and gangling, it was an uneven contest, much to be officials' frustration.

'Give it to me. It is confiscated.'

'Want to bet, bud?'

Lopes considered intervening but just couldn't find the energy or enthusiasm to bother. As it was there was already a pair of uniformed policemen in the room whose job it most certainly was but, although they watched with some interest, showed as little inclination to intervene as Lopes. They were far more interested in one woman in the waiting room. Although her hair was covered by a scarf and her eyes hidden behind dark glasses, despite the greyness of the sky, she obviously possessed a nice enough figure to attract their attention. Lopes wondered who she was seeing off. All the rest of the occupants were man, businessmen by the look of them in the main, although there was the usual 'others', probably, Lopes mused, low-level pseudo-spies, sent to watch and record who was flying in an out of the city.

Such was life in a neutral city.

Lopes was about to turn back to watch the aircraft when his attention was caught by a car screeching to a halt outside the building, the passenger door opening before it had stopped and a man dashing for the door of the terminal building. A late running passenger? Lopes frowned; No, the flight was full. Who was he then? He was tall, with a thin face and neat, short dark hair. Looking anxious, he went straight over to the airport manager, ignoring the fact that he was still arguing with the photographer.

'You chap. You must stop that aircraft,' he said.

The manager stared at him in astonishment.

'What? I can't do that.'

'I insist, one of our officials is on it and he is required urgently back at the embassy.'

The embassy. By the accent that meant the British embassy. Lopes' curiousity was raised.

'But sir, it's about to leave, look.' The manager pointed outside.

The photographer, in the meantime, was taking advantage of the interruption, quietly slipping away and making himself scarce.

'Perhaps I can persuade you,' said the newcomer, reaching inside his jacket, showing the official what was inside. Lopes was familiar with the move. He was offering a bribe.

What was in the man's wallet was clearly more than adequate, for the manager nodded and dashed outside into the increasing gloom as the light faded. waving his arms. 'Stop! Stop!'

The aircraft was already rolling but, abruptly, braked to a halt. Lopes watched in amazement as the engines were stopped, the aircraft was rolled back by the ground crew, the door opened and the steward came out, looking puzzled.

By this time embassy man was also on the tarmac, Lopes watched as he spoke to the steward who disappeared inside, appearing moments later with a uniformed officer, a briefcase chained to his wrist showing him to be a military courier. The newcomer spoke after taking him out of earshot of everyone else. The courier looked amazed, but the embassy man clearly wasn't taking no for an answer. At last, the man shrugged and headed back towards the terminal building, and from there into the car, which, once the courier was inside, headed back towards the city. The man who had arrived in the car had, Lopes noted, stayed. He checked his watch, then gave an anxious glance to another man, one of the 'watchers' who looked at his watch, nodded and then looked back out at the aircraft.

'What are you doing there?' Lopes muttered to himself. 'What are you waiting for?'

'What the hell was that about?' Lopes realised that it was the American photographer who was clearly as curious as himself.

'Good question,' murmured Lopes, looking back towards the aircraft. 'What indeed?'

The photographer shrugged. 'Hey bud, who knows? It's not for the likes of us to ask, hey?' He held out his hand. 'Howard R. Levy. I'm a reporter, freelance for now but, hey, who knows what I might get staying here. Pleased to meet you.'

'Dinis Lopes,' said Lopes. 'And sometimes it is for the likes of us to ask. Or me at least.' He strode up to the airport manager, who was counting a wedge of cash.

'Stop that aircraft,' said Lopes. 'I want it searched.'

'Do you? You can forget it chum.' The manager smiled. 'Unless you've a thick wallet. That's the only way it'll happen.'

'Oh really?' Lopes showed him his PVDE badge. 'Now do as I say.'

The man visibly paled. 'Yes, sir, of course.'

He turned ready to go out to the tarmac again.

'What's the meaning of this? That aircraft must leave. It's carrying information that must get to London today.'

The mystery newcomer had come over and stood in front of the manager, barring his way.

The latter, looking increasingly harassed, opened his arms wide in a gesture of helplessness. 'I'm sorry, sir, this man is from the PVDE, I must do as he says.'

The newcomer turned to Lopes. 'PVDE, eh? May I ask your name?'

'Lopes, Dinis Lopes. And you are?'

'Fleming. I'm sorry but in the rush, I seem to have left my papers at the embassy. I assure you I hold a diplomatic passport.'

'I'm sure you do but it doesn't matter to me here and now, Mr. Fleming. I want that aircraft stopped.' He turned to the airport official. 'Quickly, before it's too late, go and prevent it from leaving.'

'Yes, sir, of course.' The manager hurried out, waving his hands once again.

Fleming stood to one side to let the manager pass. 'I don't understand why you are doing this.'

Lopes saw him glance at the man again who was looking at his watch. 'That's simple; I want the passengers and crew off it and it to be thoroughly searched.'

Fleming sighed. 'Lopes. I've heard of you.'

'Good,' said Lopes.

'My understanding is that you are a sensible man.'

'It's gratifying I have the approval of the British embassy.'

Fleming smiled at the sarcasm. 'Indeed. But knowing you are sensible, why, then, are you interfering in the operation of a British aircraft, flying legally to Britain, with a British crew, carrying information which is vital to British interests?'

Lopes was watching the manager who was now conducting an animated discussion with the pilots, gesticulating from the tarmac up to them. 'I didn't like what I saw a few moments ago.'

Fleming raised his eyebrows. 'You mean my mission to get Major Patrick?'

'Yes. What was the urgency that caused your official to be removed from the aircraft?'

Fleming raised an eyebrow at Lopes. 'That is confidential. You can't expect me to disclose that.' He shook his head. 'And, anyway, you are stopping our flight simply because of that? On a hunch?'

Lopes held Fleming's gaze. 'It did look suspicious, you must admit.'

Fleming shrugged, 'To the casual observer perhaps. Now Lopes, I'm sure that you wouldn't want to cause any upset between the Estado Novo and His Majesty's Government would you, old chap?'

Lopes smiled 'Upset like dealing with communist agents like your colleague, Mr. Armstrong?'

Fleming gave a sardonic smile 'I don't know Armstrong personally, but I understand my former colleague went rather off piste, so to speak. Still, this surely does not mean you want to make things worse just as things are getting back to normal? Come on, Lopes, you may have acted on hunches when you were a policeman, but I know you are in a quite different role now, aren't you? One that requires diplomacy and common sense. Yes?'

'Yes,' Lopes replied in a monotone.

'Then let our aircraft leave, there's a good chap.'

Lopes puffed out his cheeks. The suave Englishman was right. He was acting on a hunch, this was a British aircraft, albeit on Portuguese territory. There was an unwritten rule, a truth that all sides adhered to, both BOAC and Lufthansa as well as his own country. The airport carried on as if the war didn't exist. It was unheard of for flights even to be intercepted, although it was within the rules of war for this to occur. The airport manager had now come back and was waiting expectantly, as, too, were the pilots, who had stepped out of the aircraft and were smoking cigarettes whilst watching the terminal. Their body language suggested both puzzlement and resignation.

Lopes wasn't meant to be here; he certainly wasn't at the airfield on official business and the Doctor's regime was trying to smooth things over between London and Lisbon. This wouldn't help. But he was suspicious, something was up, and he was PVDE. He had the power.

But power needed to be used sparingly.

'Very well,' said Lopes. 'The aircraft can fly, but,' he quickly added, 'there is something that I insist on doing first.'

***

He stepped onto the aircraft. This was the first time he'd ever been in one and he was surprised how cramped it was, as well as how steep the gangway between the seats were, one on each side. The passengers looked at him as he passed with some puzzlement.

She was in the last but one seat on the right-hand side. 'Lopes,' she said. 'What the hell are you doing?'

'You need to get off.'

'Is this a joke?' She folded her arms. 'No, I don't want to.'

'Elena, just do it.'

'No. Lopes, you're pathetic. I might have known you wouldn't let me go.'

'I'll handcuff you and drag you off if necessary.'

'You wouldn't dare.'

***

Ten minutes later, Lopes was sitting in his car. He watched the aircraft fading into the distance. He sighed and turned to his companion.

'Can I take the cuffs off now?'

'Only if you want a black eye.' Elena glowered at him. 'Why, Lopes, why? You know I had to fight to get the exit visa.'

'You had to fight? I got it for you.'

'Yes, alright, but you're showing your true colours now, aren't you? Kidnapping me to keep me from leaving so you can try and get me back.'

'Don't be so silly, Elena. That wasn't the reason.'

'Wasn't it? What was then?'

A flash lit up the evening sky. It was followed moments later by a low rolling noise like thunder. A fiery object tumbled out of the sky is the distance.

Elena's mouth dropped open in shock.

Lopes reached over and undid the cuffs.

'That was why, Elena. That was why.'

THE ASSASSINATION OF A NOBODY IS DUE OUT IN 2025

Printed in Great Britain
by Amazon